THROUGH THE STORM

There was no way to hide it. He wanted her.

"Wow," he whispered in awe. All the blood had ___ from his head and was taking up residence else-___ —which was uncool and disrespectful of her ___ house. He had to eat soon, and needed some-___ thin out the aphrodisiac he'd just ingested.

"___ really like it?" she asked, now feeling too ex-___ really look at him. She couldn't. The e___ on his face, and the way his hands had begun to ___ e again as he'd read. The way his breathing be-___ ted. . . . His nostrils flared just ever so slightly, a___ he were trying hard not to let it show—which w___ ively riveting. She hadn't had anyone ever re-spond to her work like that. Not her husband, anyway.

Forster's reaction almost made her forget where she was. But why had she even offered to do it? Her brain wasn't working right. Where was dinner?

"Like is not the word . . ."

"Thank you," she stammered.

"If you were just messing around on the pages I've read, then I'd love to see what you'd do if you were serious."

"I think I may have new, more serious material to work with, though," she daringly whispered, unable to contain herself, then immediately became shocked after she'd said what she did. "I mean—"

"Yeah," he murmured. "I hear you."

BOOK YOUR PLACE ON OUR WEBSITE AND MAKE THE ARABESQUE ROMANCE CONNECTION!

We've created a customized website just for our very special Arabesque readers, where you can get the inside scoop on everything that's going on with Arabesque romance novels.

When you come online, you'll have the exciting opportunity to:

- View covers of upcoming books

- Learn about our future publishing schedule (listed by publication month and author)

- Find out when your favorite authors will be visiting a city near you

- Search for and order backlist books

- Check out author bios and background information

- Send e-mail to your favorite authors

- Join us in weekly chats with authors, readers and other guests

- Get writing guidelines

- AND MUCH MORE!

Visit our website at
http://www.arabesquebooks.com

THROUGH THE STORM

Leslie Esdaile

ARABESQUE

★BET

BOOKS™

BET Publications, LLC
http://www.bet.com
http://www.arabesquebooks.com

ARABESQUE BOOKS are published by

BET Publications, LLC
c/o BET BOOKS
One BET Plaza
1900 W Place NE
Washington, D.C. 20018-1211

All Kensington Titles, Imprints, and Distributed Lines are available at special quantity discounts for bulk purchases for sales promotion, premiums, fund-raising, and educational or institutional use. Special book excerpts or customized printings can also be created to fit specific needs. For details, write or phone the office of the Kensington special sales manager: Kensington Publishing Corp., 850 Third Avenue, New York, NY 10022, attn: Special Sales Department, Phone: 1-800-221-2647.

First Printing: December 2002
10 9 8 7 6 5 4 3 2 1

Printed in the United States of America

"Through the Storm" is a book dedicated to all those who have suffered loss, disappointment, and grief . . . it is an acknowledgement of that sorrow, but more importantly, it is a prayer for hope and comfort, told in prose, that your storms will pass. Believe that they can, and they will.

One of the greatest things I ever learned is that in order for one to clean up after a storm, *forgiveness* is required. Forgiveness of self, of others, of circumstances . . . a spirit of gentleness is the profound essence of healing. In that regard, forgiveness is Divine.

My mother and the other wise women before her in the family used to say, "Let go and let God." In youth, I didn't understand this concept. In fact, I balked at the idea. But the older I became, and the more storms passed through my life, I began to understand the simplistic, peace-filled truth contained within those few words. One has to forgive, let judgments rest, we must have enough compassion to walk a mile in another person's shoes—even if we must stand firm with tough love—we must act with love as the basis of all of our actions, and ultimately one has to *turn it over*, and be still . . . just like the quiet after a storm.

Thank you, Mom, for teaching me how to listen to the Divine wisdom in forgiveness.

Prologue

Forster Scott Hamilton, Jr. lifted his camera to his face, adjusting the zoom lenses as he focused the shutter to capture the grisly remains of a human being. The old man had been identified as Thomas DeCicci. He scribbled that information on the empty thirty-five millimeter film container with a Sharpie pen. No matter how many of these forensic photos he took for the department he could never shake the feeling of sorrow from his bones. This was someone's relative, a person who had sired children, lived a life, and was part of a community. You'd think that by age forty-two Forster wouldn't be so sentimental about just doing a job.

He held his breath as he descended one more rickety basement step to get a better angle. The smell and flies sickened him and the medical mask he wore offered only a minute barrier to the stench. Brownish black water lapped at the soles of his heavy work boots—which he always wore for these types of jobs—and he could not even fathom how the pickup crew could wade in what was now a sewer swamp to drag the body out. As jobs on the force went, he reasoned that his was far better than most; he didn't have to dodge bullets, he came in after the fact, he didn't have to touch anything gruesome, and he didn't have to hunt, catch, see, or deal with victims or the incarcerated and their families.

"Looks like the old man was going down into the basement to check on the standing water after the storm, fell, hit his head on the stone wall over there, and landed facedown in it—then drowned. His elderly neighbor hadn't seen him in a few days, got nervous because the water was receding and a strange smell was going into the adjacent row houses, so she called 9-1-1. Just get a few shots, and you can take the rest at the morgue when we do the autopsy. Not much of a case here."

All Forster could do was nod in response to the detective. He didn't trust opening his mouth to breathe in the foul air to answer him with words. It was just another sad, routine case with awful photos to stand in tragic tribute to this person's memory.

The shutter of his camera rapidly discharged, then he made eye contact with the crime scene detective, received a confirmation nod, issued one back, and turned to leave.

One day he'd work on his coffee-table book of people in neighborhoods. One day he would pull together all of the photos he'd captured of unsung heroes, children playing in the fireplugs in the summer, old folks sitting on stoops; one day he'd compile a body of work that would inspire . . . one day. One day he'd be able to show his two small daughters the joy in people's eyes, held in tribute in black and white, or the wisdom that came with the wrinkles in a face. One day he'd be able to quit the force and take his kids to work with him. One day he'd be able to forgive and forget their mother for divorcing him and abandoning them. One day he'd be able to forgive his half brother and sister for the way they treated him and his mother, and that might even give rise to his being able to finally forgive his father. One day. But not today.

* * *

She stood patiently on the outer edge of the crime scene tape, her notepad and pen clutched in her hands. She'd made the rounds to all the shocked and bereaved friends and neighbors, and fought her way to the fore of the barrier. Cameramen from the news stations were aggressive; they had to get the shot of the body bag coming from the house for the late night news. They were not above using elbows, their strong torsos, or their huge cameras to make their presence known and gain the positional advantage; whatever it took to jockey for territory and bump other journalists out of their way.

Just because she worked for a small, local rag didn't mean she was at the bottom of the media food chain, in her mind at least. Hell no, she wasn't about to be pushed aside and give ground—she hadn't even allowed her ex-husband to do that! When she'd lived in New York, she'd learned how to just go for it—a sharp pen, a kick, or a stomp on the bridge of a cameraman's foot could get her through a throng, and a swift duck could avoid a punch, if thrown.

Lynette Graves tucked a stray curl behind her cowry-shell earring and let out her breath slowly. One day she wouldn't be hovering like a buzzard, collecting pieces of people's shattered lives for her newspaper. She wouldn't have to ask, "How do you feel," or "How long have you known him (or her)," or inquire about what the family's plans were now that this tragedy has happened. One day, she'd have a family of her own, children of her own, a full life of her own, and her own novel—instead of a collection of crime-beat articles and a ragged journal containing her poetry and stand-alone thoughts. Hopefully that would be soon, because at age thirty-five it felt like time for that one day was running out.

She shifted her body into position as she glimpsed the coroner's wagon doors open, then glanced up at the front door of the Darby County row house. The forensic photographer had come out and jumped into a sedan, which meant that the body would be coming out soon, followed by the scene's detective. She had to get to him—even though the whole sad situation always got to her much more deeply than anyone could imagine . . . but, it was her job.

One day she'd write about something positive, things that inspired, subjects that brought light into the dark corners of people's lives and minds. One day—unfortunately, just not today.

One

Forster began his after-work ritual the same as he always did, by hollering his entrance to the duplex basement of his home up to his mother and the girls as he stepped across the threshold of his sanctuary. He then dropped his camera equipment and took off his boots by the door, and put on his slippers, moving toward the only thing able to rinse off the mental grime—the downstairs shower.

It was as though the act of cleansing away invisible layers of carnage could somehow penetrate his soul to wash away the images he'd not only seen, but also felt, as well as get rid of the devastation he'd witnessed, and anything gory that could possibly rob him of peace. Each evening when he came in, he didn't even want to hug his children or touch them right away until he washed it off him—somehow irrationally feeling like his day could be passed through his skin like a virus and injure them.

The basement hamper swallowed his clothes whole as he cast them aside with disdain and turned the water on as hot as he could stand it. This was no way to live.

Immediately the water rushed against his skin and he stood under it immobilized by the sensation as it doused his injured spirit. A silent prayer for the dead man and his family began to form inside his mind, and those mental words began to fuse with the clean water until his shoulders finally relaxed under the spray of it.

"I can't be doing all this homework with these girls, and there's nothing thawed out in the refrigerator for dinner!"

His mother's voice cut through the bathroom door and the drone of the shower like a knife, scraping against his brittle nerves, flaying them until they almost shredded and snapped.

"I'll be out in a minute! Okay? Let me get this road dirt off of me and I'll be up."

"Whatever," she screeched. "But these kids need to eat soon, and so do I."

"All right, already," he boomed back, grabbing the soap and hastily applying it. He waited until he heard her footsteps return up the stairs, and he let out his breath in an angry rush. How hard could it be to walk down the street and pick up two kids from school—especially when he took them each morning before work, and they went to after-school activities each day until six o'clock? How the hell hard could it be to oversee a kindergarten-age child while she writes her ABCs, or to help a second-grader do a few math problems? And why in the world was it an impossible task to remember to take a fryer pack of chicken out of the freezer in the morning so it would be ready to prepare for dinner in the evening?

Forster allowed the unspoken indignities to become one with the water and the soap as he scrubbed his body hard and flung his washcloth into the corner of the stall. If his mother didn't drink and watch soaps all damned day. . . . If she'd gotten herself together after his father left and remarried. For God's sake, she'd had thirty-some years to get with the program: Forster Scott Hamilton, Sr. was not coming back then, and was now in his grave. If she'd just pulled her life together and moved when he'd suggested, then her home wouldn't have washed away in 1999 during hurricane Floyd. If she'd had a life, or even a real church home, then she could be like other mothers—grandmothers, and be thankful for having a decent son and precious grandchildren. If.

He rinsed the soap away along with the tenuous thoughts of woulda-coulda-shoulda. It was what it was. Just like his job was what it was. Just like his life with his ex had been what it had been. Just like his life now was what it was. Empty.

When the top step leading to the basement creaked, his shoulder muscles tensed even more and he braced himself for his mother's voice again. Quickly grabbing his towel, he dried himself and snatched a pair of old sweats and a T-shirt from the bathroom shelf, but left the water running to buy him some time.

"Scottie, what in the world is taking you so long? I told you—"

"In. A. Minute. Mom!" He hated that she always used his middle name and not his father's first name.

"Fine. Suit yourself. But if you think I'm going to just sit around and wait for you, you've got another thing coming!"

This time he didn't answer, and just shut off the running water and made his way out of the bathroom and up the steps. Taking so long? Ten minutes to get his head together and clean off after a day at work was too long? No, too long was more than thirty years of watching a woman drink herself to death. Too long was being the only responsible adult in a household since he was a boy, and then when he got married. Too long was almost a decade on the police force, seven years embattled in a bad marriage, and three years of living without any female companionship—whatsoever. Too long was living with a mother who couldn't care for herself and moving her into what was *supposed* to be a temporary living situation, but dealing with what had now become an interminable sentence. Too long was coming home daily to the mess and disarray she created, not to mention having to clean up after her drunken days. That was too long. Not waiting ten minutes until a person could get out of the shower!

"Daddy!"

A chorus of little-girl voices greeted him at the top of the basement stairs as he entered the kitchen. The sound of his daughters' cheerful squeals of delight began to smooth his frayed nervous system, but the sight of dishes overrunning the sink and the feel of an unknown sticky substance under his slippers as he approached them only unraveled him again. Why in the hell couldn't he for once walk into his home and find order?

"Hey pumpkin-lumpkins," he chuckled in a strained voice. "You girls been good at school and for Gran today?"

"Yup!" his youngest daughter giggled, snuggling into his waistline. "I got a gold star on my picture. Wanna see?"

"Yes, baby," he murmured, becoming enraptured by her upturned impish grin. "And I have just the spot for it on the refrigerator under the biggest magnet."

"Rachel ain't the onlyest one who got a star, Daddy," his seven-year-old countered. "I got a check-plus on my spelling today, too!"

"The word is *isn't,* baby. There ain't no such word as ain't." Her scowl made him laugh. The fight for his attention had brought out his better side and had made him smile despite his foul mood. "I have enough space for yours, too, sweet pea. I'm so proud of both my girls.

Gimme some sugar and go help Gran set the kitchen table for dinner, then go wash up."

"She's in her room, again, and it smells funny in there," one child protested.

"Then you girls are big enough to set it by yourselves, right?" Forster swallowed away rage and avoided eye contact with his daughters as he moved deeper into the kitchen.

"Okay, but what we gonna have? Gran said there ain't, I mean, there isn't anything thawed out."

"She's in a bad mood today," the youngest one added.

"She's always in a bad mood, bubblehead," Rebecca, the older of the two children fussed. "Can I help cook, Daddy?"

"Not tonight," he replied softly. "Just go set the table and finish up your homework. Y'all get in the tub and take a bath and put on your nights, by then I'll have rustled up some dinner and we can eat."

"But I'm hungry," Rachel whined.

"How'd the floor get all sticky?" The question was offered as a diversion while he rummaged in the cabinets for ingredients that would make a quick meal. He spied a box of Hamburger Helper and a can of mixed vegetables. Cheese on top of everything would make it a delicacy for the kids, and with the more nutritional juice gone, Kool-Aid would have to suffice.

"Gran spilled the orange juice, but I wiped it up with a napkin."

"Thanks, sweetie," he said with a sigh, knowing full well that vodka always went with his mother's orange juice. "Look. Go do as I said, and I'll get some food on as fast as possible. After dinner, we'll read a story, then I've gotta get this kitchen and the rest of the house in order. Okay. So, the longer y'all dawdle, the longer it's gonna take me."

"But you supposed to braid our hair tonight for picture day tomorrow," the eldest child protested. "And you said you was gonna let us pick out some pretty dresses to wear special, too."

"I know, I know, I didn't forget," he lied. "I'ma read while I do your heads, and you can pick out your outfits for me to iron while you get ready for bed—*okay?* Now stop interrogating me and let me get to fixing dinner."

"Is Gran going to eat with us tonight?" His older daughter held a single fork and knife in her hand, hovering by the open drawer and waiting for an answer that he didn't really have.

"Probably not, Becky—don't set for her, I'll take hers to her on a TV tray so she can eat in her room."

"What's interrorrogatin'?" The younger one looked at him, barely holding on to the three plastic cups that her small arms cradled, as though trying detect something unspoken yet palpable in her older sister and father's tense exchange.

"It means stop asking so many questions, boo-boo brain," Rebecca fussed. "Jese E Christmas."

"Okay, y'all. My patience is wearing thin. Stop name calling, squabbling, and go do what I said."

He watched two dejected forms move away from his side, one going to the table to drop her payload of cups on it and the other to resume her hunt and peck amongst the ruins in the drawer for silverware again. With his back turned to the girls he closed his eyes briefly and let his breath out through his nose. *Just some peace, Lord God, is all I ask.* . . . Then, he set his mind on dinner.

Lynette sat in her car in front of the house for a moment before getting out of it. The quiet of St. Marks Street crept into her bones and she breathed in autumn.

She loved University City . . . God was good. She reminded herself to be thankful for her health, strength, and the fact that she was still employed. She reminded herself that she'd landed on her feet and had been fortunate enough to be able to buy her own home while interest rates had plummeted during the new-millennium war. She reminded herself that she'd been spared being in New York during one of the worst days America had ever seen on its own soil. She reminded herself that she still had a mother to go home to—and she held on to that thought long enough to allow her to open the car door, exit it, and walk up her front steps. Then she paused briefly before inserting her key into the lock.

Today she would not dwell on what she didn't have. She didn't have a right to do that, nobody did, she guessed. Not after what so many people she knew had lost. The problem would be silently reminding herself of that fact while in her mother's presence.

As she turned the tumbler and opened the door, the smell of home cooking surrounded her. Scents of baked chicken and string beans enveloped her, making her stomach growl and her mouth water. Yes, God was indeed infinitely good.

"Hey, Mom," she yelled, tossing her coat on the sofa as she paced through the house to where the rich sensory treat emanated. "Seems like you've outdone yourself again."

"Aw, suga', just a little somethin' for my hard-working girl. Got some baked chicken, string beans, sweet potatoes, and a pie." The older woman chuckled as she wiped her hands on her apron and smoothed back her silver hair, which was wound in a bun. "Go set the table, and everything oughta be ready in about ten minutes."

Lynette leaned down and brushed her mother's forehead with a kiss. "You didn't have to go to all of that trouble," she said with a smile of appreciation, turning to dip a fork into the string beans, and secretly glad that her mother had indulged her. "How was your day?"

"Lynne, you tell me that each and every time you walk through the door, but you always come in here snooping in my pots just the same—but my day is like it always is, no aches, pains, no complaints," her mother returned with a sigh, whacking Lynette's hand as she sampled the hot vegetables for seconds.

Lynette paused and surveyed her mother's countenance. The sigh was her cue to press further, and it was always followed by some bad news. Struggling against the selfish impulse to allow her mother's sigh to pass, she turned and faced her, fully knowing that the pending question about what was wrong would lead her mother into unveiling the full details of a church member's ailments, someone's passing, or some situation on daytime television that neither of them could impact.

"What's wrong, Mom?" She'd nearly whispered the question as she steeled her nerves for the onslaught of tragic circumstances her mother would surely describe.

"You know old Mrs. Fisher . . . she's on the Women's Day Committee, well, she's failing."

Lynette stared at her mother for a moment and allowed her head to bob up and down with the appropriate level of remorse for the lady she couldn't place and didn't remember. "God bless her," she added by rote, and then began to search for tableware.

"Well, her daughter was up at the Thriftway supermarket today, and told me that it won't be long. You don't know her daughter, do you?"

"No, Mom," Lynette replied in a solemn tone, and then braced herself.

"Well, I suppose if you made it to church more often

with your mother, the dutiful way her daughter did, then you might know some of the young people over there."

"Mom . . ." Lynette caught herself and then retreated from the path she was about to pursue. "I'm so sorry to hear about Mrs. Fisher."

"Yeah, baby, but it's all in God's hands now."

"Uh—huh . . ."

"At least she has a son-in-law and some grands, that way she can close her eyes and go to glory knowing that her chile will be taken care of—that's all any mother wants."

"Uh—huh. She's blessed," Lynette intoned, moving from the kitchen to put the items she clasped against her chest on the dining room table. She could hear her mother dishing up the food, and she said a silent prayer that their meal wouldn't entail a full conversation regarding her own will-o'-the-wisp lifestyle.

"I'm just sorry that after your father passed," her mother offered as she entered the room with a platter, "we didn't have nothing to really leave you."

"Mom, we've been over this a hundred times," Lynette countered, taking the platter of chicken and yams from her mother and setting it on the table. "I have enough and make enough to take care you and me, and the best part of what you all had to give me goes so far beyond any money you'd leave behind. Come on, Mom, sit down and eat and let me get the rest of dinner dished up."

"I know that's what you tell me all the time," her mother murmured, going into the kitchen to fetch a bowl of string beans with Lynette on her heels, all the while ignoring her request to stop moving. "But I'd feel better if you was more involved with the Lord, and if you tithed—that way I'd be sure that anything you was blessed with just wouldn't be whisked away like me and your Daddy's house was during the flood."

Again, the storm. It had nearly washed away her parents' home, and with it washed away her mother's dreams, forcing her to relocate with her daughter and now clench her religion in her fist. Lynette sighed out loud this time.

"Mom," Lynette soothed, trying to quell the argument that was brewing in the distance, "I do tithe, but in a different way. I give ten percent of my salary to good causes, like the Red Cross, and I give ten percent of my free time helping in the community. Just because I don't do it through a collection plate in a particular church, does not mean I'm a bad person, or that I'll get the wrath upon me. Mom, bad things happen to good people sometimes."

Her mother's response was a mere snort as she sat down at the table, folded her hands over her plate, and blessed their meal.

"Thinking like that is why my soul can't rest, chile. So much trouble is goin' on in this wicked world. Everywhere you look, the devil is busy. He be seeping up into young folks, taking what ain't his, and claiming the righteous in tragedy—"

"Mom." Lynette held her mother's gaze within her own, trying to stop the tirade of fear and negativity before her mother began speaking in tongues. "Even with all that is bad, there is a lot of good. The good comes through despite the darkness. Please. Focus, tonight, on the good." The only way to reach her mother was to throw a small challenge to her faith down as a gauntlet.

"Yes, I suppose I can do that right now, since there ain't no point to trying to talk about the heavy burden on my heart."

The guilt thing her mother was so adept at was maddening, and Lynette tried to focus on the goodness of the food in front of her as she slipped a piece of tender chicken into her mouth. "Uhmmm . . ." she moaned, briefly closing her eyes as the flavors slid over her tongue. "Oh, Mom, you are the best cook."

"Pleasures of the flesh, even good cooking, can't change what is. Can only take your mind off of things till you finish eating it."

Lynette ignored the comment as she helped herself to a mouthful of succulent yams. Again she closed her eyes and allowed the sensory treat to roll over her tongue. Yet, her mother's words rang in her head. Pleasures of the flesh . . . Had her mother any idea of how long it had been since she'd indulged in any real pleasures of the flesh? A good dinner was close, but no comparison.

"Well, glad you enjoy it," her mother finally remarked, seeming quite perturbed that the conversation had stopped.

"I do," Lynette replied thickly through a mouthful of biscuit. "You have no idea how much I appreciate the fact that you cook for me and are here to greet me when I come home from work. It's nice, Mom. It's family, and not so lonely that way for either of us."

Her mother smiled, and the older woman seemed to relax her bristled countenance at the comment. "It's all I can do for my baby girl anymore. But you need more than me to take care of you, honey."

Lynette sipped her iced tea. Her bad. Her mother was focused—just on the one subject that she'd never let die.

"I mean . . . wasn't there any way you and William couldn't have tried to—"

"No."

"Well, you never know. The Lord works in mysterious ways."

"We were unevenly yoked from the start." Lynette didn't look up as she ate and searched her mind for biblical clichés that would stop the trajectory of her mother's thoughts.

"Such a shame . . ."

"Yes it was, Mom."

"You could start coming to church more, and have minister pray over you and—"

"I thank you for the offer, but I don't want my business out in the street, the congregation I mean, like that."

The two women exchanged a look, and her mother began eating.

"There's plenty of good Christian young men starting to come back to their roots now, and lots of them are—"

"Mom, we've been over this. I went out with a few of the sons of your girlfriends, and they had worse issues than my ex-husband, plus there was no chemistry. So—"

"What's chemistry got to do with finding a good suitor from a solid Christian background?"

The indignity that her mother displayed, along with the absolute absurdity of her mother's question, made Lynette smile. "Nothing at all, Mom," she said with a chuckle, ignoring her mother's glare and wishing that she'd never gone near the subject.

"You are a good-looking, hard-working, clean-living young woman, and every one of my friends who have a son that's not married or in jail or on drugs would love to have you as a daughter-in-law. I told them all you never gave me a day of trouble in your life. Never did. And, only being blessed with one child before my womb went bad according to God's will, I was thankful for that. I just want you to get on with a family so you don't get old like me, and before, God forbid, you have any female problems, so you won't be alone if I go on to glory."

Lynette leaned over and kissed her mother's cheek as she watched the elderly woman whip herself up into a frenzy, then begin to tear. She knew that the peevish tone was just a disguise for hurt, and she covered her mother's hand with her own. "Mom, you are as healthy as a horse, and should something happen, I will be able to take care of myself—with or without a man and children in tow. Please, let's just enjoy this dinner together and have some pie, then I have to get to work on a story for deadline."

"That's just it. You go out into the streets all hours of the day and night by your lonesome, then hole yourself up in that room typing on the computer, and hang out with only your girlfriends all the time . . . and you ain't getting' no younger, suga'. You won't come to church with me to get saved . . . and—"

"Mom, please," Lynette begged, becoming weary and irate at the same time. "I have been christened and baptized and I try my best not to hurt people. I pay my bills, support good organizations, and—"

"And, still got divorced, and don't have any suitors on the horizon, nor any grandchildren for me."

"Let it rest, Mom. Okay. Let's just eat in peace."

It was a stalemate. Her mother's circle logic was as intact as it had always been. But when and whom was she supposed to date? Her mother was in her space and on the phone to her aged church friends twenty-four-seven, while fastidiously cooking, asking questions, and cleaning the house. When her mother wasn't at home, the woman was at church. Other times, her mother was only gone for brief periods during the day to run small, local errands while Lynette was out on assignments. Plus, dating was an iterative process of weeding out—

it was a numbers game that she no longer had the stamina to endure.

So, if she did find a man to date, and things did heat up and go to the next level, how would that process work in the context of her life now? If she didn't come home every night, her mother would probably freak, call the police, and put out an all-points bulletin for her whereabouts, no doubt thinking that some crime-beat stalker had murdered her. Since the storm, and her father's funeral, her mother's nerves had been a wreck—which in turn was wearing a hole in hers.

Lynette pondered the possibilities as her mother picked at her dinner. If she ever had a real, hot date and told the woman the truth, she might as well come home to find her mother dead in the middle of the floor from a heart attack. Lynette chuckled to herself at the ludicrous thought and took the final bite of chicken on her plate. Yeah, when was the last time she'd been on a date anyway . . .

And, if she did want to come home after a perfect evening, and invite a man in, he'd have to parlor-sit with her mother while the game shows were on. Somehow, that didn't seem to give way to a romantic, arch your back, let-your-knuckles-turn-white-while-you-clutch-the-sheets session. Hell no. Not here. It was hard enough after living with her mother for three years in this house to remember what being with a man was like. Besides, nobody had crossed her path yet to make her risk sending her mother into apoplexy; it just wasn't worth it for a mere roll in the hay.

TWO

Lynette checked her rearview mirror at the stop sign, preparing for a turn as she watched amid the chaos for any additional stray children who might be crossing behind her vehicle while she waited for another mass of frolicking youngsters to get to safety on the curb before her. Harried-looking parents escorted some of them, and it never failed to amaze her the number of fathers that also accompanied their little ones to school. Where were these types of guys when she was looking for one, anyway?

She summoned patience as the children laughed and leisurely strolled past her, realizing that her workout session at the Fifty-second Street YMCA wasn't going anywhere in particular. Neither was she. But, it was a beautiful fall day, nonetheless. The blue sky was flawless and unmarred, and the sun's brilliant, golden rays cast a warming glare on her Subaru windshield. It was not a day to allow her mother's words and worry to continue to haunt her. Nope. Not today. She was going to work off her mother's cooking, work off her tension, and keep her body fit and trim.

As she turned up the volume on her radio to drown out her thoughts, she glimpsed a tall, attractive man with two little girls in tow. Odd, but his militarylike stride almost kept fluid time with the smooth jazz com-

ing from the WJJZ station she'd selected. The brief hesitation to move forward had made her miss an
opportunity to turn before having to wait for him and a
group of other pedestrians to cross now, which brought
an angry horn blare from the driver behind her.

Yet she couldn't advance her vehicle until they'd
passed her, and she also couldn't stop watching the man
cross with the two pretty little girls at either side. What
was his story? The journalist in her awakened as she
stared at his proud, six-foot-two carriage, his smooth,
dark chocolate complexion, and the broad shoulders
that filled out his leather bomber jacket. Boots. Work
boots. Wow . . . a blue-collar brother taking his daughters to school. Didn't see that every day. Very cool. Had
to have a solid wife, judging by the way their hair was
so neat in cute little braids with bows on the ends—a
woman's touch, or at least a grandma's touch. Matching
lunch boxes and backpacks for books . . . adorable Sunday coats and tights with dresses on, no doubt . . . black
Mary Jane shoes. Yeah. The all-American family.

Lynette let out a sigh as the crowd thinned and she
could make her turn, glimpsing the man's well-formed
backside as he bent to kiss his children and hurry them
into the school yard.

"I hope whoever she is appreciates what she's got,"
she murmured under her breath as she sped down the
block and took a hairpin turn onto Walnut Street. Without looking into her shoulder bag on the passenger's
seat, she blindly hunted for her cell phone, found it, and
clicked it on.

"Okay, Dianne," she laughed when she got her best
friend's voice mail. "It's time to come up for air and do
lunch with your girl. Call me in the office in a couple of
hours. I'm going to the gym, and I need some nonbut-

ter-dripping alternatives later in the day. Let's meet and do Thai."

The central precinct was always buzzing first thing in the morning, and as he entered The Round House, Forster stopped at Rick's desk, a ritual they always observed.

"Yo, brother, whatcha got that's good to go with coffee?"

Rick laughed and exchanged a fist hit with his buddy. "Why you always come in here scrounging for grub? Don't y'all keep no Dunkin' Donuts back there in forensics?"

"You're the detective, you tell me."

Both men laughed as Forster took a seat on the corner of Rick's desk.

"I'm just helping you out, so you stay in shape, brother. I don't have to keep the body for on the streets, you do." Forster gave his friend a sly wink as he sipped his coffee slowly through the plastic lid of the steaming cup he held. "You giving up a doughnut or what?"

Rick shook his head and finally offered Forster a donut. "You're leaning hard on this friendship and my good graces—especially since I can't get you to hang out with me no more. What's up, man? How you living?"

"I'm cool," Forster mumbled through a bite of doughnut, then slurped his coffee.

"Ain't seen you in a month of Sundays. How's my goddaughters doing, and your mom?"

"Mom is Mom, same old same old. But, the girls are fine—shoulda seen 'em today, all dolled up . . . it's picture day."

"I know you have one coming for Uncle Rick, to go on my desk, right?"

"Yeah, man. Don't I always hook a brother up? That's why you should be cool and give a brother a doughnut without static."

Rick laughed and took a slurp of black coffee from the dingy mug on his desk, then made a face. "You do, you do. Besides, I have to keep my reputation as the best uncle—since I ain't makin' no kids."

Forster grinned. "You keep running the honeys like you've been doing, and you might have to buy a frame for your own one day soon. Keep it up, and see."

Rick made a comical face of surprise, opened his arms wide, and leaned back in his chair. "Me? Oh no. You've got the wrong man. I've made it to forty with no babies, and no wife—how'd I look now getting jacked at this age? I'm a freelancer."

"That's not what I've heard." Forster chuckled, helping himself to another doughnut.

"Oh, so now you're the detective?"

"I'm just the camera guy—and I can see real good . . . like the fact that nobody can find you to even watch football. Only a woman can lock a brother down and make him forget about the finer aspects of life."

Rick laughed and hung his head, peeping up with a mischievous grin, which made both men laugh harder.

"All right. Busted. But the girl is *fine,* man. Lives with her sisters over on Parkside Avenue, you know—so, we have to be at my spot, then Saturday nights roll into Sunday, and sometimes Monday . . . what can I say?"

Forster shook his head and hopped off the edge of Rick's desk. "Enjoy, brother. Nothing else needs to be said."

"She can cook, too," Rick whispered, drawing Forster in.

He stared at his friend for a moment, opened his mouth—poised to send a zinger—and then shut it. In all of their years as friends, he'd never seen Rick appear so thoroughly happy about a specific woman. Up till now, they were all just fun for Rick, but there was something in the way his friend's eyes shone with unconcealed excitement. "You really like her, don't you?"

"Man, she's da bomb," Rick admitted in a quiet voice, then glanced around to be sure none of their coworkers could hear what he was saying.

"Deep." That was all Forster could muster.

"Look, man . . . I don't know, but . . . she keeps wanting me to hang with her and her family, meet her friends, go out in a group more than us, and—"

"Bad sign," Forster said quickly, shaking his head. "It's a dragnet. They're getting ready to posse up on you and bring you in for lockup—don't go there, unless you're—"

"Me?" Rick huffed, his bravado sounding very unsure. "Not me. I'm waaaay too smooth for the okie-doke. Uh-uh. Not this brother."

"When you going?"

They both laughed.

"She wants to do something this weekend, man. I don't know. Go to the movies, or something with a friend of hers, as a couple of couples, you dig?"

"Well, that's cool. Go see a flick, which takes two hours off of any conversation. Go for a drink or two, chitchat, and take her home. She'll be satisfied, and you've bought yourself some time."

"That's just the thing of it," Rick ventured, looking down at his hands as he spoke. "She wants to meet my friends, too. And she had this wild idea, she must have seen this mess on Oprah, about—"

"Don't even go there," Forster said with a chuckle of disbelief. "It's bad enough you've got me dispensing Love Connection advice first thing in the morning, but I'm not—"

"It would only be for a few hours, like you said."

"Dude. Listen to yourself," Forster argued. "Who's gonna watch the girls while I go with you as your body-guard? Huh? You know my mom ain't up to the challenge, and that I barely leave them with her for more than an hour after school."

"Her sisters have a bunch of kids ranging from dia-pers to eight—"

"I don't know this woman's sister!"

"But, check it out, we could go somewhere real close to Parkside where the kids would be, like up on City Line Avenue, go to a bar after, and we'd have our cells on and beepers—"

"I don't drink enough to do a bar, and I hate bars."

"I know you hate bars because of your step-brother's joint, but on this one occasion—"

"I'ma start buying my own doughnuts, the ones at your desk cost too much—"

"Wait, hold up," Rick urged, standing and following behind Forster as he walked away. "I wouldn't put my own little goddaughters in harm's way, that's for one." He placed his hand on Forster's shoulder to stop him from walking and ignored the sigh of annoyance Forster issued when they came to a halt. "For two, you're my most trusted boy, and if this ain't the one, I need you to put your eye on this sister, know what I mean? If any-body would know if a Jane was really shaky or not, I know you'd tell me . . . I mean right now, I can't—"

"You're telling me that she's got your nose opened so

bad that you can't make your own decision about this—after forty years of being in the street, dog?" Forster just stared at his friend for a moment, then burst out laughing.

"Oh, man . . . keep it down. For real, for real," Rick said nervously as he spied the other officers, whose smiles were too broad. "Look," he whispered, "it would just be one night out—and we haven't hung in a while. We can go to T.G.I. Friday's, since a bar goes against your principles."

"Now we're going to dinner? You keep adding things to this supposed package deal, man. I can't commit."

"But, for real, as your boy, do I ever ask you for anything?"

Forster had to smile as his friend's tone became plaintive. "My hedge clippers, my tools, my—"

"All right, all right . . . but still. I mean, it would do you good, too, you know."

"Now this is for my benefit? Gimme a break." Forster started walking again and his friend double-stepped behind him to keep up.

"Okay, tell the truth . . . when's the last time you've taken a lady out, much less got some?"

"You're reaching." Forster chuckled as he pushed the button on the elevator and waited for it.

"No I'm not," Rick argued. "Just between us boys, when's the last time?"

"That's my business," Forster warned, the mirth going out of his tone.

"See. It's been too long, or you wouldn't be getting an attitude."

"This supposed girlfriend that I'd have to endure for two hours, plus appetizers at Friday's, what if she's a total—"

"She's *fine,* man." Rick crossed his arms and looked at Forster with conviction.

"How do you know? I thought you hadn't met her friends? And describe fine."

"Her friend works for the newspaper with her—"

"A reporter? Are you crazy?"

"I saw her picture when I was waiting for Dianne at her house. They're best friends, went to the Islands together, and the photo was on the mantle—so I asked one of the kids who were running around, who was in the shot with their aunt Dianne, and they told me Aunt Lynne . . . so I asked D if she had another sister, and she told me that Lynette was just like her sister, so—"

"You're talking way too fast for this to be anything other than a problem, dude. No flim-flam-alacazam. Describe fine," Forster repeated, then folded his arms over his chest, keeping his line of vision on the lit elevator dial.

"She's about five-seven, pretty smile, coffee-with-cream complexion, curly hair, and a body that would stop traffic on the expressway. Satisfied?"

"How many kids does she have?"

"None."

This time Forster looked at his friend hard. "Oh, bull. Man, then, how old is she?"

"Same age, about, as my Dianne—they were in school together, same grade in high school, I think."

"Which is?"

"Around thirty-five. Why're you so suspicious? This is your boy you're talking to."

"That's why I'm suspicious, brother—'cause *I know you.*"

"That's cold, man. Totally uncalled for," Rick said, laughing.

"All right, then what's wrong with her? No kids, no man, good job, thirty-five, and down for a blind date?"

"First of all, there's nothing wrong with her. Second

of all, I don't know the sister's life story; I didn't get into all of that . . . I just sorta promised D while she was persuading me, and—"

"Wait! You already committed me because you were laying pipe and couldn't say no when your woman asked you about this? Am I hearing you right?"

"Keep your voice down, man. Chill. I was in a delicate scenario, my woman looked up at me with those big brown eyes, sighed, said that she wanted to do this, and I didn't have the heart to tell her no."

"This is a bad idea, I can tell. There's a set up, I can feel it coming, and—"

"C'mon, brother. What could go wrong? If the sister is whack, then all you did was go see a movie and spend a few bucks on some appetizers—and when's the last time you saw a movie, not on cable, that didn't have a Disney logo on it? The kids will have gotten out from under foot and away from your mom for a few hours, and you and I will have this to add to our list of laughs, if it gets crazy. Conversely," Rick added, now beginning to walk around in a circle as he spoke, "you might get lucky. She's *fine,* man, and all fine women ain't like your ex—Eva. You don't have to invest that kind of energy into it, and I'll even drive her home so you don't have to let those old guilt demons of allowing a woman to drink and drive haunt you. For real, for real, brother, you've gotta let that go and get on with your life."

The two men looked at each other for a moment as the elevator door finally opened.

"Let me think about it, okay?" Forster murmured, and then pushed the button to close the door.

"Hey, girl!" Dianne exclaimed as she entered the Thai Singha House and spotted Lynette, already seated at their favorite table in the restaurant. "Long time no see, stranger."

Lynette laughed as she hugged her girlfriend, noticing the extra bounce to Dianne's step and the sheer radiance of her expression. "You have a nerve calling *me* stranger, stranger. I have to book an appointment with you a month in advance, and even your sisters haven't seen you. Trust me, I've asked them. So, how's life, and everybody—fill in some gaps, chile."

"Oh, girl!" Dianne crooned. "Where do I begin?"

"So, you're in love again, right? Don't tell me."

"You know that brother," Dianne giggled, leaning into their table and dropping her voice an octave, "the one I met during the fund-raiser for rescue workers?"

"You snagged a man at what was supposed to be a call to arms and support for the nation . . . yeah, I do recall," Lynette remarked with a chuckle, sipping her iced tea and perusing the menu with a smile.

"That hard-body, Latino brother with the buns of steel on the police force?"

"Yeah, yeah, yeah, I remember the description."

"Girl! Oh, girl!" Dianne laughed and covered her face with her hands.

"That good?" Intrigued, Lynette fell into the humorous banter, vicariously reveling in her friend's fortune. Dianne always had a dramatic story, but there was something different about the level of excitement—it almost passed for reverence. And it made Lynette take note.

"You know with all the chaotic yang going on at our house, between Carol's newborn and new divorce, and Sharon's five-year-old twins and her eight-year-old, and her total disdain of the male species, I even had to install my own phone in my bedroom, and everything, to keep the peace and my privacy."

"What? There's enough room in your mom's big ol' house for all of you all, especially with Mom gone on to glory, I mean, the place has like six bedrooms and—"

"But, I needed my own phone, because being on the force, he works wild hours, and sometimes our conversations get a little, well—"

"No . . . on the phone, even?" Lynette covered her mouth and set down her menu, now giving her girlfriend her full attention.

"Yes." Dianne chuckled, reaching across the table to grasp Lynette's free hand. "The man has taken me out to dinner everywhere in Philly. We did Cuba Libra, Zanzibar's, Warm Daddy's, you name it . . . we've been up to The Keswick Theatre to see all the shows, chile. It took me a month to break down, because I wasn't trying to get played, and I needed to know if he had a bunch of kids, or a woman, wife, whatever."

"A month? It took *you* a month to break down?" Lynette teased.

"Shut up, heifer, and stop player hatin'," Dianne teased back. "But when I did break down . . . girl!"

"I'm too jealous," Lynette admitted with a laugh. "It's been three years of drought."

"I know, sweetie. Remember, I was on that same drought with you for at least a year, and honey, when I tell you that when you break the fast you're gonna lose your natural mind . . ."

"Order some food, girl," Lynette said with a wistful giggle. "Just thinking about it gives me goose bumps. I don't want to hear any details—I'm just glad you're having so much fun. So, this brother is all that. Excellent."

"Girl," Dianne pressed, ignoring Lynette's plea for mercy regarding the details, "after we'd exhausted every room in his apartment, which is fly by the way . . . we went to the Inn of the Dove."

Lynnette swallowed hard and decided upon Pad Thai as a lunch choice. "That's enough, kiddo. I really can't take it. I live with Mom now; you know that. I don't even read romance novels anymore to keep me focused, and I had to work out this morning to calm my nerves."

A deep giggle connected the women as they motioned for the waitress and placed their orders.

"Well, how do you think I've felt, living with my two mad-hatter sisters, kids everywhere all the time, no bathroom to claim as your own, no time alone? . . . I even had little people climbing in bed with Auntie Dianne—since my sisters don't keep them on any kind of schedule. A sistah couldn't even handle her own business and get the monkey off her back on the down low around there, so I decided to go cold turkey until I found the one. Girl, I was Jonesin' so bad by the time I met Rick, with his fine self . . . but I decided to honor my body, it's the temple, you know."

Both women laughed again.

"No, for real, I had been doing a lot of reading about spiritual principles—since all I could do was read . . . then I met him, and we just talked and dated."

"Now, see, I'd been telling you that for years and I'm so glad that—"

"But, then one night the brother backed me up against the front door, laid a kiss on me that buckled my knees, and the next thing I know, I was at his place."

"If only," Lynette sighed. "But, patience and—"

"Girl, the place we went to this weekend had a Jacuzzi," Dianne rushed in, cutting off Lynette's words and talking a mile a minute. "He broke out not only a bottle of champagne, but a bottle of this Kama Sutra edible oil . . ."

"Shut up," Lynette exclaimed, doubling over and laughing. "I live with my mother, and you're giving me the shivers, okay. Just stop right there."

"I'ma marry his butt, okay. That's all I'm going to say. Whatever issues he has, be damned."

"For real . . . whoa. . . . You have never said that about any of 'em."

The two exchanged a knowing glance.

"He has a friend, you know? Interested?"

"Tell me more about this friend of his?"

"Don't know more than I told you except that he's on the force, not married, doesn't have a woman, and is my man's best friend."

"Any chance he's a clone? A clone of what you're describing could work."

Slapping five, they sat back in their chairs.

"I could set it up so that the four of us go to the movies this weekend, if you're interested?"

"But a blind date? I mean, what if the chemistry is off, and—"

"What's the worst that could happen, huh?"

Lynette put her napkin in her lap and then toyed with her silverware.

"C'mon, girl," Dianne urged with a confident chuckle. "I want you to meet him, give me your opinion before I mentally go to the next phase—"

"But, a blind date?"

"You owe me."

"How?" Lynette asked laughing.

"I used half a bottle of oil while begging him to hook up my best friend with his."

"Oh . . ."

Three

The week had lazily dragged itself along. Time almost seemed to stand still at points, as though some unseen force were hording it. And while she'd casually mentioned to her mother that she was going out to the movies with Dianne and some friends on Saturday night, once the evening was upon her a new level of anxiety swept through her.

She didn't want to share the possibilities with the one person who could always inject a layer of guilt or too much hope into a situation. It was hard enough to keep from being nervous, or from daydreaming about it too much. But now, as she searched through her closet for a dress, she almost wished that she had sisters, or could laugh and squeal with Dianne about the appropriate thing to wear. What did one put on for an occasion like this?

If she went with a really nice dress, she might be overdressed. If she went with a pair of slacks and a sweater, she might be too casual. Lynette flopped down on the bed and stared at the opened closet and then reached for the telephone.

"Hey, lady," she said when Dianne picked up, using an upbeat tone to belie her jitters. "Okay . . . now that you've twisted my arm and gotten me to go along with this bad idea, what am I supposed to wear? What's the dress code for this?"

"Getting excited, huh?" Dianne replied with an easy laugh.

"No," she countered. "Just want to—"

"Just want to make a good impression is what you want. Look, why don't you put on a nice long skirt, a pretty blouse or sweater, some ankle boots, and go with casual jewelry?"

Lynette let out her sigh of relief quietly. "Okay. I can do that." If Dianne were there, she would have hugged her. "But, logistically, how are we going to do this? I mean the connection?"

"You tell your mom you're hanging with me, drive over here, and park. Rick will meet his friend, Forster, over here and we'll all go in Rick's SUV—since it's big enough for all four of us to comfortably fit."

Another wave of relief swept through Lynette, because she wouldn't be riding alone with a perfect stranger and going to Dianne's house provided the perfect out. Her mother's radar wouldn't be alerted.

"Okay. That's cool," she said after a moment. "But promise me that if it gets tense, you'll get Rick to bring me to your house so I can get my car and jet."

"I promise," Dianne said, drawing out the words. "And, on the positive side, if things go really well, and you all want to extend the evening, you can call your mom from my house and tell her you're with me—I'll cover."

"That will not be necessary," Lynette immediately returned. The sheer thought of what Dianne was suggesting only made the butterflies in her belly take flight again.

"You never know . . ."

"This is a blind, *first date*. Trust me, I know."

"Okay, okay, okay, I'm sorry," Dianne giggled. "But you can *trust me* that after we do this movie-dinner thing, me and Rick are going to get out of dodge with the quickness. I haven't seen my honey all week . . . and well, it's been a very long week."

"Why do I feel like I'm back in high school?" Lynette asked, laughing and falling backward on the bed. She clutched the phone to her cheek and stared at the ceiling while Dianne giggled into her ear. At thirty-five she wasn't supposed to be feeling like this, or needing a chaperone, or advice about what to wear! She was an accomplished career woman, had even been married before, and now she was trying to sneak out on a date like the old days, keeping her mom at bay, and wondering whether or not some male creature would find her witty, attractive, and worth calling after their first platonic encounter.

"Will you get off the phone and get dressed, then get your butt over here?" Dianne chided. "Don't worry. It'll be fun and he'll like you just fine, and you'll like him."

"Easy enough for you to say," Lynette sighed and sat up, recalibrating her mind to a new look and the choices her closet presented. "All right, I'm gone."

Forster looked over the seat of his Ford Taurus and gave his daughters in the back a steely warning. "All right, y'all. Listen. I want you to play nice, and not give Miss Carol or Miss Sharon any trouble. Okay?"

"Dere gonna be other kids to play with, right?" The youngest one seemed oblivious to his admonishment and was only eager to get the show on the road. "Can't we go in now, Daddy? It's cold out here in the car."

"Do they have girls or boys?" The older of the two asked. "I don't want to be stuck over here with some dumb old boys all night—and why can't we go to the movies with you and Uncle Rick, anyway?"

Two sets of eyes stared back at him, making him look away. His line of vision scanned the block for Rick's black SUV, and when he spotted it, he relaxed a bit. In truth, he hadn't thought of the answers to the kids' questions, which was perhaps why he hadn't broached the subject until midday. "All I know is that they have children your ages, Rebecca. And regardless of whether they're boys or girls, I want you all to be on your best behavior. Understood?"

"Yes, Daddy," his daughters replied in a dejected chorus.

"Good. Then, let's go in," he said with relief, glad that his daddy-voice was able to return some semblance of control and authority to the situation. Without looking at them as he got out of the car and came around to let the children out, all of his worries fused with the knot in his stomach. He should have followed his first mind. His buddy had no idea of the ripple effect that this little double date could have in his household, with the subsequent and ongoing questions he'd have to field and answer later. Then what? This was a really bad idea.

"Que pasa!" Rick boomed, opening the door and gathering up the girls in his arms as they stepped over the threshold.

"Uncle Rick," they squealed, giggling as he tickled them and made zerbert kisses against their necks.

Forster stood behind the fray and allowed his police assessment free reign. Nice environs, looked safe. Family pictures on the mantle. Three other children—two twin girls Rachel's age, and an older boy who seemed to be about Rebecca's age. PlayStation in progress on the tube. "Hey, man," he intoned flatly toward Rick when he stood up. "Whatcha know good?"

"Relax," Rick said with an easy laugh. "Come 'ere, Donell. Come on over, Tasha and Tanay—meet Mr. Forster and my two goddaughters, Rachel and Rebecca."

The children surveyed each other with timid suspicion, and Rachel held on to Rick's waist.

"I bet you have some dolls that Rachel might like to see," Rick hedged, trying to get the youngsters to warm up to each other as he helped Rachel out of her coat.

"I got some Barbies," one of the twins murmured.

"How come y'all look alike?" Rachel quipped.

"We're twins," the other twin giggled. "People mix us up all the time."

Rachel looked at them, giggled, glanced at her father and uncle, and then followed behind the two carbon copies that had immediately fascinated her—asking a hundred questions about their phenomenon as they skipped away. But Rebecca stayed put. Rick gave Forster a knowing glance, then interjected.

"Yo, Donell," Rick teased. "I told you that one day I was gonna find somebody who could whip your butt at that game you got on. See, me, I'm old, and I work all day—but my goddaughter, Rebecca, got my back." He looked at Rebecca and gave her a sly wink. "Five dollars says you can take homeboy."

"Five dollars!" Rebecca continued to stare at her uncle with her mouth opened.

"Yeah," Rick said coolly, producing the bill and waving it before the older children, who were now intrigued with the challenge. "If it's a draw, then that's two-fifty each. But, to the victor goes the spoil. No cheating, though—and no fighting."

"I'ma whip her behind, Mr. Rick. Ain't no girl gonna beat me."

Both men laughed as the boy folded his arms over his chest and Rebecca's hands went to her hips.

"I'll blow you away. You don't know who you're dealing with," Rebecca fussed, following behind her adversary as she took off her coat and dropped it on the sofa.

"See, it's in the DNA, brother," Rick laughed. "The battle of the sexes starts from day one."

"Thanks, man," Forster replied in earnest.

"Ain't nothin' to it, but to do it. Kids are easy, bro. It's the women that's hard."

Forster could only nod, and his ears remained trained on the other sounds in the house.

"Sharon is in the back getting together some popcorn and junk for the kids to munch on—pizza should be here in a little bit. Carol will be down in a minute, she went upstairs to feed and change the baby. And, as usual, Dianne is in the process of getting dressed."

Again, sudden relief swept through Forster. He needed a moment to take in the whole scene in waves. If he'd had to meet and greet everyone at once, it would have been system overload.

"You nervous?" Rick teased, going to sit in a chair in the dining room.

"Naw, man. Everything's cool," Forster lied, following his friend to take a seat.

"Then why don't you take off your coat and act like you're staying a while? Women getting dressed and ready is not something to wait on with your coat on, ya know."

"True dat," Forster said, trying to sound casual by the use of slang. He took off his trench coat and folded it over the back of a dining room chair and sat down.

"So, this is Forster?" A short, plump woman with a wide grin intoned as she entered the room with a tray of goodies for the children. "Hi, I'm D's big sister, Sharon. Your girls are as cute as they can be."

"Thank you, Sharon. Pleased to meet you," Forster said, standing and extending his hand. "I appreciate your watching the girls for a few hours—and just call me or let me know if they give you any trouble." He rummaged in his wallet to produce a piece of paper and grabbed a pen from his inside jacket pocket and proceeded to quickly scribble down his full name and cell phone number.

Sharon accepted it as he handed it to her, allowing her eyes to rove over him in a way that made him slightly uncomfortable. She had kind brown eyes that matched her hair, which was pulled into a scrunch. The twinkle in her eyes seemed to match her mischievous mouth, upturned at the corners in a pout, and she wore a too-tight, hot-pink sweat suit that showed off her ample, curvaceous figure. If this was the older sister, then he could appreciate why his buddy had been blown away. It was easy to imagine what Sharon had once looked like BC—before children.

"Chile," Sharon offered with an easy chuckle, "I have a hardheaded son and twins—your girls cannot do any more damage to my nerves than my own. Don't worry. They'll be just fine."

Her warm, homey demeanor made him relax and smile. As he sat back down with Rick and she paced away, he briefly studied her. That was all he'd wanted—a person who loved family to share his life with.

"Ooh, Rick, why didn't you tell me your friend was this fine?"

Taken aback, Forster turned and stood as a young woman approached through the dining room archway with an infant on her hip.

"You ain't right. I could've gone out with y'all—so, if this thing doesn't work tonight, I'll go next." The woman laughed, changed the baby to the other hip, and extended her hand in Forster's direction. "I'm Carol, the youngest sister. Pleased to meet you. You can come over here with Rick any time."

Rick laughed while Forster shook her hand, bewildered. This was a live one, and he didn't know what to say or do other than smile, return the nice-to-meet-you, and stand there staring back at the large gray eyes that unashamedly surveyed him from head to toe. He cast his gaze at his shoes as he became immediately aware that the woman before him wasn't wearing a bra, and her milk-laden, pendulous breasts had left a damp spot on her blouse.

Glimpsing at Rick for a rescue, he tried to make small talk with his buddy while also including Carol. "So, Dianne has two sisters? Family is good." It was trite, but he didn't know what else to say.

"Yeah, bro, there's three of them—all fine."

The compliment made Carol giggle, and she hoisted the baby up to wipe the drool from her tiny mouth.

"See, that's why we love us some Rick, around here. Too bad all his brothers are married."

Forster could only nod and discretely keep his line of vision away from the woman's blouse. "Rick's good people." He was at a loss for words. Time had become his enemy. When was Dianne coming down, and where the heck was her friend? Women.

"Well, I guess I'll go hurry my sister up, and let you all get going," Carol chuckled, issuing a wink in Forster's direction as she left the room. "I just came down here to be nosy."

Forster let out an almost-audible sigh when Carol left the room, and he sat down heavily in the chair after she was gone.

"Did you see 'em?" Rick whispered, leaning into his friend and speaking in a conspiratorial tone. "They are fine, man. All of 'em. Built like brick houses. Wait till you see Dianne, though."

Forster could only nod, as his patience was fraying along with his nerves. Whenever and wherever Rick was, it was always chaotic. It had been that way in his big, boisterous family when they were kids. His friend thrived on confusion. Yet, in his own, gloomy little home, it had been tense and quiet and lacking the joyful noise of sibling fights or interaction. Maybe that's why he indulged Rick so . . . he was like a brother and had included him in the family he'd never had. But all of that notwithstanding, there were limits—and his boy had gotten him trapped in a Twilight Zone adventure with his children as hostages.

"What time you think Dianne and her friend will be ready to pull out?" Forster cast his gaze at the kids playing in the living room, knowing full well that he couldn't just scoop up the girls and jet now like he wanted to. He'd have to explain to them, explain to Rick, and explain to two sisters, then Rick's girlfriend. . . . He rubbed his hands over his jawline and briefly shut his eyes.

"Chill, man. Relax. It'll be worth the wait."

"For you, maybe. You'll be taking your known date home tonight. Me, I'll be coming back here after whatever goes down, to pick up sleepy children, carry them to the car if they're asleep, carry them up the steps when I get home, undress them, put them in bed, then clean the house after my mom wrecked it on her at-home-alone-binge, and then have to get up in the morning when they get up to fix breakfast. You owe me, boss, for real, for real."

Rick smiled and put his hand on his friend's shoulder. "Consider it an investment."

"An investment? In what?"

"Okay. If things go well, and you like her and she

likes you, the time and aftermath with the kids will be an investment."

"Like I said—in what?"

"In getting you something to knock that chip off your shoulder."

"Man, I told you," Forster whispered. "I've got responsibilities now. I don't have time to be chasing tail. I'm just doing this because you wouldn't let sleeping dogs lie, and you wanted me to give you my opinion on your woman. That's it."

"Yeah, all right," Rick said with a wink. "But wait until you see her friend. If you still feel that way after you meet her, then I'll stand down and will even spring for a visit to your doctor, 'cause you'll need an eye exam if you can't see how fine she is."

"Whatever, man," Forster grumbled, glancing at his daughters and trying to figure out a way to extricate him and them from the evening.

The doorbell rang and Rick shot out of the chair, followed by Sharon and Carol, who had come rushing from the kitchen. The amount of commotion turned the coffee in Forster's stomach to acid, and he could feel the burn of it traveling up his esophagus. This had been a totally bad idea. By force of habit, he found himself standing up, expecting a woman to appear.

"Damn—just the pizza man," Rick fussed as he returned to the room after paying for the pies and giving them to Carol and Sharon.

Children's voices rang out as a small army ran into the kitchen behind the spicy smells. The brief hiatus from so many pairs of eyes glimpsing him every few minutes made his shoulders drop a few inches.

"Remember, dude, I had seven younger brothers and sisters. I know how to clear out a room, and I'm not above bribes or food drops. If I didn't learn how to divert attention, I woulda never got none in high school. Chill. I got this watch. We cool. The babes will be here soon and we can jet."

Forster nodded, smiling despite his original determination not to. Rick Sanchez was a pure madman . . . but very wise when it came to operational family dynamics. On that note, the brother bordered on genius, and had a heart of gold to go with it. The brief break in the action, and the reduced intensity of the family's scrutiny, did help considerably.

"I'm cool," Forster finally said, taking a seat again at the table. But he watched the front door like a cat watches a mouse hole, and then he glanced down at his Timex.

"She'll be here. Chill." Rick soothed, then jumped to his feet again when the doorbell rang. Only Sharon followed by Carol exited the kitchen, and with a much slower gait, biting pizza as they held paper plates to catch the oil running from their slices as they walked.

"Hi, I'm Ricardo. Come on in. Dianne is upstairs getting dressed. Nice to finally meet you."

Although the way the door opened blocked his view, he could tell by the way Rick had used his formal name, and by the way his buddy's voice had gone into suave, lady-killer smooth, that whatever was on the other side of the door had to be a knockout. They'd been friends long enough that he could get that much from the brief exchange, and it made his palms go moist.

Female squeals also greeted the mystery female blocked from his view, as a thinly coded exchange of finger snaps, *uhmmms,* and laughter emanating from the two sisters he could see now waylaid the person at the door.

"Come in here, sistah! D did real good," Sharon exclaimed.

"Ooh, girl, get your butt in here, chile!" Carol said through a bite of pizza and giggles.

Forster felt the blood drain from his brain. It was definitely possible to die of embarrassment.

A timid form emerged from behind the door as it slammed shut and Rick turned the locks. He could only stare at her. Wow . . .

A pair of big, doe-brown eyes set in a café-au-lait face surveyed him briefly before lush black lashes lowered over them, and a soft, sultry voice said, "Hello," from a lush, perfectly bronzed mouth.

"Hi, I'm Forster . . . nice to meet you," he stammered, still stunned by the lovely creature that had just appeared.

She looked up shyly and tucked a stray, dark brown curl behind her ear. The color of it glistened with natural highlights and looked as soft as the long, brown velvet coat she wore. "I'm Lynette," she murmured, moving her tall, graceful body closer toward him and removing her kid gloves to extend her hand.

The silence in the room was deafening as her soft palm slid into his and sent an electric current up the length of his arm. Jesus, this woman was fine. Her light scent wafted into his nostrils and he swallowed as he tried to appear calm while shaking her hand and issuing her a smile in return.

"Have you ladies decided on what you want to go see?" He'd asked the question before his brain could consult his mouth, simply because he'd wanted to hear her voice again. He watched and studied her face, totally absorbed by the way her eyes were rimmed with the barest hint of liner, making them smoky at the corners. Her skin almost seemed luminous, somehow mysteriously made radiant by a means only women knew.

"Oh, I really haven't thought about it," she replied. "It's just nice to get out with some friends and have a good time."

Check point. She wasn't fussy, and hadn't been out in a while—clue.

"Well, Rick and I will be happy to take you ladies to see whatever you ultimately decide upon."

His intestines were wrapping themselves in knots.

"Okay," she said easily. "Maybe I ought to go up and check on D, to be sure we don't miss the first shows." Then she was gone; whisked away through the kitchen door by Dianne's two sisters.

"Don't wag your tail too hard, dog—or drool on yourself. Heel. Sit. Stay." Rick commanded with a deep chuckle. "She fine, ain't she?"

"Yeah, man," Forster admitted as he slowly sat. "I owe ya."

Four

"Well?" Carol giggled as they piled into the kitchen, nearly dragging Lynette by her arm.

"Shush," Sharon warned as the children looked up from their own conversation and pizza, "take it upstairs in D's room."

Lynette glanced at the children nervously, giving each of the twin girls a kiss on the forehead and avoiding their greasy hands and mouths and she cuffed Donell and gave him a kiss on the cheek. The two quiet children sitting next to Sharon's brood were not lost on her.

"This is Ms. Lynette," Carol said to the two additions at the family table. "She's a friend of all of ours, and my sister Dianne's best friend—but she's my little bird's godmother." She handed Lynette the drooling infant, a gesture that seemed to relax considerably the wary children. As if by instinct, Carol obviously understood that Lynette might appear less threatening, and like the other moms in the room, by merely holding the baby. The two women exchanged a knowing glance.

"Now how could I forget you, peach-pie?" Lynette laughed as the baby went right for her tiny gold hoops. "Nice to meet you, ladies," she added, addressing the quiet little girls. "I'm Lynette."

"Hi, I'm Rachel," the younger of the two said with a mouthful of pizza. "You're pretty."

"Thank you, honey." The child's comment left her without much else to say, and she offered the infant in her arms a finger to grab on to versus an earring.

"Are you going to the movies, too, with my dad and Uncle Rick?"

"Yup, and what's your name?" Lynette said as cheerfully and as casually as she could to the older child, who studied her hard.

"Rebecca," the older child replied in a whisper. "My friends call me Becky, though."

Lynette was going to say that one day she hoped to call her Becky, and then thought better of it. What was she doing? "That's a pretty name—and I bet you have a lot of friends."

When the little girl smiled shyly and looked down, Carol rescued Lynette. "Give me puddin'," she said with a chuckle, "before she ruins you, and go on up to see what's taking D so long. That chile is so slow!"

Without hesitation Lynette gave up the baby and waved at the children, then bolted for the back staircase. Heaven help her. It was the same guy . . . the guy crossing the street. The guy with kids! Dianne didn't tell her she was going out with a guy that had little kids. This man had to have a wife. This was such a bad idea. She was going to kill D!

"D, you didn't tell me this man had a wife and children when you set this thing up—are you mad?" Lynette tore through the bedroom doorway and shut it as she whispered hard through her teeth.

"Re—lax," Dianne cooed, blotting her lipstick and looking at herself from behind. "You think this long, red knit dress accentuates the positive?" Dianne ran her hands over her bottom and peeped over her shoulder to glimpse her form from a rear view, then turned to face Lynette.

"Relax? Relax? Are you crazy?" Lynette began walking in a tight circle wringing her hands as she did so. "I wasn't sure when I walked in, if it was him, I mean. But then when I hit the kitchen and saw the kids—I knew. Oh, girl, I can't go out with a married man with his kids sitting at the table eating pizza with your nieces and nephew. It's so tacky. *It just isn't done.* This is, this is—"

"Crazy," Dianne giggled, hoisting up her boobs in her Wonderbra, and glancing in the mirror with a satisfied grin. "If I do say so myself, Rick is going to have a coronary when he sees me in this."

"Are you hearing what I'm say, girlfriend? Dianne—earth to Dianne, come in!"

"Relax. He isn't married . . . you saw him before?"

"Yes," Lynette hissed. "I was on my way to the gym and he was walking the children to school, and I saw him. They look too clean and neat and hair all done up not to have some woman on the scene."

Dianne rubbed her chin and then went back to the mirror to check on and primp her hair, glancing down at her four-inch platforms as though trying to decide on a shoe change. "Nah . . . Rick said he was divorced and their mother died in a bad car accident, or something. Wrapped herself around a tree after a binge, and the man's been in semimourning—I say semi, because he was divorced, after all. But, the kids did lose their mom. No current woman is on the scene, that's the good news."

Lynette could not respond for a moment and stood positively slack jawed before her friend. "How can you be so casual with information like that, D? The man, obviously, has major *issues*. And, no doubt, those poor little girls have serious issues . . ." She sat down slowly on the side of the bed.

"Look, chile, we've all got major issues. I didn't get much else from Rick other than the fact that he isn't violent, hasn't been on a date in a long time, and has a good job. He's on the force with Rick, so he's not a drug user—you know they pee test regularly down there. So—"

"So, you set me up on a blind date with a person who's still in mourning? Jesus H. Christ, Dianne . . ."

Dianne spun around from the mirror and placed her hands on her hips. Her red talons perfectly matched her dress, and she stood wide legged enough to open the slit in it to expose her black nylons. Frozen and pressed curls and giant gold-hoop earrings bobbed with the rhythm of her voice as she fussed. "Girl, the fact is the man is fine, has two cute kids, and no woman on the scene—I am not a miracle worker. Now, can we just go out, have some fun, and can you for once stop projecting so far into the future that you miss the moment? Maybe a grandma, or some auntie helps him—like your mom would if you were in the same situation, okay. Chill, and stop stressin' so we can go." Dianne grabbed her clutch and gave herself the once over again in the mirror, then glared at Lynette, but her mouth was a wide grin as she did so.

"All right, all right, all right," Lynette conceded, laughing at herself in the process. "You're right. You win. Maybe I jumped to conclusions. As long as you are sure he's not married?"

"No, he's not married," Dianne snapped, playfully sucking her teeth and rolling her eyes again. "Dag. No wonder you never get none."

She was totally grateful that Rick and Dianne had carried on with their comical banter in the car, thus saving her from having to pull small talk from the man of few words beside her. Although he seemed pleasant enough, he had nothing to say. From time to time she glimpsed him from the corner of her eye, and although his expression seemed relaxed, there was still an undercurrent of tension about him. But, Dianne hadn't lied. Rick was a knockout, and nice, and funny . . . and his friend was so handsome that it was hard to look at him.

The man smelled good, too. Although she couldn't place the cologne, it had a simplistic, woody scent . . . and he was conservative in dress. She liked that. A basic dark, houndstooth jacket, turtleneck sweater, a pair of pleated slacks, nice loafers. Yeah . . . clean-shaven, with a deep, dark chocolate complexion—ruggedly handsome. Dark, penetrating eyes, with heavy, black lashes, and a dimple in his right cheek when he smiled. But the body . . . Lynette sent her gaze out the window and refolded her hands in her lap. Thank God they could make small talk while waiting in line, and then wouldn't have to talk during the flick. Then, when they went for a bite to eat, they could rehash the movie, and then go home. She could do this.

He could do this. His buddy's crazy talk in the car helped considerably . . . after all, what could he say to a woman who looked like the one sitting next to him? Every time he tried to open his mouth, he had to swallow hard to keep his voice from cracking. Damn, the woman was all-that-and-a-bag-of-chips fine. This time, Rick hadn't lied. Plus, he liked her vibe. Conservative. Beautiful, classy . . . the way her hair was just a natural profusion of soft curls, and not too much makeup. . . . Everything about her seemed so soft. The way her fawn-colored sweater covered her and seemed to blend in with her skin, and the way her long, black knit skirt just hugged her nicely rounded hips and what had to be long, graceful legs beneath. She was so opposite from her friend Dianne, who on the other hand was short, bombshell curvaceous, and loud. This woman was soft-spoken, tall, and didn't even wear nail polish on her long, tapered hands. A natural beauty.

Forster sent his gaze out the window to keep him from staring at her. How did a brother corner a sister like this? What was the protocol? Did he ask her for her number at the end of the evening, and before they got back to the kids? Did she even like kids, and would that send him to the bottom of her prospect list? Besides, he didn't want to ask her for contact info in front of on-lookers because if he got shot down, then there was the not-too-small matter of public humiliation.

And, if he did take her out and ever wanted to bring her home, how was he going to arrange that? She didn't seem like the baby-let's-go-to-a-hotel type. His place was a pigsty, generally, when he came home from leaving his mother alone—then there was the case of his mother. That situation, all by itself, would be enough to turn off a woman. Plus, he'd never dated around the girls. What would their take on this be? How would they react? And how did one do a first night in a house with one's mother and two little kids? Scratch it, he told himself. She was just a nice diversion, and a chance to see that he still had a pulse. Oh yeah, he wasn't dead.

Trying to figure all of this out while making small talk was as frustrating as going window-shopping for a new car at the dealer's when broke. A brother could look at all the new, shiny, revved-up models and dream—but that was it. He set his jaw hard and kept his gaze out the window. Yeah, he could dream about her, that is, if he could ever get to sleep after seeing her. Why did his supposed boy do this to him?

"Okay, ladies, how about if you get the seats, and me and Forster will get the popcorn and sodas?"

"That could work," Dianne said brightly, giving Rick a kiss as the men blended into the end of the concession line.

"What would you like to drink?" Forster asked quietly, glancing at Lynette and then up at the board.

"A small Coke would be fine . . . do you need us to stick around to help you all carry it?"

"Girl, they got it," Dianne said with a wink in Rick's direction. "Let's go get some good seats. They'll be back in a few."

Once the women were out of earshot, Rick leaned in to Forster with a broad smile. "So?"

"You didn't lie, boss."

"And, Dianne?"

"Real nice, cool family . . . and, a brick house."

Rick laughed and gave Forster a high five.

"See why I've been AWOL?"

"Yeah, bro."

Rick stopped and looked at his friend hard. "Then . . . man . . . why you sound so down in the mouth?"

Forster shook the weight of his reality off and chuckled. "I hate window-shoppin', is all."

Rick nodded, glancing at the women's retreating forms. "Yeah . . . sorta like going to the Porsche dealership and having only enough to buy a bug."

"No lie," Forster admitted, his gaze now following the women as they slipped around the corner and vanished.

* * *

"So?" Dianne squealed as they found four seats together and threw their coats on two of them.

"I don't think he likes me," Lynette admitted, becoming morose as the words slipped out of her mouth.

"How can you say that?—you two barely said two words to each other."

"That's the point. Every time I tried to start up a conversation, he'd respond with a one-word answer. Not a good sign."

"Well, the man just ain't been out in the world in a while, and neither have you. Maybe he just doesn't know what to say and is warming up?"

Lynette carefully considered her friend's words and nodded. "Maybe you're right . . . but maybe I should have worn something a little more—"

"You look great. You also look like you, not like somebody you aren't."

"I suppose I'll take that as a compliment?" Lynette laughed and relaxed. Only Dianne could give a backhanded compliment and make it sound endearing.

"You don't want to play games and send the wrong signal, right?"

"Right," Lynette concurred.

"Then?" Dianne held her hands open and shrugged. Suddenly her smile broadened and she ducked her head down and covered her mouth, stifling a loud giggle. "Oh, my bad . . . my serious bad. I understand, now. Girl, don't worry."

"What are you talking about, you nut?" Lynette laughed with her friend despite her peevish tone.

"Tell the truth. This man done lit a fire in your I-don't-need-a-man-to-define-me belly. You done scoped out those buns of steel, that six-foot-two body of life and those cinder blocks in his chest under his sweater—and you're thinking about that deep, rich,

Hershey's chocolate skin, and those size-twelve shoes the brother is sportin' . . . and them big hands, and you're—"

"I am not," Lynette defended. "Just shut up," she urged, giving way to a round of chuckles. "Zip it."

"Yes you are, liar, liar pants on fire! Admit it. You're trying to figure out the logistics as we speak." Dianne's expression became comical as she mimicked Lynette and pointed at her chest. "Hmm . . . at my house, how would I get around mom; at his house, little kids and possible other family members . . . at what point do I stop saying no, because if my girl wasn't here, I'd be on this man in the dark in the theater. No. Not cool. Public exposure is a crime, and he is a cop, after all. Dianne's house is too chaotic, but a hotel for the first night is so tacky—and this one is a keeper, so I can't go down the path of tackaaaay, and—"

"Girl, stop!" Lynette pleaded, now doubling over and wiping her eyes. "Ever since we were kids you'd get me into trouble, then I'd be the one left holding the bag."

"You did think about it, though, didn't you?"

Lynette nodded and covered her face with her hands as she kept laughing. "I'll be dreaming about it for weeks, what are you talking about?"

"So, D did good, did she not?"

"Miss D did very, very well, so far. All right. Now leave me alone."

"And, is Rick all that, or what?"

Lynette took her hands away from her face and gave her girlfriend a sly wink. "Miss D did very, very well all the way around."

The two exchanged a high five and giggled some more as they saw their dates approaching.

"Not a word," Dianne warned with a grin.

"Not a mumblin' word," Lynette agreed.

* * *

His arm had ached with the inexplicable need to put it around her shoulders all during the movie—but he didn't. He didn't know her that well, and she hadn't given him any signal that he had permission to get that familiar with her yet. But seeing how comfortably Dianne had leaned into Rick, and the way they'd shared little intimate comments, just opened the empty hole within him. God, it must be nice to have someone to claim like that . . .

The woman sitting next to him in the booth seemed so relaxed, and so sure of herself. The light in the establishment turned her pretty skin a warm, rosy tone that almost seemed to match her gentle laugh and the rich sound of her voice. Every time she interjected a comment, her voice went through his skeleton—unlike Dianne's, which at times sounded like fingernails down a blackboard. Lynette's just seeped into his bones and vibrated. Now the place where her thigh occasionally brushed his was on fire. It was hard to breathe and smile and be cool.

"Okay, okay, I'll grant you that violence in movies has an impact on society—but, ladies, a good flick needs action," Rick argued.

"Now, do not get Lynne started on a sociopolitical soapbox," Dianne teased as she scooped up a nacho and began munching. "Men always want to see something blowing up in the movies."

"Well, what's wrong with that? I like a lot of action, or I get bored. You do, too. At least that's what you told me last week." Rick beamed as Dianne slapped his arm and giggled.

"Boy, shut up. See, now you didn't have to go there."

Lynette laughed easily and looked down at the mushrooms stuffed with crabmeat and selected one. Rick and Dianne's exchange, and the overtly sexual tone between them that had been building all night, made her cheeks warm, and she didn't know what to say. She searched her mind for a witty segue to include Forster in the conversation, while distancing it from anything too physical. But every time he spoke his voice connected to a forgotten, yet smoldering ember within her, and her stomach did flip-flops, making it hard to respond to the man.

When her leg accidentally touched his beneath the table, she thought she'd jump out of her skin. It was like brushing against smooth, polished stone. When Rick made him belly laugh, and the dimple in his cheek dented in, and his thick, soft lips parted to show off a dazzling, perfect white smile, she almost coughed and nearly choked on her wine. But she was cool, though. Lord, where did this man come from?

"So, what kind of beat do you handle at the paper—given that Dianne claims you have a soapbox? Political news?"

He'd actually asked her a direct question. His gaze was so intense when he finally did so that it held hers for a moment. And what a redirect! The man had a gentlemanly save to the direction of the conversation. Touché for the man of few words!

"I wish," she said with a slight grin. "I do crime—the local crime beat. I guess we're in a similar line of work?"

He could only nod momentarily as she stared at him with those gorgeous, penetrating eyes that looked all the way down to his soul. She seemed to be taking in shallow sips of air, which made her breasts rise and fall in a hypnotic rhythm that he dared not succumb to but could only study from his peripheral vision as he reached for his beer.

"I just shoot the photos after the bad guys have come in." It was the only answer he could muster while looking at her.

"You're a forensic photog?"

When she gasped and smiled more broadly, and her eyes sparkled with appreciation, he took a swig of his beer. The gasp had run down his spine and nearly made him shiver.

"It's not glamorous, trust me."

"My boy is the best in the business," Rick offered, glancing between the two and then back at Dianne.

He didn't know how to signal to Rick to back off. It had taken him all night to muster up the courage to get her attention and go for it, and he was rusty . . . so he didn't need to lose the scent of the hunt—not on the first howl.

"Really?" she replied, her line of vision leaving his and going to Rick's.

"They call him to log everything that goes on in the Delaware Valley. The brother has the eye."

Bad move, Rick. He mentally cursed his friend's timing. Then her smile and return gaze rewarded Forster.

"Do you shoot anything else, when not doing crime-lab stuff?" She waited and toyed with her thin, gold necklace. "I only ask because I write during the day for the paper, but have my own projects that have nothing to do with crime and gore—keeps me balanced."

It was like a gift from on high . . . a connection, something to talk about, and she'd let him in.

"Yeah . . . I have a collection of black and white shots of people in neighborhoods, people overcoming odds, and people just living life. I started working on it to cleanse my palate after some of the stuff I see during the day."

"I know what you mean," she added in brightly, leaning closer to him, her expression now more open and solely focused on him. "You ever think of putting your work in a real nice coffee-table book? I know some folks in publishing who might be able to do that, especially if you've got some significant community shots."

"My girl can write her butt off, too," Dianne interjected. "You should read some of her poetry and her haikus. She's deep. Very deep."

What was Dianne doing? Lynette's mind screamed out as her smile remained frozen on her face. The man had thawed out, she'd found something that he was really interested in, that she loved too, and that they could talk about—and now her girl was stepping all over it in an effort to help.

"You write? I mean," he chuckled, "of course you write—but not for the press? I know you said that, but, well . . ."

Help him out, girl, her mind chanted. Help the brother out.

"Yeah, I do. It's what I do for relaxation."

"Funny, I go out with my camera and shoot when I need to relax."

"See, here we are sitting with two artists, D," Rick chuckled, swallowing his beer and grabbing a Buffalo wing.

Not now, his mind yelled at his friend. Chill, brother.

"Maybe I can show you some of my black and whites sometime, to get the honest appraisal from a person who has an eye? I mean, before I'd consider sending my work off to a publisher . . . I'd want somebody objective to look at it."

He held his breath as he watched her lids lower and

her beautiful lashes dusted her cheeks. Please, he prayed, don't anybody else say a word, except her.

"Tell you what," she murmured, gathering up her purse and digging into it. "How about if I let you read some of my pieces when you show me your work? Fair exchange?"

His heart was slamming against his ribcage as she produced a small white card and a pen and put her home telephone number on the back of it.

"Sounds fair," he remarked as casually as one could while battling dry mouth. "Like they say, fair exchange is no robbery."

Damn right. He wasn't that rusty after all.

"Good," she said with a smile as he reached into his jacket breast pocket, produced a business card, and borrowed her pen.

"Yeah, y'all, it's *all* good," Dianne giggled as she sipped her drink. "I need to fix my face and hit the ladies' room. Lynne, you comin'?"

Forster moved over and stood so Lynette could exit the booth. He felt as though a ten-ton weight had been lifted from his shoulders, and he sat down hard after the women had walked away.

"Why do they always go to the bathroom in, twos, man? Answer me that? You never see two guys ask each other when they have to pee."

Rick laughed and shook his head. "You obviously never had sisters, dude. It's a ritual. They travel in pairs. We don't have to go to the bathroom together, because we can work out whatever we wanna talk about while they're gone."

"Oh." Forster finished his beer and looked into the bottom of the glass.

"Big move, brother. Good sign. You're in."

"Think so?"

"Yeah. D just went to make sure that she doesn't get spooked after making the first move—since you was taking so long to flush her out of the bushes, hombre."

"I couldn't get a word in edgewise around y'all. You can't just rush up on a sister like that."

"True, but you also can't let her get away. So, now what?"

"Beats me."

"Think long, think wrong, bro. Call her, now that you got the number—don't sleep on this."

Forster looked toward the ladies' room and picked up a nacho.

"Yeah. I won't sleep on it. Not this one."

Five

Sitting in front of Dianne's house in Rick's vehicle had not only returned them all to the place where the evening adventure had begun, but also to that awkward place where no one was quite sure of what to do. What was protocol here?

It was obvious that Dianne and Rick were now straining to make small talk. The sexual tension between them had begun to escalate markedly ever since the couples had left the restaurant. Forster seemed to be holding his breath for a moment as he stared at her, and then glanced up to the house. What was that about? It was as though he were torn between the kids and prolonging . . . no. . . . A tiny tremor claimed her, now making her hold her own breath for a second before releasing it. She was imagining things!

"I want to thank all of you guys for a really fun evening," Lynette said in a chipper voice, attempting to break the awkward silence and announcing her departure.

"Don't you guys want to come in for some coffee or some dessert or something?"

Lynette leaned forward from her position in the backseat and gave Dianne a peck on the cheek, declining the insincere offer. "No, sweetie. You know my mom is probably pacing a hole in the floor, and besides, I have a story deadline due for Monday. I need to get some rest."

Dianne nodded and returned Lynette's kiss. It was best this way. Everything could end on a high note. Plus, it was as plain as day to everyone in the car that, while Dianne had spoken, Rick hadn't taken his eyes off her, nor had her friend stopped stroking the nape of his neck. Could she blame her girl? Could she blame them?

"Rick, Forster," Lynette added in her most professional yet warm tone, "it was truly a fun evening, and I thank you gentlemen for including me." She exchanged a handshake with Rick and held his palm a moment and smiled. "You take good care of my best friend—everything she said about you is true."

Rick beamed and leaned over to offer Lynette a kiss on her cheek. "Thanks, sis. An endorsement from you is worth more than you know. And, she was right about you, too. Good people, through and through."

"Forster," Lynette quipped, adjusting her purse over her shoulder as she extended her hand and got ready to exit the car. "It was a real pleasure, and I hope I get to see those award-winning photos some time." When his palm slid into hers, she steeled herself for the electricity that was sure to surge up her arm. "You take care of those two precious angels in there." Then she quickly pulled away and opened the door.

"I will, but hang on," Forster said with a chuckle. "This might be the new millennium, but chivalry is not all together dead. At least let me walk you down the block to your car?"

She waited as he thumped Rick on the shoulder and got out on his side upon receiving her nod. When he came to her side of the car and closed the door, she had to laugh at herself.

"I'm sorry. It's just been a long time since anybody did that." She could feel the smile widen on her face despite her attempts to seem ultracool. It was nice that he also smiled back in a wide grin.

"Been a long time since I've done it, too . . . which was why I was slow to the draw. My apologies."

They both chuckled as they made it halfway down the block and she stood by the driver's side of her car. Somehow she could tell that they were laughing at more than it just being a long time since they'd experienced dating rituals.

"I really enjoyed myself tonight, too," he finally said as they shared another awkward moment while she hunted for her keys. "I just hope my girls left Dianne's house in one piece."

Lynette looked up into his easy expression, noting how it softened when he talked about his children—just like it had when he'd briefly exposed his creative work. "Trust me," she said with a smile, "your girls couldn't have done a thing in that house that hasn't already been done to it. Dianne and I marvel all the time about how it's still standing, after she and her sisters and I put a hurting on it when we were kids, then twins and a knothead, adorable nephew—whew!"

They both laughed again. "Yeah, boys, I hear tell, are rough and tumble. The girls are a trip enough . . . between bickering, hair, and clothes, what do you do but love them?"

Again a silence fell between them, but it wasn't so strained this time. This man was giving her information. Clues that she knew he wanted to give her, without coming right out to say so. Or, was she just reading more into the benign statement than warranted?

"Well, it was really fun . . . I hope we get a chance to try this again," she finally offered as she inserted the key in the lock and turned it, this time waiting for him to reach for the door to open it for her. They both grinned when he did so, and she hopped into her Subaru, but allowed him to shut the door. Only when he stepped back did she turn on the engine, and then wave as she pulled off.

He stood in the vacated parking space for a moment, watching her car vanish. Twice now she'd given him an invitation to connect with her again. Trouble was, how would he arrange that? He took his time and leisurely strolled back to Rick's black SUV, noting that the windows were steamed up. Okay, now what? He didn't know Dianne well enough to just knock on the window, but being almost midnight, he definitely needed to get into her house to collect his kids. He opted to rap on the back window and walk up the front steps.

When the passenger-side window came down, Dianne's flustered expression made his line of vision dart between the car and the front door.

"Er, uh, listen I'll just be a minute. I have to get the girls."

"Oh, yeah . . . the kids," Dianne said with a giggle as she peeped out of the car at him.

He could only shake his head as his buddy leaned over and gave him a sheepish look.

"Uh, I'll catch you later, man. Thanks a lot. Excellent evening."

"Yeah, man," Forster said with a smile, then waited as Dianne extricated herself from the SUV and scurried past him to open the door.

When they entered the house his eyes immediately went to the tangle of bodies on the sofa. Both of Dianne's sisters were dozing and watching a cable-station movie through half-closed eyes, Donell was fighting sleep and trying to act like he was awake while reclining in a La-Z-Boy chair under a big blanket, and Carol's infant was sprawled across her lap. His two girls and the twins had curled up on the sofa between the two women and were asleep. Dolls, board games, and parts of plastic toys were strewn everywhere, along with stray popcorn kernels, juice boxes, and cookies. It had obviously been one heck of an evening festival in there. And, despite the total chaos that the children had left the house in, the scene instantly made him relax. He smiled.

"They didn't give you too much trouble, I hope?" It was all he could offer as he glanced around the living room and Dianne's sisters yawned and smiled up at him.

"They were angels," Sharon said in a sleepy voice.

"They had a ball," Carol yawned again and then laughed. "Pure kid Heaven . . . and, what about Daddy?"

"I had a really good time," he answered in earnest. "Thanks Dianne, for suggesting the evening, and ladies, I don't know how to repay you for keeping my girls while I went out."

"No problem," Sharon said warmly. "Lynette is just like a sister to us, plus, me and Carol know what it's like to be on parental lockdown and not be able to go out."

"Yeah," he chuckled, going to collect the children's coats from the side of a stray chair. "Truth be told, I haven't been out in years." As soon as he'd made the admission, he wished he could have retracted it. Somehow, it was a little too personal, but in this setting, he oddly felt like family. There was a calm sense of completion that swept through him. This was indeed what he'd wanted all of his life. "Well, look, I don't do a half-bad job with kids—maybe I could take them with me, especially Donell, to some of the PAL activities . . . I mean, the Police Athletic League does a lot with kids during the year, and they might enjoy it?"

"Wow, Dianne . . . where did Rick find this one?" Carol crooned. "You sure you don't have a brother somewhere?"

Forster laughed, shook his head no, and shrugged off the quick dagger that went to his core at the mention of having a brother. Reginald Hamilton was no brother; he had been more like a vicious contender for his father's legacy. In that regard his halfbrother hadn't been a son anymore than his halfsister had been a daughter to their mutual father.

"I'd better get these girls out of here," he said quietly, struggling to get the coats onto two sleepy, immobile children. The adults all laughed as they flopped about and whined.

"Let me take the little one," Dianne offered, discretely collecting an overnight bag from inside the closet door. "I can carry the peanut, you take the long-legged load."

"She's heavy," Forster warned. "Just let me get the big one over my shoulder first, then if you help me hoist the little bird up, she naturally clings."

This time they all laughed as the two adults tried the contortion almost to no avail. Walking wide legged, Forster nodded to the two sisters, who seemed to be thoroughly enjoying his plight. "I bid you adieu, ladies," he said with a deep chuckle. "And I promise to return the favor soon."

Wobbling out the door with Dianne on his heels, he gave Rick a wink as his buddy leaned out the car window and waved at him.

"I'll catch up with you soon, man," Rick called behind him.

"Cool," Forster grunted, making his way down the street.

"Well at least you could go help your boy open the car door and get your goddaughters buckled up?" Dianne fussed as she paced behind Forster.

"I got it, I got it," Forster protested, even though what

he was saying made no sense. How the heck was he going to get his keys, much less manage the locks?

"My bad, dude. My bad. Hold up."

Rick jumped out of the car, fished into Forster's pockets for his keys, and opened the car door, helping him with the rag dolls he struggled with.

"I don't know what was on my mind, bro. Sorry."

Forster only smiled and let the comment slide, understanding full well what was on Rick's mind—nothing but Dianne. "It's cool."

Once the children had been stowed in the backseat and buckled in, Forster stood and stretched, and to his surprise, was kissed and hugged by Dianne.

"You are such a nice brother," she said wistfully. "I hope things work out for y'all."

Her honesty and excitement once again put him at a loss for words.

"She likes you, you know."

Why did he feel like he was back in high school, and why did what Dianne had just said given him such a rush?

"She's a very nice sister." That's all he could say.

"You like her, don't you?"

"D!" Rick fussed, pulling her against him. "Mind your business, woman, and let the man get his kids home out of the cold." He issued a wink to Forster, who chuckled in appreciation of the save.

"Yeah," Forster murmured, giving Dianne a sly wink. "Let her know how much, too."

"Ooh, see, *I told you* they'd be good together!"

Dianne did a little jig and spun around, making them laugh as Forster got into the car, turned on the ignition, and hit the lights.

Now the trouble was figuring out how not to like Lynette Graves so high-school hard.

* * *

Lynette was floating on air as she crept into the house, trying not to wake her mother as she tossed off her coat, turned off the downstairs lamp, and made her way to her bedroom. This evening had made her feel like a schoolgirl again, and it required an aftermath giggle fest. But, alas, her mother had never been one to share those kinds of moments without a serious sermon that would blow her natural high, and her best friend was otherwise indisposed.

She sighed as she slipped through the bedroom door and quietly hooked the lock. They'd already argued about the fact that she was going to be out late on a Saturday night, and probably wasn't going to make it to church again this Sunday. The two had lived together far too long for her not to know that her mother would come barging into her bedroom in the morning anyway, holding a cup of coffee and a plate of toast as her excuse for waking her.

The sudden sense of confinement made her want to grind her teeth. While she thanked God that she still had a mother who was warm and genuine, she also knew that it had become way past the time for her mother to begin to have her own life. Dianne had called it a codependent relationship at one point. As with most things, D was right. But how could she help the person who was so dear to her find a way to stop manipulating her life without hurting her? Now, sitting in the dark, as a grown woman, trying to keep the light from under her door from being spotted and hiding from her mom like a kid who'd sneaked in after curfew, she undressed slowly, silently, and with mixed emotions swirling in her head.

At first coming home and moving in with her mother

had been her refuge. It was balm to her tattered spirit after her husband had made a child with another woman and left. She'd told herself that she was coming home to help her mom after the storm, to provide for her now that her father was gone. But that was only half of the truth.

Lynette slipped on her nightgown after quietly dropping her clothes on the chair and removing her boots. What was the truth, then, really? That she had fibroids so bad that she couldn't easily conceive, if at all? That her self-important, record-label husband couldn't wait, and didn't want to go to fertility specialists; his fragile ego being too damaged by the prospect that something could be wrong with either of them . . . so much so that he needed to fall into another woman's arms and make a baby?

Lynette sat down on the bed carefully, ensuring that the mattress didn't make a sound, and slipped under the covers. Cool, crisp sheets caressed her and she hunkered down under them and pulled her pillows to her. Five years of ugliness in total. Two years of separation during a bitter divorce—during which time she'd had her heart ripped out while another woman got to have her husband's baby. Then she'd left the city and come home—home to her mother's open arms, comfort cooking, and safe but boring life. Three years of self-imposed, solitary confinement of her own choosing. Five years.

It was time for her to have some space. It was time for both her and her mother to heal. It was time for both of them to move on. That didn't necessarily mean a total move out of each other's lives—but they were two very different people, with different needs, and now they both needed some space to be those individuals. Why couldn't her mother just accept that without drama?

She let her breath out hard in despair and closed her eyes against the dampness forming in them. Her mother wasn't to blame . . . she was—just as Dianne had told her . . . just as her post-divorce therapist had once told her. She'd been the one who had allowed things to go on this way; she'd returned to become the child in the cocoon of her mother's protection again. So just like birthing pains . . . she might have to hurt her mother to get out of her womb, to try to sustain her life on her own again, and to cut the safe yet confining umbilical cord between them. The hurt would be done with care, if there had to be hurt. Separation, equidistance was healthy; smothering was not. She cringed at the thought of having to be reborn, and having to hurt her mother again in a long, protracted labor. Life had already hurt her mother to the bone.

But why did it have to be an either-or choice? Nature forced the issue of coming into the world with hard contractions, a cry for life upon a breath of air, and eventually a disconnecting of the placenta from the uterine wall, making the two that had been joined separate—however always bound by the relationship and experience of closeness they'd shared.

Oddly, that's what she'd wanted to share with a husband . . . her husband. What she'd dreamed of was being half of a team of two separate yet complete people, coming together as one, but with cosupportive, in-unison goals. She'd wanted a big, unruly family, one like Dianne's, with room enough for people to make mistakes, fight, and patch it up again afterward—with love never in question. Instead, she'd been robbed by betrayal and a situation that would never go away. A baby. Thus, a woman and a constant reminder of his affair, which would be a constant reminder of her own failing to do what she'd always taken for granted she could do: be a mother.

She clutched her pillow to her chest and buried her face in it. So much had been taken from her in such a short time, and still, even alone in the dark, she felt guilty for being angry with that. Yes, she was fortunate to have a job, to have good friends, to have a good mother, to have her health and strength and a home. . . . She repeated those words to herself like a mantra, and had done so every day since her life unraveled. She was not a direct victim of a terrorist-haunted world, and had only been a tertiary victim of that. Then why was she so tense and angry right now? Especially after such a wonderful evening out—which was also another blessing?

She focused her mind on the positive, and slowed her erratic inhales to deep, cleansing breaths. She would not be tense. She would not keep revisiting the failure of her marriage. She would not keep rehashing her frustrations about her mother. She would take ownership of her role in all of these issues. She would take control of her life, be firm, and not feed into guilt. She would concentrate on the things that made her happy. Tomorrow she would go running along the Kelly Drive, down Boathouse Row, past her favorite place—the Art Museum. She would not be held hostage to rage or haunting memories . . .

Forster Hamilton's smile came into view behind her closed lids. Mentally she replayed his deep, warm voice and shuddered as it sent ripples of anticipation through her. Her mind scavenged for every memory of the evening . . . the way he dressed, the way he smelled, the way he looked, every detail of the things he'd said and the expressions on his face when he'd spoken. The way he'd stood so close to her as she got into her car . . . that brief awkward moment that begged for a kiss that was too soon to be delivered.

As her mind wound around the thought of what a kiss from him might feel like, she felt her body respond to the fantasy. It had been so long since she'd even had a person to dream about . . . three years, plus two very angry ones made a total of five years without the luxury of human touch, of pleasure, of feeling like a full woman. Now that time was bearing against her inner thighs, spreading up to her moistened valley, burning a hole in her lower belly, forming goose bumps on her arms, and making her nipples sting in outrage about their neglect.

The gentle kiss she envisioned at curbside gave way to a more passionate one in her mind. Her tongue slid across her teeth, as she imagined what doing the same within Forster's might feel like. The mental kiss melted into his imaginary touch . . . his hands seemed so strong, yet gentle, and she fought against the urge to touch those points on her body that were now burning.

No. She would not go there. She'd overcome that need ever since men were no longer a part of her life, and her religious mother had taken up residence with her. There was no way she could release herself the way she wanted to with someone else in the house—especially her mom. The need to do that had ebbed while she was in New York, before she'd moved back to Philly, and she hadn't given in to those feelings for years. Three years, and counting. Giving in to that, being consumed with quenching that need, had only driven her out on ill-fated dates during her harrowing separation, and only left her depressed after she was done.

Work, exercise, wholesome healthy things were a positive outlet. She didn't need to go there or to torture herself with these thoughts.

Lynette cradled the pillow more tightly against her, trying once again to force her erratic breathing to a place of calm so that she could sleep. Forster was a nice man, and obviously a dedicated father. He was the kind of guy that her husband should have been, but wasn't. Renewed anger began to douse the flame of her arousal, and oddly that was relaxing. Yes, he was a good brother, indeed. Still, there were issues, logistics, children, and probably things she didn't even know about to get in the way of any possible relationship, much less passionate touching.

However, just the internal words alluding to his touching her made her shiver with anticipation. It was just a time thing, she told herself. If it hadn't been so long, the chemistry wouldn't be as strong. Three to five years . . . the words rang in her head like the sentences the judges on her reporter beat issued. Three to five years . . . her body screamed in defiance as she tried to ignore it. Three to five years, her hardened, distended nipples whispered as the pillow rubbed against them, making her catch and hold her breath for a moment. He's so handsome, her lower belly quivered in protest as she inhaled deeply, remembering his scent.

His thighs brushed against hers in her mind as she squeezed them together tight . . . just as they had under the table in the restaurant, where nobody else saw it, but they both undoubtedly felt it.

The memory made her hips begin to move ever so slightly against the edge of the long pillow despite her mental admonishment for them not to. Their arms had touched in the theater, the warmth emanating from his running up the length of hers, covering her left breast like a molten palm, forcing both her nipples to pout and sting during the entire movie, dampening her panties, making her squeeze her knees together hard, increasing her desire to rhythmically tense and release the muscles in her thighs for friction . . . just as she was doing now, silently, discretely, unseen.

Agony gripped her as she clutched the pillow needing release, but still too conditioned, too inhibited to seek it. Small gasps seeped past her lips as the burn between her thighs became unbearable, and the slow, quiet rub of her breasts and mound against the pillow became too soft to satisfy her, yet too painfully teasing to ignore. How did she let her thoughts take her here, to a place where she was so close to thrashing that she wanted to moan and cry out?

Mind over matter . . . she'd gone to therapy, taken yoga, read all the self-help books about positive visualization and imagery . . . she didn't have to give in . . . it would pass. People were celibate and happy. People lived for years without touch, or self touch. If she could just get her thighs to stop their damnable rhythm . . . if she could switch thoughts, and think cleansing thoughts long enough to get her rim to stop burning and to stop sending shivering contractions deep inside her well. If she could just stop her nipples from caressing the softness of the pillow, and could wrench the too-sensitive skin around them away from the back and forth motion that sent waves of pleasure through her. All she had to do was stop envisioning his lips pulling at them, suckling them, making her pant . . . all she had to do was make the little nub of skin between her legs stop throbbing, and to stop begging her to touch it. All she had to do was stop recalling how the man made her feel.

Begrudgingly, she pushed the pillow away from her and rolled over on her back and stared up at the ceiling in the dark. Her breaths now escaped her lungs through her mouth. A thin sheen of perspiration covered her, causing her nightgown to cling to her body like a second sheath of skin. She'd be all right. It had just been too long, and she had allowed herself to get excited by the presence of a handsome man. Foolish. She spread her legs to stop her thighs from committing any further egregious acts of torment against her. If they didn't rub together, didn't tense and release, then everything between them would eventually cool off and calm down. If she lowered the blankets, then her overly sensitive breasts could get some air, and also cool off. Without the torment of friction, this would soon pass—just like her momentary fantasy of being alone with Forster Hamilton would pass.

Yet the supposedly calming minutes without the pillow against her dragged out her torture. Instead of the cool air offering refuge, it danced across her swollen breasts as though a breath coming from his heated mouth. The lack of rhythmic rubbing of thigh against thigh sent a sharp tremor through her middle that contracted her belly so hard she almost sat up. The stinging at the ends of her breasts had angrily transformed into an ache. She covered them with both palms, and nearly moaned as the craved warmth released a rush of new moisture from her valley. Her hands, no longer her own, became his as they played against the distended flesh, and rolled the pebble-hard tips with her fingers through the sheer fabric, whispering to them harshly their need for skin-to-skin contact. And her fingers listened to them, since they we no longer her own—they were his, and they found the opening of her buttons, peeling away the gown, and lavishing attention on where it now hurt so badly.

Drawing in air through her mouth, she licked her lips, then her fingers, and the sensation of wet skin touched hot, angry areolas, nearly making them sizzle as they circled them, flicked against them, becoming his tongue as her eyes closed and her hips secretly, quietly, rose and fell to the rhythm she missed so much.

And the rest of her body begged her for that same attention until her hand slid down her abdomen and found its way under her gown. Tentative at first, her palm investigated her inner thighs which burned so hot with fever that her hand trembled as it approached her quivering, wet valley. She couldn't stop the gentle stroke down the seam now engorged and slick with want, and each pass by the region of discontent drew her finger deeper, bolder, until it swiped the nub that licked back at it in defiance.

One hand clutched her breast hard as the other darted in and out of the flooded center of her anguish, and soon it took on the missed rhythm of man fusing with woman. She breathed him into flared nostrils, thrust hard against a relentless palm, and remembered all at the same time why she missed this part of life so much.

Six

He was thankful that Rebecca had awakened enough to practically sleepwalk as she followed him into the house carrying Rachel. Tonight there'd be no requests for extra sips of water, no whining about the need to go to the bathroom, or pleading to stay up to watch one more television show. Whatever had happened at Dianne's house while he was away from the girls had been enough to total them.

Forster chuckled to himself as he yanked off kid clothing and pushed small, flaccid arms and legs into pajamas. The seven-year-old only halfway objected as he first slipped her nightgown on over her head, to protect her budding privacy, then yanked down her jeans and helped her thread her arms out of a sweatshirt and into the gown—pulling it through the neckline like a magician. The pants came off with the sneakers as his daughter flopped backward onto her bed without a fight. If it could only be this easy every night, he thought, feeling extraordinarily upbeat as he swept their brows with kisses and tucked them in good. He stopped at stared at them for a moment as he turned on their night-light and shut the bedroom door. That's what it was all about. Family.

Then, why did everything have to be an either-or choice, black and white without shades of gray? The errant thought almost stopped him midstride as he made his way to his mother's room. He'd learned about shades of gray from her, he mused, resuming his focus to move down the hall. Perhaps that was why he so enjoyed working with monochrome film: it had so many variations that could be brought out by accessing the shades of gray. Nothing was absolute. Especially not his relationship with his mother.

Checking on the constant source of his vexation, he gently tapped on her bedroom door, which was ajar. She didn't answer, and as per usual the television was on and watching her sleep, a cigarette was precariously smoldering in the ashtray, and her best friend, vodka, had obviously paid another evening visit.

By rote he kissed her forehead and covered her up, damping out the cigarette butt and removing her pack, the bottle, and the glass. He switched off the set as he shut the door behind him, wondering how long it would take before there would be a night when sirens might race to his home to find it engulfed in flames from a stray ash. As he made his way to the kitchen, he glimpsed his daughters' room.

It was bad enough that he had student tenants in the upstairs apartment that probably didn't make safety a priority . . . and it was bad enough that he'd grown up with the constant fear of the house going up when his mother smoked and drank herself to sleep—but he'd never wanted that terror visited upon his children. That part of it was black and white, and Forster let out a grunt of disgust as he went toward the kitchen. But after her home had been flooded out in '99, what was he supposed to do, abandon her?

At one point he'd convinced himself that his endurance of such a life with her as a kid had made him strong. He'd told himself that on the upside, it had made him able to subsist on little catnaps, and it had served him well in the military when he had to work military-police guard shifts. He'd made himself believe that it had helped him to adjust to the sleep depravation required for patrols. But now, as much as he loved his mother, his children were again at risk. What purpose did it all serve now? Where was the strength in constant worry?

The issue of Eva was once black and white, but as with his mother, it eventually developed on its own, in hindsight, to include all sorts of shades of gray produced by love, devotion, and responsibility. Perhaps too much responsibility took it out of focus like a rack shot.

Everybody knew that confirmed alcoholics did not stop drinking until they wanted to. His mother never wanted to badly enough to seek help—nor did Eva. Yet, he told himself as he let his breath out hard and began clearing away the mess that his mother had left in the house, she was his mother—and life had given her enough of a reason to drink. Funny thing was that, just like his ex-wife, he hadn't been able to turn that relationship into easy black and white.

He'd felt like he owed them both. The gray part of what he could never shake. His mother had given him life, had cared for him as an infant, and somehow had kept a roof over his head as a kid when his father walked. And for all of her toxic behaviors, she loved him—and he was her son. Period. But, now he was a father, too, and there would soon be a black and white choice in the matter for the sake of those who couldn't make choices on their own, just the same way it had come down to a clear choice with Eva. Get help or leave.

Forster worked furiously at the dirty dishes and then made quick work of the kitchen floor. The living room and dining room then became his mission as he tried to shake off his memory of Eva. She was toxic, just like his mother. Then after all this time, why couldn't he shake what was then a clear decision?

Fury made his hands work quickly against the offending mess in the house. He had to get up in the morning, and didn't have time to think about this old tale. They had to go to the PAL Run for the Rescue Walk at the Art Museum. The girls would be exhausted, and he had to find some clean clothes for them so they wouldn't catch a cold, and he had to make snack bags with water, juice, and oranges so the kids wouldn't dehydrate.

What did he care about his mom's condition? She'd lived like this for years and wasn't going to change. Eva had been the one who'd had an affair, and had been the one who had abruptly served him papers, and then left them for two years to seek greater fame and fortune than he could provide. His mind ricocheted against his will from one indignity to the next as he worked.

She had been the one to put his children at risk as she gallivanted to the other side of the country. And she'd been the one who'd come home drunk to wrap her car around a tree a year ago—killing herself and traumatizing the little girls who still adored their mother who'd left them. She was history. But he'd been the one who had to clean up after the mess!

Forster went to the refrigerator and searched for snack items to put in Ziploc bags, ignoring the fact that his hands were trembling. So what his ex-wife had given him two beautiful girls, then immediately wanted time to find herself and her wanna-be acting career in Los Angeles? She'd simply left them, and told him it was better that he keep the kids until she *found herself.*

Who the hell has to find themselves once they became a parent? It wasn't in the job description!

He stopped what he was doing and stood still, trying to collect himself in the process, and remembering what Rick had once said—over the long haul, she'd probably saved his life.

Working at the task more calmly, he tried to wrest his mind to the positive. Because of Eva he wasn't enlisted any longer, having to constantly move and uproot, nor was he in harm's way during the Gulf War. Because of Eva's devil-may-care attitude toward their marriage and family, he had even removed himself from the Reserves because he was the sole custodial parent, therefore had missed active duty in Afghanistan. But, because of her insanity, he'd missed a chance to be a frontline part of what he'd been trained to do—to serve and protect his country. And, because of the beautiful daughters she'd given him, he'd moved into forensics on the police force, the lesser of the evils presented by his career of being in harm's way.

Forster wiped up the juice that had spilled from the sides of the cut oranges and placed the plastic bags of slices in the refrigerator. He then turned his attention to the pile of ashtrays that he'd carried back to the kitchen, a habit developed to make his mother have to get up and fully wake up to search for her cigarettes if she wanted to smoke.

The smell of ashes in the double sink made him want to wretch. Wetting the overflowing ashes before he dumped them into the garbage, he watched the filthy water run down the drain. Black, white, gray. Why was he thinking about his mother and Eva when he'd just come in from a great night out with a fantastic woman and good friends?

Maybe it was just like what the fellas had told him the

effects of helping out at Ground Zero during the aftermath would be—something that would forever haunt him, sneak up on him when he least expected, something always with him to tear away at any sudden joy. The crisis counselor that had assisted his unit had said that some images stay for a very long time, and one could only hope that they become muted with time, less vivid, more gray so one could live with them. He was living with his mother that way. He'd have to learn to live with the memory of what Eva had done in the same manner. Wash it out. Make it turn gray so he could move on.

While he felt robbed, he had to admit to feeling blessed at the same time. The ultimate catch-22. What did he have to complain about? He wasn't in the rubble, nor were his children missing him . . . nor were his buddies torn up as they tried in vain to dig him out. He still had his best friend, who was like a brother—Rick.

Forster shut his eyes hard to fight the images of what he'd seen. It took a moment to steady himself as he gripped the edge of the sink. Being on the bucket brigade would always stay with him—just like certain smells would be . . . ash was one of them.

Yet, being there had also made him find God and settle his longstanding grudge with the Almighty. Yes, he was blessed—healthy, lucky to be alive, and he had a good, solid way to provide for his family and serve his community. He was a decorated vet with an honorable discharge, had a nice home, and even though he had to constantly clean behind his mother and the kids, at least it was a place to call his own. At least he had a family. Most of all he had his girls. Eva hadn't been able to rob him of them. Although her sudden death almost did.

He said a quiet prayer of thanks and allowed the tension to unfurl itself within his shoulders as he began turning out the lights and doing a once-through security check. Had his daughters been in the car with her that day when she'd come back to Philly to reclaim them . . .

Mere chance—maybe it was God's hand—had made the day-care center workers wary, and Eva's actions had given them pause; that day alcohol and Eva's drunken condition had been his friend—it had bought him time to get to the center after they called to verify the children's release; it had bought him time to argue with her, it had sent her off alone and left his children at his side. But it had wrapped her rental car around a tree on Belmont Avenue . . . and it had left his children with inner wounds that God only knew how they'd ever fully heal.

Forster's gait had considerably slowed as he entered his bedroom and shut the door without turning on the light. He leaned against the door and closed his eyes, praying for an answer to stop the inner turmoil.

He counted his blessings again, as though reciting a rosary. He had gone out to see a flick, a beautiful woman had sat next to him, his children were happy, they'd returned home safe and secure. His mother hadn't burned down the house while he was gone. A beautiful woman had momentarily taken him out of the hell that always settled in his mind. A funny, witty, intelligent, nice woman had shown interest in him . . . and his libido had awakened, but the gray ashes in the house had put it out.

Maybe if he called her tomorrow, she'd make him feel that sense of excitement that he'd almost forgotten even existed. Maybe if she would come over to look at his work, and he could talk to another adult about the second love of his life beyond the girls—his photography, maybe he could feel the warmth again that she'd created in his body and soul. Maybe, if she wasn't put off by his mother's condition . . . maybe

if she could deal with the fact that he had kids . . .
maybe if she could see life in all of its shades of gray,
and could see him, really see him . . . maybe if she
would just smile for him again to make his stomach
tense in a way that it hadn't in years . . .

Yet, that was a lot for any woman to deal with—any
person, for that matter. Stranger things had happened,
though. . . . Maybe she was sent to him through a friend,
through mere happenstance, maybe as an olive branch
from the angels above . . . as one more repair in his rift
with God. That was insane to consider; there was no
bargaining with the Alpha and the Omega—what He
gave you was a gift, and not because you'd earned it.

A deep sigh of fatigue pushed its way up from his
lungs. There were too many unknowns, despite how
mind-blowing the evening in her company had been.
But maybe, just maybe, if he could trust not to get
burned. Maybe, just maybe, he could stop living like a
monk, and find the joy of holding a woman in his arms
again—a thought so dangerous that it sent an immediate shudder through him.

Or, maybe, like so many times before, he was just
dreaming . . .

Seven

"You're up early." Lynette's mother beamed as she came into the kitchen. "I thought you weren't going to church this morning? And tell me you are not going in that jogging suit—you young folks take casual to a whole 'nother level. Did you eat yet?"

Lynette could feel something fragile within her begin to unravel, but she smiled and kept her voice calm as she looked up from tying her running shoes. "Good morning, Mom. Yes, I'm up early, and no, I'm not going to church, and yes, I just had a very light breakfast of fresh fruit and juice—would you like some?"

"Oh," her mother replied, not bothering to hide her disappointment or simmering anger as she began to fix herself some toast. "You can get up early enough to go out to exercise, but you can't accompany your own mother to church."

Her mother had made the comment without even looking in her direction. She'd given Lynette her back to consider. And in that very brittle moment, something within Lynette snapped. Today was going to be her birthday. It was time for the first contraction to begin.

"Mom," she said in as pleasant a voice as she could muster. Then she waited until her mother turned around to face her. "I love you very, very much . . . and I do go to church with you upon occasion—just not every Sunday, the way you would like."

"It's not what I want, it's what the Lord wants."

Lynette counted to ten before she spoke. "True. But, from my understanding, He wants us to communicate with Him everyday, not just on Sunday, and I do that—as well as have fellowship in His name. Am I right? And, I do my daily meditation without fail."

Her mother seemed to relax, as though a victory was in her grasp. "Yes, child. Praying regularly is good, and a person can't argue with fellowship in His name. At least you do that, and I'm glad you've finally changed your mind and gotten some sense into your head."

Lynette let her breath out slowly and chose her words carefully. "I am not going with you to find church in a building this morning. I'm going out on the PAL Run for the Rescue event on Kelly Drive, and I'm going to use the gift of good health He gave me to help raise money for the ongoing New York rescue effort. Would you care to be a sponsor . . . or to ask some of your friends, in church, to make a pledge?"

Cornered, her mother turned away and went back to fixing her toast and began preparing coffee. Tense moments passed between them, and it was obvious to Lynette that her mother wasn't going to respond. Lynette stood and approached the woman who was once again ignoring her.

"There are all kinds of ways to do the Lord's work, Mom. My way is more out-and-about in the community, yours in more under the formal auspices of the church—both are valid, and it's all good. I respect yours; I'm just asking that you respect mine. Okay? So, you have a nice day at church and I'll see you when—"

"Respect?" Her mother's voice boomed as she spun on Lynette. Hot tears were in her eyes and she nearly trembled with repressed rage. "Respect! You call how you treat me respectful?"

Taken aback, all Lynette could do for a moment was stare at her mother.

"How do I, and when have I, ever disrespect you?"

Her mother's breast rose and fell with inhales of sudden fury. "You are just like your father! You never come home—are always out in the street. I never know where you are, whom you are with, or when you're coming back. You don't talk to me, you talk at me—telling me what you want, what you're going to do, and it's always about what you want, never what I want. What I want is always an after-the-fact consideration, or no consideration! Just like last night. It's not fair."

A new, painful awareness began to swirl within Lynette as she watched her mother battle with a person no longer alive on the planet. The unfinished business between her parents had entered the room and taken up residence in the house. Now it was unsettling things, rattling things, like a displaced haint in the kitchen.

"No, it's not fair," Lynette finally said in a cool tone, reining in her own temper. "It is not fair for you to coop yourself up in the house, to totally involve yourself in activities that do not necessarily make you happy—but you feel compelled to do out of some sort of misguided guilt . . . and it is definitely not fair for you to lay that at my feet. I am not Dad, but I am his child. Just like I'm yours. And there was nothing wrong about me going out to the movies with a few friends last night. Nothing!"

What she didn't say to her mother was that she didn't do half of what she wanted to do last night. She never got to do what she wanted anymore! Not since she'd become a child under the roof that she paid the mortgage for. That was unfair. That was frustrating. It was like having the constant behavior police on her case, and she hated it.

"I am happy doing what I do," her mother finally snapped after a moment, turning away quickly, and then walking to the refrigerator to get milk for her coffee. "I'm not happy about how you conduct your life, is all. That's the issue."

"No," Lynette nearly whispered, summoning the strength not to scream. "You are frustrated, and angry that dad died, and angry that he lived his life the way he wanted to—despite your view of how he should have lived it."

Her words sliced through the room leaving a terminal silence in their wake.

"How dare you . . ." Her mother was now facing her, her eyes no longer shining with tears of hurt but with glittering resentment. "You don't know *anything* about what went on between me and your father in our marriage—which is, and never will be, any of your business! Frustration is having a daughter who cannot keep her own marriage together, much less dispense advice about her mother's. Frustration is having a child who you send to college, give everything you have to allow her a chance at the world on a platter, but who comes home for you to cook for her, clean behind, wash and iron for, and then always having to be the one to straighten out the messes other grown folks make—and to watch people who have been given every opportunity in life, on your back, stand in your face and be ungrateful when you've asked for so little, like going to church once a week, in return. That's frustration, baby girl—so, yes, maybe, you are right. I am deeply frustrated."

Mortally wounded by the reference to all of her failures within her life and marriage, Lynette opened her mouth, then shut it, then turned to walk out, and stopped

and spun on her mother. Her own voice had become so
calm that it scared her. "No, Mom. Frustrated is to have
a cord of guilt wrapped around your neck. Frustration is
doing things for the sake of others, because you love
them, but being afraid to be who you really are—because you might offend them. Frustration is having your
parents push you to do well, demand that you excel, and
then tell you how much you owe them because you simply did what *they* wanted you to do!"

When her mother didn't respond, but simply stood
there, staring at her, mouth agape, Lynette pressed on.
"Frustration is being thirty-five years old and afraid to
bring a date home, because you're afraid of what your
mother might think, afraid that your choice might not
pass the third degree, or make it past a church Inquisi-
tion!" Her voice had escalated beyond what was
reasonable, and she could feel her temples pounding as
sudden fury claimed her until her ears rang.

"Frustration is being afraid that you might mess up
again, in anything you do—that you might not have
made a good choice, and your nose will be rubbed in it
when you get hurt again, hurting you twice—once by
your lover, then by your own mom. I've been trapped in
this house, afraid to do anything, for three years . . .
three, whole, years after being a married woman, living
on my own, having a life and a husband—and you be-
grudge me the movies, and say I disrespect you?"

"Baby . . ." Her mother began to reach for her hand
then retreated, her words trailing off, giving Lynette an
opening to rail on as her mother stood transfixed in the
middle of the kitchen floor.

"Frustration, Mother, is knowing that your deepest,
darkest hurts will be hurled back into your face, all because you made the choice, as an adult, to spend your
Sunday doing something that brings you joy, for once.

That's not fair. Frustration is having a person hide behind religion to manipulate you into doing what they want you to do all the time, rather than just being honest and coming out and say—"

The slap stung her cheek and jettisoned saliva out of her mouth. Stunned, Lynette looked at the woman who had struck her, and who now had tears streaming down her face.

"Don't you ever question my faith—or dare to call me a liar!"

"You just questioned your own faith, Mother, when you struck me. But I have enough respect for you to turn the other cheek. I did learn something in Sunday school after all."

Her mother paced away from her, leaving the coffee and toast where it sat on the drain board, and went to fetch her coat. "I'ma pray for you, chile. That the demons in you—"

"Stop it!" Lynette shrieked, hurrying behind her mother and slowing her retreat by holding her arm firm. "Just stop it. Listen to yourself."

"If you don't mind," her mother replied coolly, "I am going to church."

"Not before we finish this. Let's pray right here and now then for clarity, mutual consideration, and some much-needed Grace—but today, Mom, I'm going to tell you the truth, and I am sorry if it hurts."

Her mother crossed her arms over her chest and closed her eyes. Lynette waited until she opened them again, not sure if the woman had begun praying or was counting to ten before deciding whether or not to strike her again.

"So, what brings on this so-called truth according to Lynette Marie Graves? What am I to listen to this morning? Some bar-stool epiphany you experienced out in the streets with your girlfriends last night?"

"You hit me—"

"You sassed me, chile, and spoke the Lord's name in vain. I am still your mother!"

"You hit me," Lynette said as calmly as she could, "because you are frustrated. You said yourself that you are tired of doing for other people who do not appreciate it. Well what does a person have to do to show you that you are appreciated? Huh? How much is enough? Is there some mystical, invisible scale that I am not weighing in on correctly? You're tired, I'm tired, we're both tired—so why are we doing this?"

"I am tired of all of you all," her mother admitted cautiously. "And, I do know what it's like to be young and trapped in a house, I never asked you to—"

"Listen to what you just said. *All of you all*. Dad is gone. There's only me. I have never required that you do for me the things you do. You don't have to clean this house, or cook every day, or wash laundry . . . you are not the maid, Mom! I'm grown, and can do it myself, and for you. If it's frustrating you—then *stop doing it*."

"Oh, sure," her mother scoffed, "and this house would be a pure disaster if I didn't do what I do."

"I want you to get still for a moment, Mom. This house, the condition it's in, does not have to meet a certain standard. I have not imposed that standard on you—you've done that to yourself. To my knowledge, Dad never imposed that standard on you . . . it was how *you* wanted to keep house."

Her mother swallowed hard and began putting on her coat.

"Mom, if you want to go on trips with your friends, go. If you want to be active in your church, do it. If you want to just go out and have fun, do that . . . just leave me a note about where you are so I don't worry, but go with my blessing and my love, and my greatest wish for you to be happy. If I can give that to you, why can't you give that same respect back to me—and why did I have to get the taste slapped out of my mouth for telling the truth, in my own home, as a grown woman? Fair? You talk about fairness?"

Her mother's lip trembled as she buttoned her coat, and Lynette wiped a large tear away from her cheek and placed a kiss behind it. She held her mother by both arms and looked at her squarely. "You don't have to be the martyr," she whispered. "There was only one to save the world, it says so in the Bible."

"Trapped . . . you say? You have no idea what it was like in those days," her mother murmured. "Everything now is so free, but people judged a woman, then."

"People may have, but I didn't and don't. I love you, unconditionally. But you are taking it out on me."

"We had to keep a nice house. Cook, clean, do everything at the highest standards. He got to do as he pleased, and your father did—trust me. Then, when it was supposed to be our turn, my turn, all those years of him abusing his body took a toll, and he got sick and left me." Her mother's voice cracked, and the expression in her eyes became wild, as though she were a small, trapped animal looking for escape. "He left me, Lynette!"

"I know," she whispered, gathering her mother in her arms, stroking her back as the older woman shook with sobs.

"It wasn't fair!"

"I know, Mom . . . no, it wasn't."

"Keep your eye on the sparrow, they told me. Wait on the Lord, they said. Every nice dress I ever wanted . . . I passed up for the household, to make ends meet when he burned up the money having good times. I didn't do like the other women. I sacrificed so my child could have. I didn't go on little trips. I didn't buy new shoes. I put my family, my household, and my chores before all my good friends . . . I worked, and worked, and waited for my turn! Three years, try thirty-eight . . . and then tell me about waiting your turn."

Lynette's fingers found the silky hair at the nape of her mother's neck, and she tried to stroke away the pain.

"He owed me that. I never slept with another man than him—no matter what he did. Then he got sick and that was taken away, and he died and left me with Social Security and my schoolteacher pension. We didn't even have enough to rightly bury him; he'd drank it all away, save a few dollars. But, I was supposed to understand, I was supposed to make up for World War Two, and be patient with his leftover demons. I was. But he left us, Lynette—how could he do that?"

Her mother's sobs cut through her skeleton to the marrow. All during the funeral, her mother had politely, silently wept, yet never sobbed. During every family crisis, even the flood, her mother had been the rock. And, yes, the woman had given every shred of her life, the very fabric of her DNA to make a secure quilt to blanket the family—and her mother had been robbed.

The lump in Lynette's throat gave way to tears and she wiped at them angrily, and then gently lifted her mother's chin to look into her eyes. "It was not fair, Mom. It wasn't."

The elderly pair of eyes that now stared back into Lynette's was startling to her. The transformation that the truth seemed to cause appeared to age her mother's face by ten years. Now she could see all the wrinkles, all the fatigue, all of the work, all of the hurt, and yet, her mother's eyes searched her own with the furtive quality of innocence that broke her heart.

"It was not fair," Lynette repeated, "and you have the right to be angry about it—all of it. That's okay . . . it's okay to be angry about an injustice." She waited until her mother nodded, and she dabbed at the tears on her withered cheeks. "It's just that, after getting angry, you have to decide what to do about it."

A pair of elderly eyes left her gaze and their line of vision went toward the window as her mother sighed.

"It's too late for me to do anything but go to church and come home."

"Not true," Lynette whispered. "That's an old myth—a lie."

Her mother's eyes searched her face again. Hope shone within them, and her smile was sad and gentle. "That's because you are young and vital and have the rest of your life ahead of you. One day, you'll leave me again for a new husband, or a boyfriend, or a better job. You've still got enough time for a second chance. Wait till you're my age . . ."

Lynette put her arms around her mother's shoulders and brought her to the living-room mirror. "I see a beautiful, gorgeous, highly intelligent, kind woman," she murmured, stroking her mother's hair into place. "I see a pretty woman who still has a figure, a woman who is mobile, and energetic . . . a woman who could be out in the community, who could teach children in the public library's after-school programs, or go to senior dances, go on cruises, ride the bus with her girlfriends to the casinos, and be on the arm of any eligible deacon. I see a woman who could go on a date."

Her mother appraised herself and laughed. "My child needs glasses, too. As well as her head examined."

"Not letting you off the hook that easy," Lynette said

with a smile. "Remember that time in school I came home and told you I was ugly . . . you did this for me. You stood me in front of this same mirror, and made me see all the possibilities in myself when I could only see a nappy-headed little girl, with scarred up knees and two missing front teeth. I see a woman who tried her best, and gave us all her best—no matter how hard that was to do sometimes."

Her mother covered her mouth recalling the memory, stifled a sob, and closed her eyes. Two big tears wet her lashes and spilled down her cheeks. "I never meant to make you feel trapped by me," she whispered on a hoarse breath. "God in Heaven knows I know how terrible that feels."

"We were both overwrought and upset," Lynette murmured, "and said things . . ."

"That were true."

"But that could have been said more gently."

"But that needed to be said," her mother pressed, opening her eyes and staring at Lynette. "I am so sorry . . ."

"Me too."

This time the silence between them was a comfortable companion, like the calm after a hard rain. Much had been shared, not simply washed away, as though the shed tears had been water sent to nourish the dry spots in their souls.

"Tell you what," Lynette finally offered, softly kissing her mother again. "You go fix up that pretty face, dab on just a little blush and lipstick again, and I'll go change."

Her mother looked at her and began tearing up again. "You don't have to go, if you don't want to. Anyway, after this, I already feel like I've been to church."

"Yeah, me too, but I'm not ready for our time together this morning to end. I want to spend the rest of this gorgeous day with my mom—my best friend, doing something she truly enjoys. Just so long as she can appreciate the fact that, sometimes I might not want to do what she wants to do, but as a friend, I can compromise and hang out with her—enjoying the fact that she likes doing whatever . . . and sometimes, just sometimes, I'd like it if she hung out with me trying some of the things I like to do . . . like going to the movies, going to the theater, going to see an art exhibit . . . albeit, she has already probably done a lot of things I wanted to do, just by going to all those kiddie events that she had no interest in whatsoever. Deal?"

Both women chuckled. A warm hug surrounded Lynette, and her mother simply laid her head on her shoulder for a moment.

"Deal," her mother whispered. "That's all I ever wanted from him."

"I know," Lynette whispered back. "But, we both got left . . . so, now, it's just us girls. Let's have a day of it. We'll go to church, and we'll go out to eat for brunch—away from church—and we'll laugh and just have a good time. Today is the day of rest, so we won't cook dinner, we'll do something radical like order out . . . or simply stay out in the streets until we're both weary . . . maybe we'll go for a drive, or something? I don't know. We'll let the breeze blow us around. But, you will not clean, I will not write, we will not worry about the laundry, and we will enjoy this day God made."

"And, you'll tell me all the fun you had out with the girls last night . . . maybe even tell me about the double date you went on?"

"Mom!" Lynette laughed.

"You got dressed too many times, and kept getting on the phone with Dianne . . . I remember what that was like. So?"

"It was so much fun, Mom. He was so nice. . . ."

"I love you," her mother whispered tenderly, putting a stray curl behind Lynette's ear. "And, I'm happy for you . . . and I promise to try to stay out of your way, and not to judge so hard, despite my ongoing concern as your mom . . . as long as you share every juicy bit of gossip with me so we can giggle. I haven't girl-giggled in so long . . ."

"I love you, too," Lynette murmured. "Neither have I." And then she left her mother's embrace to take the stairs two at a time before she broke down and wept.

All of the years of misunderstandings, all of the things that had been taken for granted between them, all of the unspoken hurts that had given their fights a life of their own, became so clear, yet so unimportant. Age and rank and role made no difference. All that stood between them was so vastly the same. They were both women, both injured, both healing, both confused, both in need of human interaction and love and understanding, both were made of flesh and blood.

Lynette threw cold water on her face, splashing away the hot tears that would not stop flowing. If she had only known . . . if she had only listened. . . . If she had only seen past her own pain to be able to connect with her mother's, and yet, she firmly told herself, this morning was a necessary first step in the birthing process. Guilt had no place here. It was no longer needed.

She dried her face roughly with a towel and looked in the mirror. A day out with her mother was in order, not because of guilt, not because she had to, but because it was wanted and needed for both of them.

Today, after all, was their birthday.

Eight

The muscles in his legs twitched with the repressed desire to run. A surge of adrenaline coursed through him as he watched the diverse groups of joggers get smaller and smaller, easily pulling away from the parents, kids, and elderly people in the walkers' section. God, he missed the exertion of a good, clean run. The last time he'd been able to do so daily was in the service, then at the Police Academy. He shifted Rachel's weight on his shoulders and slowed his gait so that Rebecca could keep up with him. Maybe he'd get back to jogging, then serious running again.

But, mornings were out—before-school logistics didn't allow for it. Evenings were out—his mother's condition didn't allow for it. Weekends were not his own—that was PAL volunteer time and activities with the girls, which had turned him into a chauffeur. His most current athletic regime had consisted of hoisting his daughters from his side to shoulders. Most days his free weights collected dust in the basement. Well, one day, he'd get back . . . maybe he'd start a junior track team for the neighborhood kids, that way he could stretch out his legs, too, instead of just being a spectator coach all the time.

By late afternoon the girls were beginning to get cold and hungry. They'd done well, though. Despite the need

to stop ten times during their leisurely stroll to hit the
Porta Potti stations, to sit and have lunch, to kick the
leaves, their little threesome had made progress enough
to log a few miles for the cause. He was proud of them.

"Okay, troops. Let's just make it to the main sign-
out table to have our sponsor sheets stamped, then how
about we call it a day?"

"Can we go to McDonald's?" Rachel begged.

"Pleeaaase?" Rebecca chimed in.

"No junk food on Sunday."

"Aw, Dad," Rebecca pressed. "But whatcha gonna
fix, huh?"

"Maybe some chicken, or—"

"Hot dogs and baked beans?"

Rachel's question made him laugh. He did feed them,
but even he had to admit that it was a standard military
issue diet.

"I haven't decided, but we need to eat something nutritional after this," he chuckled as he cajoled them to
keep moving. "March."

Her mother looked positively radiant as the late afternoon sun caught in her hair while they drove. Ever
since they'd left the restaurant, she'd been humming one
of the big band tunes that she'd heard at the jazz brunch.
Getting out of the house, together, had been good for
both of them.

"Now wasn't that better than being stuck in one place
all afternoon?" Lynette teased, thoroughly enjoying how
happy her mother seemed. "A break in the routine is
good for the soul."

"But they gave you such small portions for so much
money," her mother fussed. "I could have fed an army
for what that lunch cost."

"You always dish up everybody's plate like you're feeding an army." Now they both laughed as Lynette chided on. "These folks have to make a profit, or people will lose their jobs."

"They make it all look so pretty, that I'll grant you—"

"And, it was very good."

"True."

"But?"

"They just don't give folks enough to even take some home for later."

Lynette laughed harder and shook her head. "But, you can't discount the atmosphere."

"Atmosphere? If you have the right people in your home, and some good food, and good laughs and good music, you've got all the atmosphere you need."

"Mom," Lynette chuckled, drawing out her title like a whining teenager.

"You know what I really love," her mother said in a conspiratorial voice. "A good house party."

"A house party?" Now Lynette really giggled hard. "Since when?"

"I love to entertain . . . to have people over. I miss the big family dinners we used to have when everybody was living—all the old folks are gone now. Used to get a kick out of you girls all running around, cleaning up, putting out pretzels and chips and rolling back my rugs to boogie-down. Then your dad and all his buddies would come over to supposedly chaperone, but they got in more trouble playing cards and drinking their spirits in my kitchen than you kids ever could have. They were more work than you all . . . and their wives would come too, which meant it was really a party for both sets. Don't you remember how much fun that was when things were lively in the old house?"

The wistful tone of her mother's voice sent them both

time traveling for a moment, and she felt a bittersweet pang of joy mixed with loss for the era gone by. Yes, things had been lively in the old house, and that was what was missing in the new one—laughter, noise, and music. Determined not to allow her mother to lose her girlish smile, she brought them back to the present.

"Well at least, today, you didn't have to worry about us thumping on the floors so hard with our dance steps that we shook your china cabinet."

Now her mother laughed in earnest. "But, I still could've fed you more at home than that bird-ration-sized meal they gave us at that fancy-shmancy restaurant—even though I am very proud that two young black boys own it."

"And where else can you hear smooth jazz, plus the masters' . . . like, tunes from Monk, or big band sounds like that anymore—all in the same place?"

"On my stereo at home," her mother countered with a chuckle. "I've got all the greats on seventy-eight platters—Dizzie, Count Basie, Duke Ellington, and the songbird Sara Vaughn . . . and Madame Holiday—Billie, of course."

Lynette's mother-friend was back, with bragging rights. She loved it, and decided to keep the happy banter going by egging Ida Graves on.

"But to hear the music live, Mom? Be honest . . ."

"Okay, okay, you've got me. This was so much fun, Lynette!"

Her mother's face shone with the excitement of a schoolgirl, wide-eyed with expectation and wondering where next the breeze might blow them.

"Mom, look," Lynette urged as they turned off Broad Street and took the scenic route home, going down Benjamin Franklin Parkway. "Have you ever witnessed anything so pretty, with all the flags of every nation, the fountains going, the library, the Franklin Institute, all the pretty, old buildings with gorgeous architecture . . . with the Art Museum as a centerpiece and the sun beginning to drop just at the apex of the building? It's only a little after three now, but by five o'clock, the whole sky turns rose-orange-pink—we'll have to come back and see that one day. You can't imagine how majestic that looks, and it's right here in our own backyard."

There was so much in the world that she wanted to show her mother . . . so much her mother deserved to get a chance to see for herself. As she watched the smile on her mother's face become serene, she knew she had to get her to experience some of it while there was still time.

"No . . . I can't imagine anything so beautiful as that sounds," her mother finally murmured in awed appreciation. "I don't think I ever really stopped to look at it, not even after living here all my life. It sounds like a postcard . . . pictures I've seen in books. Lynette, you are making me envision things with brand-new eyes. This is spectacular."

An easy silence enveloped them as they rode, sharing the beauty before them and the quiet camaraderie of just being together.

"Look, there's the Run for the Rescue event," Lynette pointed out. "All the runners and walkers are coming back in. We'll probably have to go around the diverted traffic, because the museum's front steps are always blocked off for these things. We can catch it on the news tonight—see the news vans?"

Her mother became still and her once-radiant smile vanished.

"Lynne, baby, I am so sorry . . ."

"For what?" Perplexed, Lynette brought the car to a slow stop at the light and looked over at her mother.

"That event was something you wanted to do, and it was for a good cause . . . look at all the people who came out for it. I just didn't understand—"

"Mom," she replied with a soft smile, touching her mother's hand as she applied pressure to the gas when the light changed. "We laughed more, and talked more, and had more fun together than the law allows, right?"

Her mother nodded and smiled, but it still contained a haunting sadness.

"Didn't you enjoy being out and about a little?"

"I did," her mother whispered. "But, you should have been able to go with your friends . . . honey, you can't baby-sit me forever. I know that."

She wanted to hug her mother—to just stop the car, lean over and pull her close, but traffic patterns didn't allow for that gesture. "I do not call having a girls' day out, baby-sitting. And, I do go out with my friends, plenty. We were supposed to do this today."

"Well," her mother reasoned, but still not sounding sure, "I suppose God works in mysterious ways."

"Yes, He does," Lynette said brightly, making a turn that would take them off the Parkway before they got trapped in event traffic. When the light changed and held them, she turned to her mother. "So where to—"

"What's the matter?"

Lynette double-checked what her peripheral vision had initially only glimpsed.

"Oh, no."

"What?" Her mother urged. "What's the matter?"

It had to be something subconscious, some subliminal thing that she'd pushed way down . . . but how could she explain to her mother that at first she'd thought she was just going out for a good cause, that's why they'd argued about space and respect for privacy—it had not been a planned stalker attempt . . . but he had mentioned the PAL organization in passing . . . it must have taken root in her mind, so when she woke up . . .

"Oh, man . . . Mom, I know you're gonna get angry, and be hurt, and really, and truly, I didn't know and that wasn't my plan this morning . . . I don't even know where to begin."

"Lynne, you are not making any kind of sense. What is it? Hurry, before the light turns green and you take off babbling and unfocused while you're driving."

"Okay, you're right." Lynette drew in a quick breath and discretely pointed to the thick crowd of pedestrians entering the wide intersection. "See that guy crossing the street with the two little girls?"

"Yes," her mother shrugged, worry lacing her brow.

"I know him. I mean . . . just the other day he was crossing the street and I saw him . . . but the crowd of crossers was smaller, now its huge . . . then, come to find out, he was a friend of a friend of Dianne's . . . and he just showed up as my blind date because of some crazy scheme D cooked up, and—"

"Then roll down your window and holler hello to the man."

"What? All in public like that? Look at all these people out here. I don't know the man well enough to presume, Mom. I can't just do that, he was going to call me one day, maybe, but now he's with—"

"What's his name?"

"Forster Ham—Mom! Don't. Roll up your window this minute." Lynette could feel the blood draining from her face as the elder woman in the passenger's seat ignored her.

"Yoo-hoo," her mother waved, making about twenty heads turn at once. "Forster!"

She was going to die. Her mother was having a second childhood—possibly brought on by a senior moment. Right out in the street, only blocks from the historic Benjamin Franklin Parkway. Action news vans were in the offing and could get it on tape. Film at eleven. Her mother, a prim schoolteacher, was hollering out of her Subaru window like a teenager in a way that would have gotten her grounded twenty years ago when she was fifteen. "Mom! Please!"

"He saw us. Wave and pull over."

"Are you out of your mind?"

"Well," her mother said with mischief twinkling in her eyes, "I messed up a possible chance meeting . . . I was the one who disconnected the angels' work—but I can help fix it."

"Don't fix it; let it be, and—"

"You just said yourself that the Lord works in mysterious ways, did you not?"

"Yes, but—"

"Then let Him work. I'll be the vessel for the moment. You worry too much—where's *your* faith? Haven't done this with the girls in years."

"Mom! This is insane, plus there's nowhere to pull over."

"Yes there is—in that bus zone. Just go right over there and put your flashers on so they don't give you a ticket," her mother urged, pointing her finger and insisting with more authoritative instructions.

"Your mother-voice is not working on me because you are not acting like my mother." Lynette didn't know whether to laugh or cry as she saw Forster perk up, wave, and move across the street to where her mother was animatedly pointing.

"See," Ida Graves chuckled. "It's my turn."

"Your turn?"

"To embarrass the bejebbers out of you, and to help.

He seems like a very nice man . . . so handsome, and two gorgeous little girls."

"Stop it," Lynette whispered as she watched, mortified, while Forster and his children made their way to the side of her car.

"Hey, Lynette," Forster said with a wide grin of recognition. "Ma'am," he added, nodding in respect to the older woman in the vehicle as he body-shielded the children from any traffic in the double-parked lane. "Girls, say hi. You remember Miss Lynette."

"Hi," a singsong chorus replied as the two little ones peeked through her window and waved.

"Hi," Lynette squeaked. "Uh, you should get the kids curbside—this is so dangerous out here. Sheer mayhem."

"Traffic is all moving slowly, don't worry, I've got 'em. I didn't expect—"

"Pleased to meet you," her mother interjected, extending her hand through the car window.

"Oh, I'm sorry," Lynette stammered. "Where are my manners? Forster Hamilton, my mother, Mrs. Ida Graves . . . and his girls, Rachel and Rebecca."

"Well, the pleasure is all mine," her mother crooned as Forster's smile broadened. "And such beautiful, absolutely darling little girls."

"It's nice to meet you, ma'am. You two look like you've been to church or somewhere special . . . forgive the grubby appearance, we were—"

"Don't you dare apologize for being out in the sunshine with your children and helping a worthy cause. Please."

"Well, thank you," he said in a voice that almost seemed shy, "the girls were real troopers, and they did very well today."

"You all must be fall-down tired and hungry, to boot?"

Lynette almost groaned as she watched her mother begin to go down a very familiar path of attempting to feed people she barely knew.

"It was a long day for the girls. I know they're starved and need a bath."

"Just look at them . . ." her mother crooned. "You hungry, sweetie birds?"

When the two heads nodded, her mother made a clucking sound like a hen calling chicks. "Then a hot piece of butter pound cake, after some pork chops and gravy, with mashed potatoes, and a little bit of string beans to keep you strong like your daddy, sounds in order."

"Oh, ma'am, I couldn't impose on you and Lynette's Sunday like that with my brood all dirty and—"

"Gorgeous. I tell you those children are simply gorgeous and I won't hear another word."

Forster chuckled, and his five-year-old tugged on his sleeve.

"I want some cake, Daddy."

"You don't make all that stuff for Sunday dinner, and Gran is always sick and can't cook . . ." Rebecca chimed in.

As her mother's smile deepened, Lynette imagined a giant, kindly spider spinning a cotton-candy web—but it was still entrapment, no matter how gentle the ruse.

"Aw . . . I'm so sorry to hear that your Gran is sick . . . well, then, we'll have to just fix her a plate to send home."

"Gran likes cake," Rachel pleaded, making all the adults chuckle.

"Ma'am, I couldn't ask you to do something like—"

"Now, you just think nothing of it. It's the only Christian thing to do . . . plus, it's Sunday. I wouldn't hear of not sending something home to the children's ailing grandmother."

With her mind she willed her mother to stop to no avail, nonetheless sending telepathic gamma rays to the woman who charmed Forster Hamilton back to boyhood. The man had lowered his eyes, and now seemed all bashful, and was practically eating out of the woman's hands. It was her mother's tone . . . slightly southern drawl from her once-removed North Carolina roots, mixed with a singsong clear brand of diction that only schoolteachers owned. And, the cherry on top was her effusive, unrelenting, feminine adoration. The scary thing was, it was working. And the way her mother just took over the conversation . . . there was no getting a word in edgewise.

"But," he stammered, "I don't want to be a bother, and I'm sure Lynette has—"

"It's no imposition whatsoever, and Lynette and I were just going to spend a nice, quiet, boring dinner with just the two of us, as always. Fixing dinner is my Sunday ritual anyway, and there's always room at my table—especially for one of Philly's finest—I take it you're on the force from the sweatshirt?"

"Oh, yeah, yes, ma'am . . . been on the force for years."

"Now see there, Lynette. I have to offer a plate to one of our nation's heroes. Bet you were also a military man at one time."

"Mom . . ."

Forster chuckled. "It's all right. Yes, ma'am, for a while."

"I could tell right off by your straight carriage. My late husband was in the service. Always know when a man was in uniform. So, there. It's settled. Lynette, give the man our address."

The woman was unbelievable! Forster had become putty. Embarrassment didn't even begin to describe . . .

"Last night," Lynette broke in, "I gave him my—"

"Hush and write it down for the man again, child," her mother chided with good nature. "Can't you see that with all the other things, like little backpacks and such, that he had to tote down here today that he probably doesn't have it at the moment, and may have left it home?"

"I have it in my wallet," he offered quietly. "But just the number."

"Well give the man the address, Lynette!"

She accepted the card he produced for her, secretly pleased that he still had it on him, and she scribbled their address under where she'd placed her home telephone number.

Forster inspected it and smiled. "Wow. You all live right around the corner . . . we're on Pine near Forty-third—"

"Now what a divine coincidence. We live on St. Marks, between Forty-second and Forty-third. That settles it. You're a neighbor."

"But, you all weren't expecting all of these extra mouths to feed, plus we'd have to at least wash up, and—"

"We have water at our house," Ida Graves said pursing her lips, then laughed. "All I require is for you to wash your hands, bless your food, and dig in. Now is that too hard?"

"No, ma'am," Forster replied with a chuckle. "Only if it's not too much trouble . . ."

"None at all. See you in a little bit. My, it has been a pleasure."

Lynette opened her mouth then closed it and waved good-bye as she watched Forster move his brood to the curb. She continued to wave numbly while she pulled into traffic, not sure of where to begin her complaint first.

"What did you do . . .?"

"I invited the man and his children to dinner."

"Again, I will ask you, Mom . . . what did you do!"

"That man was—"

"You don't know him!"

Ida Graves covered her mouth for a moment and her eyes became as wide as saucers. "He's not married is he?"

"Well now is a fine time to get the facts."

"Well? Oh, Lynette . . . did I mess up?"

"Yes, even though he's not married."

"Of course he's not," her mother said shooing her with her hand. "Or you wouldn't have gone out with him.

"He's divorced—"

"God is merciful."

"Mom!"

"Well, God *is* merciful. One person's old shoe is another person's shiny boot."

"Where do you come up with this stuff?"

"All right . . . an ex-wife can be a problem—"

"His wife passed—"

"A widower? God rest her soul in peace."

"Mother . . . I don't believe you—"

"The man is coming over to dinner. First stage of courtin' is through a man's stomach. Did you hear it growl when I went through the list? I heard it, you heard it, so, that means—"

"People are coming over the house, and when did you cook all that—"

"Saturday night, I didn't want you to be upset because you wanted to order in, but I never save all my cooking for one day, plus, you were out and I was bored, so I started making the string beans, then the cake, and potatoes don't take no time, and I can run slices of cake in the oven for hot—"

"Mom!"

"See, sweetie, this is why a girl should always be prepared, and that's why I never let the house go to total ruination—you just never know. So, all you have to do is pull out the good plates, and—"

"But—"

"I seasoned up enough meat for the week, like I said, I had time on my hands, so we'll just eat it all in one day, and he can take some home—"

"Mother!"

"Well, you gotta make enough so the man can take something home to his ailing mother, but send it in a casserole dish so he has to bring it back and see you again. Plus, meeting up like this for the second time was a sign. Divine intervention."

It was hopeless! Who captured and wrote down these mystical signs, or better yet, who held the playbook for master ninja, female secret agent? Double talk, circle logic . . . totally outrageous . . .

"Where do you come up with this stuff, Mom? You cannot go around just rolling up on people like you're in a gang, hollering to a man out of a car window, and offering him dinner in a female drive-by! It's just not done."

"Since when?"

Her mother's laughter made her see stars. It was the most off-the-wall, exasperating, out-of-order, unvarnished display of—

"You know what your problem is," her mother giggled, cutting off even her mental dialogue.

"Yes, I have a basic idea. It's five-feet-five inches tall, seventy three years old, and—"

"Somebody lied and told you young girls that you had to go for it alone and do this courtship thing all by yourselves. Nonsense."

"Heaven help me . . ." Lynette lifted her gaze toward the car ceiling.

"Heaven is trying to help you, suga', but you are so stubborn." Her mother shook her head and looked out the window. "See, in my day, everybody got into your business, and helped you land a beau. Your mama provided the venue, the atmosphere, the food, and your girlfriends plotted along with you—like that sweet child, Dianne, did for you."

"Wait, now Dianne is sweet? You never even liked Dianne, and always told me she was fast and would get me in trouble."

"Well, I was wrong," her mother said decidedly. "I have misjudged her exuberance for life."

"You are sitting here telling me, my bad, after how many years—"

"Dianne was just spirited, and you were the conservative one, so I worried. But the past is the past. That child has redeemed herself. She could've been greedy, you know?"

"Greedy? Mother. Her boyfriend Rick is Forster's best friend and she would never—"

"No, no, no," the older woman corrected. "Not to keep him for herself, but she has two other sisters that she could have passed him off to, but she thought of you first—now that's a true friend. Soul sisters can be thicker than blood, sometimes. My goodness what a gift. Had one of them myself, once."

"Mom, you are not going to divert this conversation by going onto a tangent about play-Aunt Sylvia."

"God rest her soul."

"Okay."

There was no use and Lynette knew it—so did her mother, who sat smugly in the passenger seat. The excitement in her erupted every so many blocks, bursting out in little giggles as she'd bring her fingers to her lips and send her gaze beyond the car window. And although curious about what drove her mother's private mental conversation, she knew better than to ask . . . because only Ida Graves and God knew what outrageous thing could happen next.

Nine

Her mother had burst through the door like a SWAT squad, taking the pins out of her hat so fast that she wielded the long instruments as though weapons. She stabbed them into the brim and then tossed it in the top of the closet quickly, hung up her coat, and brushed past Lynette on a mission.

"Now what?" Lynette followed her mother's breakneck pace around the house, talking to her in rapid-fire questions as they tried to tidy up. Forster and his children would be ringing the bell at any minute! This was a very bad idea. She'd strangle her mom later.

"Just slick up the downstairs powder room, and stay calm, don't panic," her mother urged. "If he's a gentleman, they'll be about a twenty-minute lag."

"What does being a gentleman . . . never mind."

"Because, if that young man was raised right, he will come in here with something in his hands."

"But *you* invited *him* to dinner, Mom! He was out in the street—"

"A gentleman would stop along the way and bring something. That's how it's done."

Her brain was on fire and she could not argue any longer with her mother's invisible knowledge base. There simply wasn't enough time.

"Hand me my two big skillets," Ida Graves commanded, as though she were an emergency room doctor doing triage. "I'ma get these chops on, fast, then the string beans can heat up while I do the potatoes. The cake's already done, just needs warming for dessert. Gravy . . . bring down the flour so I can make it in the pan from the drippings when the chops are done. Be sure to put on a nice tablecloth, and use real napkins— only set down the plates and glasses, no silverware, though. Hand me an onion, then make some iced tea."

Lynette was breathless as she scampered behind the woman who was turning the kitchen into an efficient ER and the dining room into a cozy restaurant. How did she do it? And all that business about being tired, having arthritis. Humph. Her mother looked rosy, healthy, and like she could run a marathon. It was hard to keep up with her!

"Okay, last question. Why no silverware?"

"So those little girls will have something to do while you and your suitor talk on the sofa. Gotta keep children occupied to keep them out of grown folks' business."

Her mother never turned away from the stove as she answered her, and she tied the knot on her apron without even looking at it—a real pro.

"Lynette, don't be silly. They can help."

"Oh." The infinite wisdom in her mother's plan had left her momentarily stupefied.

"Don't just stand there gawking at me—go put on something more comfortable, and bring me down my slippers."

"I don't have time to change, they'll be here—"

"You won't have time if you keep arguing. Now do as I say. I'm the one who answers the door, not you— you'll seem too anxious. You must display calm. Plus, it's bad manners, and will only make your guests feel uncomfortable, if we're all in church clothes and they just came in from a day in the park. I can be dressy, I'm your mother and the cook, and I'm not the one courting. So, go change so you'll put that man at ease when he comes in here."

"Now I can't even open the front—"

"No. And hand me that flour!"

He pulled the car into a space on the tiny, one-way street that he'd driven past a hundred times without notice. He surveyed the neat row of houses that had yards in between them and wide porches, thinking somehow this was the kind of place he had imagined Lynette Graves would live. Why that came to mind, he wasn't sure. But he did know that he needed a moment to gather himself. This was not what he'd planned on today, even though it had the makings of everything he'd ever hoped for.

However, there was just no way he could resist Mrs. Graves's charm, much less her daughter's, and as his mouth and stomach were saying yes in the middle of the street when the offer was being made, his mind was telling him that this was a bad idea, too soon, and way too fast. A date was supposed to be a solo mission, and so far, the woman he was trying to get next to might as well have been surrounded by palace guards—her mom, his children, and two of their friends. A brother couldn't get a break.

Forster took his breath in slowly, let it out, closed his eyes, and rubbed his face with his hands.

"What's the matter Daddy? Are we here yet?"

"Nothing," he murmured to his five-year-old. "Just tired. And, yes, we're here."

"I'm hungry," the seven-year-old protested.

"Why'd we have to buy flowers, and stop at 7-Eleven

for ice cream? That lady said she had cake. Bet she had ice cream, too."

"You don't go to people's houses without bring a little something along, pumpkin."

At least not when you were meeting their mother for the first time, his mind added. Not when you were going to see a woman who you wanted so badly you couldn't even dream about her—'cause it scared you to even get your hopes up that high. It just wasn't done.

"Look," he warned, turning toward the backseat. "I want you all to be on your very best behavior in there. They didn't have to invite us . . . and, don't break anything, or start clowning around in that lady's house. I want you all to mind your manners, and remember to say thank you when offered something. We got that?"

"Yeah," the oldest child sighed.

"Can we eat now?" the other child whined.

Forster steeled his nerves and got out of the car, and then collected the children while pulling out the bag of ice cream and the cellophane-wrapped floral arrangement he'd been lucky to get from the dwindling choices of a downtown street vendor. What was on his mind? He should have passed on the invitation. He wasn't ready. He'd never had to formally do this before. It was something out of a fifties movie!

"Ring the bell," his whispered. "Once. And don't lay on it, you hear?"

"Okay," Rachel giggled, pressing her nose to the glass in the upper pane that Forster had raised her to. "The window is all pretty colors!"

"It's stained glass, sweetie."

"Lift me up so I can see, too, Dad! I wanna see."

"Wait till they open the door, okay?"

"You always pick her up first," Rebecca said sullenly. "Jus' 'cause she's the baby."

"I am not a baby!"

"Cool it, y'all. What did I say in the car?"

The kids grumbled but fell silent, and stuck their tongues out at each other in defiance. Seconds turned into minutes, which felt like hours . . .

"Come in neighbor," Mrs. Graves said warmly as she opened the outer door and led them into the vestibule. "Now what did you go and do?"

"Just a little something for the house," Forster said quietly, closing the outside door behind him and handing her the flowers along with the bag with ice cream. The immediate smell of home cooking made saliva come to his mouth and his stomach gurgled with anticipation. God it had been so long since he'd enjoyed such a simple pleasure.

"Now you *know* you didn't have to do that."

Then she smiled and kissed his cheek and let them in past the vestibule, locking the second door behind them once the children had tumbled over the threshold and touched the stained glass in it.

"Ma'am, I really appreciate your invitation."

"The pleasure is all mine. Now, you all take off those coats and put them in the closet over there, have a seat, and let me get back into the kitchen . . . make yourselves at home. I have all sorts of music over there that you can feel free to put on, and there's some paper and pencils on the coffee table to occupy the girls. I need to get back to my pots, and Lynette will be down in a moment. She just went up to put on something more comfortable."

"Thank you, again, ma'am."

"Stop thanking me; it's nice to have company."

He watched the very attractive matron recede into the depths of the house, and he better understood where Lynette got her graceful manner and classic beauty. In her heyday, her mother must have been something else.

His eyes scanned the terrain. Everything was so orderly, neat . . . This was what a real home was supposed to look like.

Moving with caution, he removed his daughters' coats and gave them *the eye* to get them to sit down on the overstuffed floral couch, draw, and not to dare smudge anything on it. Once the telepathic order was received and obeyed, he went to the closet and hung up the coats. Dag . . . even the closet was orderly. This was the type of home that had pictures on the mantles, brick-brack, and he knew it had to contain a proverbial china closet somewhere. Deep. And no man had snatched up the fine woman now descending the stairs like a princess? What was wrong with the brothers!

The intoxicating smells coming from the kitchen and the sight of Lynette Graves moving toward him almost buckled his knees.

"Hi," she said shyly, then came nearer holding a pair of pink slippers. "Look, I have to apologize for my mother. She's a very determined woman . . . and . . . I know this was an unplanned imposition on your Sunday, but . . . well, I appreciate your stopping by."

Was the woman crazy? An imposition to be treated like a king and to have his children fed and loved up by a grandmotherly type . . . and to get to see *her* again?

"Lynette, this is real nice—especially for the kids. It's a treat. I'm just sorry that we've imposed on your Sunday quiet time."

Was he kidding? To have a chance to see *him* again, and to have him and his children meet her mother, and to get a Good Housekeeping seal of approval on a guy that was making her blood boil . . . he had to be joking.

"Hi, Miss Lynette," Rebecca chirped. "Can we put on the television?"

"No," Forster commanded. "They have on the stereo

now. Just draw some pictures like Mrs. Graves gave y'all the paper and pencils for."

Lynette stifled a smile, and dared not go against his parental edict despite how dejected the girls looked.

"Good, you're finally down," Mrs. Graves said brightly, returning from the bowels of the house with flowers in her hand, swapping them with Lynette for her slippers. "Why don't you put these in some water on the dinning room table? They are so lovely. Forster brought them—wasn't that sweet?"

Her mother was amazing. The woman had timing like a Swiss watch, which she was beginning to appreciate. Lynette lowered her nose to the spray and looked up and smiled. "Yes, these are very lovely. You didn't have to do that."

Oh, yes he did. The smile it brought to her face was worth ten times the small gesture.

"It wasn't anything." His heart slammed against his breastbone and he glanced away. Watching her in mixed company was too hard at the moment.

"He also brought ice cream to go with the cake," her mother added, slipping away into the kitchen again.

"I'll just be a minute. Make yourself at home," Lynette said in a shy voice. This man was making her crazy. Flowers. Her mother had to be a psychic.

"I'm hungry," Rachel whined.

"I told you all—"

"It's all right," Lynette chuckled. "I'm hungry, too. How about if you ladies help me finish setting the table?"

"Okay!" a chorus chimed.

"I do that all the time for Dad," Rebecca said proudly.

"I help, too," Rachel fussed, skipping behind her sister as the three women left the room.

Data point. She was learning how to read the signs

like her mother was just now teaching her to. No woman in the house, obviously, other than an elderly grand-mother—the kids set the table for Daddy . . . which meant that, more than likely, Daddy was the one cooking. Yeah . . . it was Sunday, and the girls said Gran was too sick to cook. Then who did hair? Daddy. Wow. She needed cold water for the flowers—fast.

Wow. Forster sat down slowly on the couch and stared behind their retreating forms. He'd heard about stuff like this. He'd always envisioned a family like this for him and the girls. Packaged with a princess and a real, honest-to-God, cooking, loving grandmother, too? The trajectory his thoughts were taking made him edgy. Why would any woman of this caliber want to deal with all the baggage he was carrying? One visit to his house to meet *his* mother, and poof, the fantasy would be gone. But, good Lord, the woman was fine. The fact that she was so nice and so real just made the thought of not being able to win her all the harder to bear.

Again, time became his enemy as every female in the house left him to his own devices. The rich aromas coming from the back of the house were making him dizzy, and the insistent day dreams about Lynette that were plaguing him made him stand up and pace. Flashes of her in the long layers of knit fabric from the night before were commingling with the way her wool slacks clung to her backside when she'd left the room. And, her mouth, and those eyes . . . he had to get his mind on something else, or risk his sweatpants giving his thoughts away. Not in Mrs. Graves's house under the auspices of a Sunday dinner. Don't go there, not even mentally!

That reality became a cold dash of water, and he

moved to the stereo to look at the album collection of old seventy-eights, and thirty-threes, in order to get his mind off of the unthinkable, and to his surprise he was completely spellbound.

They had all the greats, and apparently Lynette had added to her parents' choices with the seventies masters. Dag-gone . . . The O'Jays, Tower of Power, Brass Construction . . . Earth, Wind & Fire . . . Minnie Riperton, The Isleys, The Commodores, and LTD . . .

"Mind if I put on an album?" He'd hollered the question as though he were home, settling on Jeffrey Osborne before he heard the answer.

"Make yourself at home, I told you!" Mrs. Graves yelled back.

Dust crackled on the needle as he set it down and stood beside the old technology. It had been years since he'd actually heard some of these songs. Now he was feeling them. Every pore of his body soaked the music in.

"Listen," Mrs. Graves whispered, glancing behind the little girls as they left the room to put out the knives and forks while Lynette stirred the iced tea.

"What?" Lynette whispered back, now more humbled by her mother's ability and acumen, and desperately wanting to make sure the evening went off without a hitch.

"Listen to the man's music choice. A slow, beautiful love ballad."

"It's just calming music, nothing loud because we had on smooth jazz on the radio before. He's just being respectful of—"

"Will you for once give me credit for knowing something?" Her mother hissed back with a smile. "Their mother is gone, the grandmother is sick, the children are neat and mannerly and obviously adore him, and the man's stomach growls at the mere mention of food."

"But what's that got to do with music?"

"He's lonely. Have you seen the way he looks at you?"

"How can I see how he's looking at me when I can't look at him?"

Her mother laughed in earnest this time and shook her head while tending the meat on the stove. "For goodness sakes, Lynette. Go keep him company on the sofa. I'll keep the girls distracted until I finish these chops. Trust me on this."

For the first time in a long time, she didn't argue or question the wisdom of the sage. It was liberating to have someone there who knew more than she, and who hoped as much as she did. Needle points of anxiety prickled the tips of her fingers as she nodded, glanced away in embarrassment, and took up the vase instead of the iced tea and left the room.

"The flowers look lovely on the table," she murmured, finally garnering the courage leave the dining room to sit beside Forster. She picked up the cover of the album he'd selected and tried to seem casual. "I haven't listened to some of these songs in years."

"I know what you mean," he said with quiet appreciation lacing his voice. "But, are the girls okay back there? I hope they aren't under foot and bugging your mother? I know what it's like to try to make dinner and have them in the way, bickering, and asking a million questions."

"Are you kidding? She's probably teaching them how to make gravy by now, and she's in hog heaven."

"I don't know about your mom, but I sure am."

Wow . . . he couldn't believe he'd said that. It sounded too anxious, too corny. Damn!

"To be honest, I am too."

Lynette could have kicked herself. Way too bold! The truth just slipped out, and it sounded too desperate, too anxious . . . oh God!

Forster swallowed hard and looked out the window. She was feeling it, too. He had to remember to breathe or he'd pass out. Only six inches between them, kids running around, and a mama in the kitchen. She smelled so good . . . that fragrance again. Her smile was so shy, and her skin looked so soft, and the music was running through his veins as Jeffrey sang everything he wanted to share. His hands were trembling as he surveyed another album. "That's good," he said as calmly as possible. "Then when you come by to see those photos, I'll know what kind of music you like."

Oh, boy . . . years of abstinence were making him stupid! He needed a diversion—fast.

"I thought you were going to let me read some of your work, too? Remember last night—fair exchange is no robbery?"

Remember last night . . . remember last night! Was he out of his mind? How could she forget the way the man had made her wet her panties by merely brushing her leg? And she'd been so wound up that she'd practically breathed the offer to him—but now? Right here and now, with her mom in the kitchen, Sunday dinner pending, little girls running from room to room . . . now, he wanted her to bring down her poetry, and to share some of the most sad and intimate, erotic, steamy parts of herself?

"Yeah," she murmured after a swallow. "I remember." Then a self-conscious chuckle worked its way up from her throat.

"Well," he said leaning in so close their noses almost touched.

"I'll go get it," she whispered back, briefly shutting her eyes as a tremor went down her spine and lit a fire in her belly.

"I can't wait," he said, his voice now husky.

"I'll be just a minute."

She shot up from the sofa like someone had burned her and tried to walk calmly up the stairs, reminding herself to breathe on each step. Jesus help her, she had to pull it together before her mom read the undercurrent between them. This time there was no mistake—the man was on it. She was on it. Problem was, space.

Grabbing her journal from her nightstand, she made her way back downstairs and returned to Forster's side, noting that the man stood each time she or her mother entered the room. Old school was working overtime, and it was chipping away at her inhibitions. No, it had pulverized them.

"Some of it is really rough, and not anywhere near ready . . . some of it is sad stuff I was going through when I was dealing with the whole divorce thing . . . some of it is just little daily epiphanies . . . and, well, some of it is a little racy . . . but I was just messing around with thoughts on paper."

"Stop explaining away your work," he said with a smile. "To the artist, nothing is ever truly finished. I just want to check it out—no judgments, deal?"

"Deal," she said relaxing with a laugh. "And, when you get all nervous when I look at yours, I'll remind you of the same thing."

"Deal. You show me yours, I'll show you mine, okay?"

The double entendre sent another tremor through her, and all she could do was smile and nod. Where was dinner? She should have been back there helping her mother . . . she needed a break in the action—fast!

Divorced with no children . . . the man had to have been a pure, unadulterated fool! As he read some of Lynette's words, they held him in a vice grip—her pain was so familiar, the sense of loneliness pouring from her prose . . . then he turned the page. Her description of wanting to be touched, the sensual ache that came from needing to feel the burn of human skin-to-skin contact, the fires within her soul . . . and yet not accepting to have them quenched unless her soul and spirit could also be touched. The descriptions, the way she told the unvarnished truth, the imagery on those pages. . . . He took his breath in hard through his mouth. There was no way to hide it. He wanted her.

"Wow," he whispered in awe. "I'd better put this down for a minute to get my head together." What the hell else could he say? He had to do Sunday dinner any minute now, and he was going blind. All the blood had drained from his head and was taking up residence elsewhere— which was uncool and disrespectful of her mother's house. He had to eat soon, and needed something to thin out the aphrodisiac he'd just ingested.

"You really like it?" she asked, now feeling too exposed to really look at him. She couldn't. The expression on his face, and the way his hands had begun to tremble again as he'd read. The way his breathing became stilted. . . . His nostrils flared just ever so slightly, as though he were trying hard not to let it show—which was positively riveting. She hadn't had anyone ever respond to her work like that. Not her husband, anyway, and she'd never really allowed any other guy she was dating to see it. It was too private . . . but Forster's reaction almost made her forget where she was. But why had she even offered to do it? Her brain wasn't working right. Where was dinner?

"Like it, is not the word . . ."

"Thank you," she stammered. His voice had entered her ear and nibbled at the lobe of it. Just the vibration from the sound alone sent an electric current through her. "I was just messing around, like I said. It all needs to be cleaned up."

She glimpsed at him, but this time his gaze held hers.

"If you were just messing around on the pages I've read, then I'd love to see what you'd do if you were serious."

The comment had been delivered two octaves lower than what she remembered as his normal speaking voice. The baritone vibration connected to her skin, and caused gooseflesh. Her nipples stiffened beneath her blouse, and she noticed that he noticed when his lids had lowered by a quarter. The man had swallowed hard before he'd spoken. He now openly displayed raw hunger, which was no longer a subject of mental debate—it was beyond the question of did he or didn't he. That guessing game was over. He clearly did.

If her mother hadn't been banging pots in the kitchen . . . if two little kids weren't a giggle away . . . if she hadn't been raised by Ida . . .

"I think I may have new, more serious material to work with, though," she daringly whispered, unable to contain herself, then immediately became shocked after she'd said what she did. "I mean—"

"Yeah," he murmured. "I hear you."

Damn. This was getting too deep for the venue. It wasn't supposed to go here—not yet.

"It's been a really long time since . . . I've enjoyed . . . since I've had somebody come by."

Nothing she was trying to say to clean up her comment was being delivered with the right amount of discretion! It all sounded too forward, too . . . too . . . too something! What did her mom put in the iced tea, truth serum? All she wanted to do was let him know that she was definitely interested in him, but while also keeping the right distance protocol so he didn't think . . . damn. The years of celibacy were wearing her out, and she was so rusty at this dating thing, which was all about pacing . . . and now the man had breathed, "I hear you," in a way that had made her wish they were alone!

"I hear you," he murmured again, but this time he'd almost panted out the words on a whisper. "You have no idea how long it's been."

The sound of children bustling into the dining room with her mother on their heels made both Forster and Lynette sit back. Both gave each other a sheepish glance as they then stood, and both discretely let their breaths out in unison.

"Well," Ida Graves said brightly, calling to them from the dining room brandishing a platter. "I sure hope everybody is hungry?"

Ten

His belly was so full that all he could do was sit back in his chair at the table and puff and blow with total satisfaction. Mrs. Graves had outdone herself, and no matter what he'd told her, she kept piling succulent chops on his plate like it was Thanksgiving. In many respects, it was. He and the children had laughed at the funny stories that Mrs. Graves had shared about having teenagers in her house against Lynette's protests, until finally Lynette broke down and told some comical stories of her own. And then, there was Lynette's laughter . . . and the way her eyes sparkled with mirth. Thanksgiving had indeed come early this year, just in time for the fall leaves to change.

Watching his daughters' lids grow heavy from the long day and now overfilled stomachs, Forster begrudgingly began the slow process of extricating his brood from the ebullient hospitality that he could have enjoyed all night.

Almost as though sensing his departure, again Mrs. Graves jumped in before he could form the words, and extended the evening with one more treat—homemade butter pound cake.

"Now I know you are not about to take these children out of here without dessert," she fussed, standing and removing a decimated platter from the table.

"Ma'am, I don't know if any of us have room for dessert after this fabulous meal. Lord in Heaven . . . I haven't eaten like this since I can remember."

"Daaaaad," a sleepy Rachel whined. "Can't we have some cake and ice cream? You promised."

"Yeah," Rebecca fussed, her face growing alarmed and looking like her father had committed a felony. "You even bought the ice cream. C'mon, Dad . . . pleeaaase?"

"You are simply overruled, Daddy," Mrs. Graves said with a chuckle as she moved toward the kitchen.

"But where do these two skinny little girls put it all? That's what I wanna know." All he could do was shake his head and relent while sucking in air to try to make room for what he could only imagine to be a heart-stopping end to the meal.

"Children always have room for dessert, and they did very well with their plates," she countered, hollering from the next room.

"Your mom is something else," Forster sighed with a grin. "They broke the mold."

Lynette laughed and stood up slowly, practically wobbling from the fullness in her stomach. "That they did—I told you and warned you, but you didn't believe me, brother."

"No," he said, growing serious. "I didn't mean it like that . . . she's a peach. All mothers should be like her. You're really lucky."

His words briefly halted her retreat to the kitchen and she studied the genuine appreciation in his expression, which went with the wistful tone in his voice. "Yeah . . ." she murmured. "I love her to pieces. There's nobody like Mom."

He nodded, and she walked away, trying to imagine what comparison he was making. When she entered the kitchen, her mother was carefully arranging slices of cake on a cookie sheet in the oven, and had already taken the ice cream out of the freezer to soften on the side counter.

"Thanks, Mom," she whispered, coming up beside her mother and hugging her when she stood.

"Now wasn't this just what the doctor ordered?" Her mother looked so fulfilled that all Lynette could do was hug her tighter.

"You're a genius."

"Just experience."

"I love you."

"I love you, too, suga'. Now go back and keep your company occupied while I bring out dessert. After you all eat, I'll take the girls on the sofa with me to piddle around, and you let that gentleman help you clear the table."

"But he's company . . . I mean . . ."

"Yes, and you want the man to feel at home—like family. And, you want to give him room to say a few words to you without all eyes on him . . . so, go with me on this one last little request, and then I'll get out of your business. Plus, it wouldn't hurt for him to see that you know how to wield your weigh in the kitchen, and aren't just all degree—some things ain't changed since Adam and Eve. Now scat."

Lynette laughed and nodded, although totally doubtful of her mother's claim to get out of her business. But somehow, at the moment, she didn't mind that her mom wouldn't.

"I'll just take these dirty plates away and make some room on the table for dessert," Lynette said efficiently as she swept into the dining room.

Before she could protest, Forster was on his feet and

it made her smile. Her mother was a master, a psychic one at that!

"No, no . . . you're company," she said quickly, almost bumping into him to relieve him of the soiled plate he held.

"I've imposed enough, and I sat here and ate like a yard dog," he said with a deep chuckle. "Plus, I have to stand up to shake four chops, half a plate of mashed potatoes and gravy, and a mess-kitchen pot of string beans with biscuits down into a leg, or I'll burst at the seams when the cake comes."

"Mom has a heavy hand when it comes to dishing up for people," Lynette admitted with a giggle. "For her, food equals hospitality, and I think she enjoyed cooking for a man again."

"Well, I'll be much obliged any time your mom is feeling the need to put on the pots, as she says. Have mercy, the woman can burn."

"Yeah," she said with an appreciation. "I had to double my exercise routine when she moved in here."

"No doubt," he sighed as they walked back to the kitchen together. "Let me take those in to the girls," he said to Mrs. Graves, who was holding small saucers brimming with the treats. "Then, afterwards, you, ma'am, are going to take a load off and sit down, while me and Lynette clean up. Like I said before, you've outdone yourself."

Lynette stifled a smile as her mother put on her most innocent expression.

"Now, son, I am slowing down a bit, and I do appreciate the offer, but I certainly couldn't ask a guest to my home to clean up all of this fracas I've left in here. I'll just pace myself and get as much of it done as I can . . . then, in the morning—"

"Ma'am, please, let me do that. Lynette, tell your mother to let me help. It's the least I can do."

"Mom, why don't you go on in and have dessert? You've been fluttering up and down and you've been out all day, then cooked . . ."

"Well, if you all insist. Maybe I will just set a short spell . . . then I can show the girls how to make little vests out of crocheted squares. I am getting on in years, and after I eat, I just don't have the same energy as when I was a young woman."

"Then, it's settled," Forster said with a smile, pecking her on the cheek.

"Oh, all right . . ." her mother sighed and smiled brightly. "But so long as you know that you are welcomed any time. I haven't had a man around the house, or little children to do for, in so long I can't remember. It was nice to have you—and I don't want you to think any of this was a bother."

Her words poured over him like warm butter and melted him down to the soul. "Ma'am, I haven't been done for like this in years, if ever. And I want you to know that the hospitality goes both ways. If you or Lynette ever need anything, I'm a phone call away and right around the corner. Anything in here breaks, needs fixing . . . or if you hear a bump in the night—I am a policeman, and public security is my business . . . even help with bags at the market, just so long as you call me first. Deal?"

"Deal," Mrs. Graves crooned, moving to Forster and holding both of his cheeks with her hands. "Now I'ma put your telephone number and address right up on my refrigerator under a magnet, and you do the same— make sure the children have it. I am home all day with nothing to do. So, if you have to work late, and want me to walk around to the school two blocks away to pick up those two darlings, you have but to ask."

Forster simply blinked and stared at the woman for a moment. God was answering so many of his prayers at once it was making his head spin.

"I mean it," she said, dropping her hands and standing back a ways to make him understand she was serious. "I've taught children for over thirty-some years, and had an ailing mother when Lynette was a small girl. I know what it is trying to keep a house, watch your own child, and do for others all the time, and tend to the ailing. Besides," she scoffed, "I haven't felt this useful in years—would do me as much good as those children. I taught second grade—what is elementary school homework to an old school teacher like me? So," she said with added conviction, walking to the counter to dish two more saucers of dessert, "it's settled."

"But—"

"No buts. You'll call me if you need me. I'm going to fix up a plate for your mama *then* I'll sit down. See if she'll eat just a little if she's real sick—you have to keep her fed. And, if you have to work late, or just want to go out on your own for a while to clear your head . . . or need a little time to yourself for a change . . . or just need somebody to put together a meal for you to take home—you have my number. You buy the food, and I'll prepare it . . . Sunday is my cooking day, so all you have to do is drop off a selection of groceries, I'll tell you what to buy, and I'll fix so you can freeze for the week. Just let me know, and *it's no bother*. All you have to do is ask."

"I . . . I . . . I don't know what to say, ma'am . . . I mean . . . thank you so much," he stammered. "But, I can't let you do that—I mean, going to all that trouble. The girls are used to—"

"That's just it. *You have girls,* son. And, if their grandma is ailing, then you need some female help. And, only the Lord can tell Ida Graves what she can and cannot do. So. It's been said, and the offer has been made. Suit yourself as to whether or not to take me up on it. But, you are letting those children's ice cream melt while you stand here in the middle of the floor gawking. Lynette, help the man get the saucers on the table, since he seems to be having difficulties, would you, suga'?"

They both laughed and followed Ida Graves's orders. At least Lynette had a witness now to the fact that there was no arguing with Ida Graves.

Again he found himself in the position of having to sip in air after his stomach took another load of a mouthwatering treat from Ida Graves's kitchen. Unable to stifle a yawn, he simply covered his mouth and gave in to it.

"I'm sorry, y'all, but I'm done. Totaled."

"I'll take that as a true compliment," Mrs. Graves said with a chuckle, standing slowly herself as she called to the two nearly limp little girls at the table. "C'mon sweetie birds. Let's go let this cake rest while your daddy and Miss Lynette clean up. You all put on the music and I'll go fetch my crochet basket, then you can pick out your favorite colors."

"What's crochet?" Rachel asked through a wide yawn.

"Oh," Mrs. Graves replied, as though it were a big secret, while glancing at Forster in triumph and exchanging a wink. "That's a way to make some really pretty things that all girls love. You do it with yarn. What's your favorite color?"

"Mine is purple," Rebecca chimed in.

"I like pink," Rachel added. "But what you gonna make?"

"How about if we start by working on some little squares, and then we'll hook 'em all together and make some pretty vests—like the kids are wearing now?"

"You can actually make them out of thread? Here, yourself, I mean? Not from the store?"

"Yup," Mrs. Graves said with confidence. "Might even have some of those colors, too. I know I have pink, but we might have to compromise on the purple. I think I have a pretty dark blue in my basket, though . . . but I will be sure to pick up purple, just for you, the next time I go to the store. Shoo now, let's go sit in the living room and I'll get my basket. Your daddy can help you put on a record while I hunt for my supplies, then he and my Lynne will clean up the table and the kitchen."

Pure amazement nearly held him midstep as the older woman enraptured his daughters. She was right—there were so many things he hadn't a clue about how to teach young girls, and in that moment he realized that the day would soon come when there'd be things that he wouldn't be able to.

But there were some basics that his own grandmother had taught him, and he'd be sure to pass on what cursory knowledge he did have. "What do you say, ladies?"

"Thank you, Mrs. Graves!"

Forster nodded, approving of their response.

He made quick work of cajoling the girls to listen to Chaka Khan, and laughed as they tried to convince him that she'd stolen her hit from the rappers, instead of it being sampled the other way around.

"All right, all right, ask Uncle Rick, then," he teased, leaving them to shimmy and shake in the middle of the living room while he went to help Lynette.

"Can you imagine that?" Carrying silverware to the sink, he dropped it into soapy water and shook his head.

"Chaka Khan is not one of the original divas, and she stole music from some young boys?"

"No!" Lynette laughed. "Heresy!"

"That's what I told them, girl. We oughta go out there and show them the real moves . . . remember The Abby, The Old Man, The Slide, and The Bump?"

"C'mon, c'mon," Lynette belly laughed, shaking suds from her hands and running ahead of him into the living room.

"See, now we old folks is gonna show you how it was done," he boomed. "Aw sookie, sookie, now, girl . . . show 'em the bump, Miss Lynne!"

"I got chure move, boy," Lynette boomed back. "To the left, to the side, spin around, awwwww, don't hurt chur-sef!"

"Nah, to the floor, oops, psyche-your-mind," he teased through hard chuckles, jumping away from Lynette when she went to bump him, then coming at her low on the down beat.

The kids were rolling on the sofa with belly laughs, which drew Ida Graves down the steps, and she joined in the merriment, watching Lynette and Forster perform moves from yesteryear.

"I thought you all were washing dishes—you're as bad as the children," she giggled, pulling out her yarn and wiping tears of sheer glee from her eyes.

"Oh, no, ma'am, we had to address a challenge to the great music masters of the seventies, first. We gonna do them dishes, pots and pans, too, but first we had a score to settle with two nonbelievers," Forster huffed through a dance step, spinning and bumping Lynette so hard that she bounced away and almost lost her footing.

"Dag, boy! Oh, so now you want to go Soul Train serious, huh? Well, a sistah's got something for you!"

When Lynette started doing The Penguin and took it

to The Funky Chicken, everybody howled. Forster lost his composure, doubled over and waved his arms. The girls were now sliding off the sofa onto the floor, and Ida Graves was wheezing for air.

"Enough, enough," he laughed hard. "Point made!"

"You better come wash my mama's pots and pans, den, boy," Lynette teased with her hands on her hips. "My mama don't allow no partying in her house lest you clean up, ain't that what you used to tell us, Miz Ida?"

"Sure as rain," the older woman laughed. "Sho 'nuff."

"Then, let me hightail it into the kitchen so I don't get put out and can come back."

"That's just what you need to do—trying to show out on me on *my* dance floor, brother. Who you think you is, anyway?"

They left the children and Mrs. Graves laughing behind them as they ran to the kitchen and started mimicking bump dance moves in front of the sink.

"Oh, those poor children," Lynette sighed with a hearty laugh. "I remember my parents barging into our parties with some old mess they used to do from the fifties, trying to tell us all about how we didn't know music. I can't believe we just did that—you know it's a sickness that comes with age!"

"I hear you," he laughed from deep within his chest. "My uncles and aunts used to cut up the rugs down at my grandmother's house in Georgia. Dag, I miss those days. Thanks, Lynne, for bringing them back this evening."

The two fell silent for a moment, the mirth dissipating, as they stood side-by-side at the old double sink.

Wow . . . he had called her Lynne, not Lynette . . . and had told her something about his past—which until this moment, she hadn't realized that he hadn't mentioned anything about it.

"What's your mom's favorite ice cream?"

"Strawberry. Why?"

"Might have to stop down to Reading Terminal to get her some of the good homemade stuff from the Amish vendors . . . I have to do something—"

"You have done enough, trust me." She added more hot water to the sink and then stopped her task to look at him. "Do you know how long it's been since I've had my mother back?"

When he didn't respond, she pressed on.

"Tonight she had a man to feed, little girls to dote on like they were her own grandkids, and she laughed, Forster—really laughed. The woman is in seventh heaven. Ever since my father got sick and passed—and I was gone, went right from school to New York, then a storm flooded her out of the home they'd built together, the woman has not laughed—not the kind of laughter that comes up from your soul."

"Then fair exchange is no robbery," he murmured. "Used to laugh like that when I was a kid, and my dad and mom were together . . . and when we'd go down South every summer to see my grandmother. She had the kind of home like this—one filled with food, commotion, family, and a lot of laughs. Then, one day, she passed, my parents split, my mom started drinking, and it all stopped. I was eleven when I stopped really laughing."

The look of sheer heartbreak in her eyes made him turn away and fetch a pan from the stove.

"I'm sorry," she whispered.

"Hey, it's cool. That was a long time ago. I just really appreciate you and your mom giving a little bit of that to my kids . . . and to me. Kids should know times like this—it holds them together when things aren't so cool."

When she didn't respond, he rattled on, searching for anything, something to say that would restore the groove he'd just blown. Why did he even go there? He always sabotaged himself, and after a wonderful evening, what would make him just completely spoil it with the information he'd shared!

"How about if you leave the silverware and the pots for me—I just don't want to do your mom's good plates. Heaven forbid I drop one with my clumsy self, and . . ."

The look on her face made his words trail off. Her gaze held him with so much warmth and compassion, and yet pity was nowhere to be found in those wide, brown irises that soaked him in.

"I can see the genetic resemblance, inside and out," he whispered. "You and your mom are good people . . . inside and out. It's always in the eyes, my grandmother used to say. You can see a good heart there . . . through the eyes."

She looked down at the suds bashfully and spoke as she began to work. "My mother meant what she said, and I second her offer. We're neighbors . . . and you and the girls have a couple of friends around the corner, now. I was blessed to grow up the way I did—we didn't have much money, and we lived in a tiny little row house, but we did have plenty of good times. I certainly don't mind sharing Ida Graves, God bless her, while she's still here."

"I meant what I said, too . . . about you being able to call on me if you hear a bump in the night, or need something fixed, or whatever . . . your leaves raked, ya know?"

"Yeah, I do," she said softly, stepping aside as he

hoisted a large skillet into the water to begin scrubbing it.

Without speaking, they had fallen into an easy rhythm in the kitchen. It was as though they'd worked side-by-side like this for years. There was an indefinable simpatico. She dried and moved the delicate plates and utensils and made room for the heavy cast iron that her mother was so found of; he scrubbed the heavy metal and rinsed it, putting it on the drain board when she was done. No words were necessary.

"This morning, I called Sharon—Dianne's sister," he said offhandedly after a while. "I told her that I'd take her kids, the twins and her son, to a bowling party PAL is having next week. It's up on City Line and Haverford Avenues . . . Saturday, like three to six . . . didn't know if you'd be interested, but it might be fun? No pressure, or anything . . . just thought, well, you can let me know."

"Bowling?" A wide grin came out on her face.

What was he thinking? By now he should have been angling to ask her out on a real date! He could have kicked himself.

"I know it's corny, but—"

"Oh! Do you know how long it's been since I've done that? When were kids, the church used to hold bowling parties all the time for us, and we used to go in big groups, and chew gum, and talk about the boys, and have the music blasting, and we'd run into the bathroom, giggling," she exclaimed, making a twirl in the middle of the floor. "I'd love to!"

"If you're sure?"

"Ooh, is Dianne going, too, with Rick?"

He had to laugh. God, he liked this woman, who made him feel so good . . . so young . . . so everything . . . so alive.

"Truth be told, I don't know. My man was AWOL at the walk, as I'm sure your girl has him indisposed," Forster confided with a deep chuckle. "Those two . . ."

"I hear you," she giggled back, moving closer to him. "That's all right, we'll take the crew and feed 'em good, and spoil 'em up, and give Sharon a break—but Carol is on her own until her little bird is weaned. That's my goddaughter, but I can't give the baby nothing but love until Mommy stops breast feeding."

"I feel sorry for the girl," Forster added with a smile. "She fussed so hard in the background when Sharon told her and started teasing her about being on lock-down until her baby went to the bottle, and Sharon just rubbed it in like salt in a wound. Those two are a trip."

"You don't have to tell me," Lynette chuckled, shaking her head and accepting a dripping, clean skillet from Forster. "They used to bicker like Frick and Frack since we were kids."

"But," he hedged, "are you sure you're up for a whole bowling alley filled with hollering kids for three hours? Seriously, girl, you don't have to go there, if you don't want?"

The hopeful expression he held made her want to wrap her arms around him, but she didn't. Instead, she just waved him away as she paced across the room to put the pan back where it belonged. God, how she liked this man. "I'll be too through if y'all leave me."

"I don't know if my Taurus is big enough, though?"

"I can drive," she scoffed, taking another pot from him and putting it on a shelf. "Besides, you need another car, really, to belt the kids up right and get them there safely."

"True . . ."

"What were you going to do, anyway, especially if Rick was on the lam?"

He laughed. "I was going to put Donell in the front seat, Rachel on one side in a belt, Rebecca on the other in a belt, and strap the twins in under one on the hump in the middle."

"Riding like The Beverly Hillbillies? Ain't that against the law, officer, to overload a car with kids like that?"

"I just had to make it a few blocks from Parkside to—"

"Thoroughly bogus," she huffed, and then burst out laughing, making him laugh again, too.

"All right. Deal."

"Deal."

With no more dishes to wash, they stood for a moment staring at each other. Now what?

"Well, it's getting late . . . and it's right before a school night for the girls," he murmured, wiping his hands dry on the end of a dish towel, and glancing at the clock on the wall. "I'll bring your mom's plate back over, soon."

"Okay," she found herself whispering while drying her hands . . . and now finally understanding the wisdom of getting to know a man from the inside out, first. The old dolls had been right. There was a certain wisdom in taking one's time.

"Okay," he murmured back, but did not move.

Hope for someone like this had once seemed like a birthright, and then it became too dangerous to even consider. And the man that she once thought was handsome beyond words, had transformed into something even more breathtaking as he stood before her like a gentleman . . . a man who'd allowed her to be herself in her own home and had given her a glimpse of his soul in the kitchen . . . a man that respected her family, her friends. A man that she found herself twisting a towel into a knot because of as she stood there like a girl of sixteen. This was a man that made her want to run upstairs and call her best friend.

If only she had had a series of chaperones to guide her when she'd met her husband . . . if only there had been plenty of group activities before they'd gone straight from meeting each other to sleeping with each other . . . if only they had been able to become comfortable friends, first . . . learning how to share what she'd just shared in the kitchen with a man she barely knew. If only she'd listened to her mother.

"Next Saturday, then?" Her voice was so soft that she wasn't sure if it wasn't just a thought.

"Yeah. I'll come by to your house first, and we can drive together . . . follow each other over to pick up the kids from Dianne's. Maybe you can even convince her and Rick to go?"

"I'll try," she offered with a smile, "but I think it might take the Jaws of Life to pry them away from each other. I hear tell that policemen carry such equipment in their trunks?"

"Not us forensics guys. But, I can't blame the man, either . . ."

He had replied with a quiet chuckle, but his gaze penetrated her in a way that made the butterflies take flight in her belly again. He'd left his statement hanging, just dangling like a hint to allow her to know that he could envision the possibilities. But he'd also covered it enough with subtlety to show her respect. If he hadn't glanced away, her knees would have turned to jelly.

The way she looked at him, he couldn't keep staring at her, but being in her presence had rooted him to the kitchen floor. Did she have any idea what a night like this, and her mere presence alone, was doing to him? Watching her wring and twist a dishtowel in her graceful hands like that . . . the sign of being just a bit nervous, tinged with a bit of anticipation, and she hadn't flinched when he'd commented on their friends' passion.

If only . . .

Eleven

When the spray from the shower hit him, he almost groaned with relief. The girls had been easy to get in and out of the tub and tucked into bed, and mercifully, his mother was out like a light when they got home. All he had to do was clean up and leave her a note about the food he'd brought in from Ida Graves's house—his mother would eat later, as per usual, when she got up in the morning. But at the moment, he could finally relax, without worrying about any of that.

The walk, the food, the laughter, the dancing, and Lynette Graves, had frayed every nerve in his body while satisfying almost every muscle in it at the same time. As tired as he was, he should have simply gotten through his nightly routine, then crashed and burned. Yet, he didn't feel sleepy—just fatigued, in a sated sort of way.

It was odd, but the woman made him feel jumpy, but also her countenance and her mother's warm hospitality had made him feel so comfortable. And, for the first time in a long time, problems were the furthest thing from his mind. It was a strange sensation, since worry had become his constant companion. Almost like a starved lover, it normally clung to him, made him constantly roll around tasks and responsibilities in his brain. But, tonight, where was worry? Perhaps she had left him in a huff, being displaced by another woman. "Good riddance," he murmured and put his head under the spray, feeling the water pelt him into oblivion. Lynette Graves gave rise to a whole different set of issues that paled nagging worry. She owned doubt.

But, God, a hot shower felt so good on a full stomach. This was the sort of night that should have been shared with a bottle of wine and soft music . . .

His mind drifted with the suds that fought to disappear down the drain. Fix dinner, eat and laugh with the kids, bathe the children and read stories before tucking them into bed, a grandmother saying good night and going to bed, cleaning up the kitchen as a team, then asking the wife if she wanted to sit on the sofa for a while . . . putting on the easy sounds, then open a bottle of wine . . . sit next to a soft woman under low lights . . . listen to her tender voice . . . laugh together as you rehashed the evening . . . "Yeah."

But did he say, "Wife?"

Maybe . . . touch her beautiful face, and stroke her velvet-soft hair, pull her in close and feel her breathing through your chest . . . placing a kiss on the crown of her head, making her look up to receive one against her mouth.

He shuddered and closed his eyes. Lynette Graves was making him dream things he'd stopped dreaming, and feel things he'd stopped feeling . . . and worst of all, she was making him more than hope—she made him wish.

To no avail, he commanded his mind to stop wishing for what was too soon to be. That would only become a source of frustration, he told himself as he put his hands out in front of him to balance his weight on his palms against the cold tiles. He turned his face into the full blast of the spray. Forget about it. Dwelling on how much he wanted this woman might make him make a false move, do something stupid, like rush her, and then he'd be doomed to the male purgatory of being considered just a dog. For her, he wanted to be more than that—and a woman like Lynette Graves just wasn't to be rushed. Especially if you wanted the entire package deal. . . .

He wanted to be able to sit on the sofa with her one day and have her look up into his eyes with respect . . . admiration. She had that kind of eyes. Those beautiful, big brown eyes that he could drown in. The kind of eyes that made a man feel like he could do anything in the world, was invincible . . . the kind of look that her mother had given him, the same look that his grandmother used to give him as a child, same look his daughters gave him, the kind of eyes that told a person he was somebody. They were not the kind of eyes that saw flaws, or hardened around the edges to reflect back disappointment. They were the kind of eyes that one wanted to see admiration reflect back from . . . and Lynette had shown him that so many times tonight.

But when would be the right time? Finding out how much he liked her had only seemed to make time stand still. Finding out how good they were together had made him wish, and seeing that her eyes could penetrate him with passion, unlike the other eyes he'd just thought of, made waiting all the harder. Oh yeah, she'd made it hard . . .

He turned up the hot water and stood flat-footed in the spray. He could wait for a woman like that. Actually, he had no choice. If he could just get his body to cooperate with his mind, and to get off the subject, then he could hang. He wasn't a teenager; he was a grown man with kids. He'd been through worse than waiting for a woman to feel comfortable with him . . . there were a lot worse things than having to kill an erection.

If he could just stop thinking about the words on the pages she'd written, and stop his mind from seeing the way she'd sipped shallow breaths while they sat on the sofa alone. If he could just push away the glimpse he had of her nipples getting hard under her blouse . . . or stop remembering what her leg brushing up against his under the table had felt like. Pure, smooth butter . . . Jesus, make a way that won't take too long . . .

He turned his back to the spray and let it pummel the tension out of his shoulders. He took in his breath through forced, slow inhales. He had to shake this out of his mind. Tomorrow was a workday. Tomorrow he'd take her mother's plate back. Tomorrow he'd stop by Reading Terminal and pick up strawberry ice cream and some purple yarn . . . tomorrow maybe he'd see her again. Tomorrow, maybe he'd get to see that pretty, shy smile again. Or maybe she'd belly laugh with him again . . . perhaps her eyes would grace him with an expression of appreciation one more time? He'd pick up some roses at the Terminal . . . and find out when she could come by to see his photos, and maybe she'd come and sit on his sofa in the basement . . . maybe late, one night, when the kids were in bed.

And maybe he'd get to feel that private sigh of hers reverberate through his skeleton again. And maybe she'd take in tiny sips of air for him . . . and maybe her eyes would say it all, just as they had for a moment, too brief a moment, on her mother's sofa. . . . And maybe without a chaperone this time, she'd allow him to sit nearer. And maybe she'd allow for just one gentle kiss. And maybe she'd allow him to deepen it with his tongue . . . she'd said it had been so long for her, too, and he'd heard what she implied—but was too much of a lady to state.

And, just maybe he was wishing, but if it had been anywhere near as long for her as it had unbearably been for him, she'd return the deepened kiss with her tongue. And maybe, if there was hope, she'd wear a soft cotton blouse, one just sheer enough for him to see the outline of her sexy, rounded breasts . . . and maybe, if they both had been as starved as he so clearly was, then she wouldn't object to his touching what pouted for his attention . . . brown or pink? he wondered, as an unrelenting throb made him suck in his breath quickly.

Maybe her thigh would brush his again . . . maybe her blouse would have buttons on the front . . . maybe her bra would unclasp from an easy hook in the front center, and he could find out if the color on the tips matched her pastel mouth or not. Maybe they were dark like her eyes. And maybe she wouldn't be too offended to simply let him love her, just a little, on the rec-room sofa . . . not all the way, just enough to hold him over, to bring him closer to his wish.

But what if there were time and space and a place to give her all he needed to give her? The fantasy fractured him and his hand covered the source of the ache. Instead of his palm ebbing the pain, it burned it, branded it, sending a coursing agony through the entire length of his groin. A groan echoed and bounced off the tile back at him, the sound of his voice foreign even to his own ears. It had been so long . . . and the contact of skin against skin tightened his grip, and its request for friction became a demand.

What would she feel like . . . ? Wet, breathless woman . . . responding to his thrusts, calling his name, her legs locked around his waist, her hands holding on to his shoulders, her moans sending shafts of heat into his ear, making him thrust harder . . . making up for all the nights in bed alone. What would her throaty call sound like, her breasts against his chest feel like? What would her firm, high, round bottom be like, cradled in his palms . . . and those long, shapely legs, twining within his, his hands in her hair . . . and a spasm rippling up from her center, clenching him, holding and releasing him, drinking him, until he just couldn't stand it . . .

The convulsion began in his stomach, took his breath as it fought to exit him, forcing him to reach out and hold on to the shower wall to keep from falling. Wave after wave of spasm rocked him, and he sucked in air through his mouth, trying to steady himself, trying to remember where he was . . . home alone.

"So?" Ida Graves didn't look up as Lynette flopped onto the sofa next to her.

"He asked me out, in the kitchen, to go bowling with him and the kids . . . next Saturday."

"Uh-huh . . ."

Her mother hadn't taken her gaze from her needle as she'd made the casual reply.

"Do you like him?"

This time Ida Graves looked up and smiled. "The question is not if I like him, but do you like him?"

Lynette found an idle ball of yarn and began fiddling with it, winding and unwinding it.

"Well?"

"Mom," she murmured, "I just don't want you to get your hopes up, then be disappointed. I mean, he seems nice, and everything . . . but, you never know how these things go . . . and, now he's got you hooked on him and the kids, and what if we fall out, then you'll be all sad because they don't come around anymore, and you know what I mean."

"I know that you're messing up my skein, for starters," her mother laughed gently. "And, for two, I am way grown, Lynette. I can fend for myself."

"No, but for real, Mom . . . we don't really know him, and what if there's something that makes us fall out, or the chemistry is wrong, or whatever . . . he finds some-body else—a million things can happen. And, here you are—"

"Nope. Here *you* are. Lynette, I don't have to date the man, you do, sweetie. And, if y'all fall out, well, we'll cross that bridge when we get there."

Lynette chuckled and looked at her mother, search-ing her eyes for any wisdom that would make the butterflies calm down. "I suppose you're right. I'm pro-jecting the worst, rather than thinking about the best . . . but do you think he likes me?"

Why did she feel so totally, entirely undone by this man . . . so much so that, she was back to sitting on the couch with her mom asking questions from an era gone by? Does he like me? Coming from a grown woman? This was not a good sign.

"I think he more than likes you," Mrs. Graves said, setting down her hook and yarn and holding Lynette in her gaze. "I think, no, correction, *I know* that this man is absolutely crazy about you, and after a few more of these group dates, out of respect, you'll need to have in your mind a very clear picture of where, and how far, you want this to go. Am I making myself clear?"

She could not be having this discussion with her mother!

"I . . . I . . . ur, uh, Mom!"

"I thought that man was going to absolutely slide off the sofa—just melt away, from looking at you and talking all cozy, when I left you two alone. You could have cut the so-called chemistry with a knife. I wasn't born yesterday, you know."

Lynette opened her mouth and closed it, but no words came out, and the fact that her mother chuckled, adjusted her reading glasses on the bridge of her nose, and took up her crocheting again, didn't help matters.

"Well," the older woman said, "I guess that means it's time for me to make a little space in here. Can't fight nature, that's like boxing with the wind." Then her mother sighed as she cast a sheepish glance at Lynette and went back to the task in her lap.

"Mom . . . I'd never . . . I mean . . ."

"When you were sixteen, and the fellas would come sniffing around, some I'd clear out for, some I wouldn't. Ain't nothing changed since Adam and Eve, like I told you before. But, like all things, discretion is the better part of valor, and this time, instead of just allowing for some kissing time . . . well . . . I guess I can go on down to the casinos with my girlfriends, or take a trip to Lancaster to shop. . . . That one, Lynne, I'll clear out for."

"Mom, no, really, it isn't like that . . ."

Her mother's gaze held hers as the older woman looked up at her again.

"Baby, for that man . . . that one . . . your mother will clear out. You understand what I'm saying to you?"

"I . . ."

"Only if you want me to, now mind you, and I'll know when."

"You . . . wait . . . how?"

"'Cause you'll get all evil, and start pacing, and start talking about needing your own space again. Lordy, chile, if I had know that was what was in your system from last night, I'd booked myself on a dang cruise for a week. He's worth it—I was young once, tol' you that."

"Mom!" Lynette covered her face and laughed hard, too embarrassed to do much else.

"Yeah," Ida Graves sighed. "I remember what that was like . . . feeling all out of sorts, not exactly knowing why . . . too shamed to just say it plain, because you hadn't made it plain in your own mind yet, much less enough to tell somebody else—not that a lady would tell anybody else, even though, today, you young women tell all your business. It just wasn't told, in my era, but that doesn't mean it didn't exist. There's nothing new under the sun."

Lynette glanced away, her mother's casual truth almost too much to take in one sitting, especially after an evening in Forster Hamilton's presence.

"Do you ever miss . . . never mind. I guess, what I'm asking is . . ."

"Yes," her mother said so matter-of-factly that Lynette had to stare at her. "Yes," she repeated with emphasis. "Very much. If what you had with your husband, or any man, I suppose, was good, you will miss it. That's normal. By my count, it's been three years, and you're a young woman . . . that's an awful burden, youth."

It had to be the surprised expression on her face, the one she couldn't now control, that had made her mother giggle.

"Do you know how long I waited to be able to say that? Have you any idea of what being a widow is like . . . when everybody thinks you're this dried up, old prune, still in mourning? And, do you know how long I've waited for my daughter to grow up enough to talk honestly with? That's why I cried harder when my mother died than when my husband did . . . because she was my rock, my friend, my everything. I wanted that with you, too . . . a good friend to go with the good daughter I already had."

"You talked about stuff like this to Grandmom?"

"Close your mouth, child, you're catching flies," Mrs. Graves chuckled. "Suffice to say that we spoke in metaphors and parables, but we understood each other, and she taught me a lot. So, what I learned, I'll pass to you . . . and you pass it on, and so forth. That's how life is supposed to go—but, today, parents are burying children, and such . . . everything is all turned around and not in the order God made things."

Again, all she could do was stare at her mother.

"So," Ida Graves said as though passively resigned, "I think I may take Deacon Charles up on his offer, now, and might accompany him to Atlantic City to play the slots on a Friday afternoon. May even go around to the school and do a little after school volunteering, or maybe read to children at the library on Fortieth Street—would do me good to go out."

"Deacon Charles . . . ?"

"That old buzzard has been pestering me for years— even before your daddy passed. But, he's still sorta handsome, and I can still see the good looks left over in him from when we dated in high school."

"What!"

"I told you, I wasn't always your mother, and I did have a life . . . quite a colorful one, as I recall. But, that's my business." Ida Graves laughed hard as she fumbled with her yarn and readjusted her glasses on the bridge of her nose. "You are catching flies, again, Lynette," she teased without glancing up.

"I'm not asking you anything else, Mom . . . but all I will say is, you and Aunt Nellie and Aunt Suzette must have been a handful for Grandmom."

"Uh-huh. But, what about this fella? You *really* like him?"

Lynette paused, and her voice became a mere whisper. "Yes, Mom. I do. I'm just afraid that . . ."

"He's not William, rest assured. Don't be afraid of him for that—there's other reasons, but not that."

Puzzled, she again searched her mother's expression until the sage decided to speak once more.

"I know he's not William because of the little things. The man has good home training, Southern style to be exact."

"His grandmother was from Georgia, and helped raise him for a while—how did you know he had roots down South?"

"Well, there you go. Lynette, there is *nothing* on the planet like a Southern gentleman, trust me—and on that one, no, you cannot ask me how I know, but honeychile, I do!"

This time they both laughed hard, but many questions still remained and she pressed for wisdom, now helping her mother make a new skein as they sat.

"But, you said there were other things . . . things to worry about. He did say his mother and father split when he was little, eleven." She held back the part about his mother drinking. Oddly, her mother's opinion of him mattered now very much, and she just didn't want to damage Forster in her eyes.

"Now, that's a shame," Ida sighed, clucking her tongue. "That poor child . . . But, that doesn't have a thing to do with it. Couldn't you tell how much he values family by the way he wrapped his arms around it in here? Most likely, his wife did the messing up, God rest her soul, but she had to be crazy. He's not the leaving kind of man, and doesn't seem to be the type to leave a girl, either. Forster is solid—permanent."

"Then, if that wasn't it, what do I have to be worried about?"

"You have to worry about that man seeing the diamond in the street that you are, snatching you up so fast, and popping the question. That's what you need to worry about, suga'. It's not him, it's you—I don't think you're ready to try your luck again. He is."

"Oh, Mom, come on . . . see, that's what I meant about you getting your hopes up too high, wishing too hard—"

"You are as blind as a bat," she laughed, taking off her glasses and setting them on the bridge of Lynette's nose for comedic effect. "Here, you wear these."

Lynette giggled as her vision blurred, but she kept them on for a moment to make her mother giggle harder. "Okay, now that I am truly blind, tell me what I can't see."

"You didn't see the man glance around and do a house check—"

"A house—"

"That's right, a house check, to see if you were good mother material—the kind of woman to bring up his girls right. I have a child, so I know. You, on the other hand, wouldn't even know how to discern the look."

"Deep," Lynette murmured, regaining her original awe for her mother.

"Second of all, he kept watching you, seeing if you approved of his manners, his conversation, and if the little ones took to you. Then, he eyeballed me, to see if I'd be a help or a hindrance, and was trying to see if I approved of him. The poor man looked like he was on trial, went all ashen from time to time, such a shame, too, because he has a handsome complexion. Good looking young fellow."

"But—"

"Don't interrupt while I'm schooling you, baby. Now, the topper was, before I had to say a word, he was helping you out, and trying his best to earn his keep for his supper—sweat equity. A man that's just passing through don't put in sweat equity. This one did, and he kept after them younguns with *the eye,* making them behave, and they did . . . then, at times when he'd glance at you, daughter, I'm telling you, the heat was so thick I could have used it under a frying pan. Then, he'd catch himself, and look away. Respect. Numero uno, is to respect a lady before her mother in her house. Impressive . . . don't see it anymore these days. But, just the same, I probably got a hole in my dining-room drapes from him looking at you, then quickly looking away toward them. So, that's what I'm basing my judgment on . . . all the signs that only a mother can see."

"Wow," Lynette murmured, flopping against the back of the sofa.

"Yes, wow," her mother said, shaking one hand like it had been burned on the stove. "And, if I were you, at your age, with a second chance around like that, I might have to disrespect my mama—just don't put it in my face, is all I ask."

Lynette covered her mouth and laughed as the older woman looked up toward the ceiling and spoke to it.

"Sorry Mom," Ida Graves said, "but you know the truth is the light."

"You are so crazy, Mom!" Laughter temporarily stopped her words, and abiding companionship filled her heart. "If wishes were fishes. . . . Well, he and I have both been in bad marriages, he's got little kids to worry about possibly taking through another one—if he decides on me—but that's too crazy and too soon to even think about. Plus, we haven't even been out alone, yet, on a date, and you've got me going down the aisle, raising children, and jumping in the sack. Mom . . . you talk about me projecting. . . . And you got all this from a Sunday dinner?"

Her mother just chuckled and began to put away her crocheting and then stood. "I'm going to bed now . . . when you get to be my age, you just know when to speak your mind and when to let it rest."

"I love you, Mom."

"I love you, too, baby."

"Thanks for everything."

"Don't thank me, say your prayers tonight, hard, and just thank Him."

Lynette smiled and kissed her mother good night. "I will."

"Good . . . and a little wishing, too, never hurt anybody."

Twelve

It helped his sullen mood considerably that Rick was out on assignment when he got to work. This morning, he wasn't sure if he could take a chipper disposition, a relaxed vibe, or the normal digs comparing his monk status to Rick's playboy existence that came with the friendship, especially if Rick started in on questions about Lynette. Not this morning. Not after tossing and turning all night, and not after waking up with another blinding erection for her that had to be dealt with through mind over matter. He was just not in the mood for ribbing.

And, as expected, the day crawled like a lazy turtle in the Georgia sun.

Finally able to get out from under the ever-present mountain of paperwork, he'd almost prayed for an assignment—anything to get out beyond the four walls, even though when they sent him out it was for tragic reasons.

The crisp fall air, however, did him good, and he found himself in front of the Reading Terminal, then parking, and then wafting through the large covered farmer's market like a zombie. Despite the press of the normally heavy lunch crowd and shoppers, he was in and out in moments, back in his car with his vehicle headed toward West Philadelphia. Still in a semidazed state, he once again found himself on the front steps of the Graves residence, ringing the bell with the full intention to hand over his parcels and a plate to Ida Graves—then he could bring closure to the night before and deal with the long week ahead of him without Lynette.

But instead of an elderly woman answering the door, fate had played a cruel trick on him. It sent a mirage to the door, an oasis, and all he could do was stand there for a moment, parched, clutching his packages as she smiled at him.

"Hi," she said brightly. "I thought you were the courier. I decided to work on my assignment from home today, because I hadn't done a thing yesterday—Mom and me hung out. . . . Oh, where are my manners, look at me just babbling, come on in. Forgive me for . . . well . . . this is my work-at-home-and-comfortable outfit."

"No apologies needed. You are home, and I am the intruder. This is just a quick stop by—I've gotta get back to work."

He had forced himself to smile, tension made that nearly too painful to accomplish. Sunglasses hid his eyes, and he was grateful that he hadn't taken the full blast of her warm rays without that protection. Because if she had seen his face, unmasked, there would have been no doubt, and there would have been no way to hide what his expression surely told on him. And there was no way to prepare himself for her natural beauty. She was more gorgeous clean-scrubbed without makeup than with it, just as he'd imagined. . . . What was a man supposed to do?

The woman had thrown open the door, her face had lit up, and she'd stood there with her hair somewhat tussled, and she was wearing a thin white, sleeveless T-shirt—with no bra—and a pair of black, ballet-style stretch pants that hid nothing, and she stood there in bare feet.

"Normally, I would have called first," he managed, but didn't trust himself enough to cross the threshold yet, "thought your mom would be home. Didn't see your car when I pulled up, so—"

"Come in, come in. Can you believe it, she took my car to go run some errands and to have lunch with her girls. My mother hasn't driven herself around in years. Boy oh boy, I don't know what you did to her, but it was all good."

Then she laughed, and the melody of her voice sent pinpoints of light behind his eyeballs. He briefly shut them and tried to banish the image of her shiver, and the way she ran her hands up and down her arms, and the way her unharnessed breasts squeezed together when she did so . . . and how the goose bumps on her arms had formed tiny pebbles that stood up and challenged him at the ends of them.

He shivered, too. Then followed her inside.

"I wanted to get her plate back to her and bring her that strawberry ice cream, plus that purple yarn she wanted . . . figured, at my house, her good plate was in jeopardy."

"Oh, she is going to be so thrilled when she sees these, too," she added with a giggle, liberating the dozen long stem roses from him. "Forster . . . these are beautiful."

The way she'd intoned the last part of her statement of appreciation was practically making him weave in the middle of the floor. The way she drew out his name, and breathed it out after lowering her nose to the blossoms. There was barely enough blood left in his brain to summon speech.

"Those are for you . . . the ice cream, yarn, and the plate are for her," he said hoarsely.

"Thank you," she murmured. "You really didn't have to."

Yes he did . . . oh hell yeah, he did.

"I just wanted you to know I really enjoyed your company last night." Holding out the ice cream to her, he tried for an evasion to his senses. "Better get this ice cream in the freezer before it melts, though." Yeah, before he and the confection became a puddle in the middle of the living-room floor.

"You are just so thoughtful," she cooed. "C'mon back in the kitchen while I put these in some water and the ice cream away." She poked in the bag and chuckled when she spied the yarn.

Then she nearly skipped ahead of him. All he could do was follow her and watch in agony as her long legs took full strides, which made her behind hypnotically bob and sway before him.

"Okay . . . but I've gotta get back to work."

"I know, I know, and I'm not going to keep you," she said laughing as she puttered and he stayed by the door frame. "It's just such a nice surprise on a Monday, you know. I promise not to hold you long."

Hold me hostage, baby . . . his mind yelled out, as she dipped and swayed and sashayed around the kitchen like a dancer. Then, there was the voice again.

"Oh, these are so pretty . . . just gorgeous . . . do you know how long it's been since someone gave me roses?"

Then she looked up at him with those eyes—slightly sad, full of wonder, and sparkling with more than he dared to imagine.

"You deserve to have a flower shop in here," he murmured. "I'm just glad that you like them."

Then she came near him and stood on tiptoes and

brushed his cheek with her luscious mouth. The burn from it made him swallow hard, and he inhaled her as discretely as he could. God, she smelled so good and felt so soft. He had to thrust one hand in his pocket, and hold out the plate, ice cream, and yarn in a plastic bag with the other to keep them from shaking, or reaching out to pull her to him hard. He needed something to do with his hands.

"Oh, yeah, the ice cream and Mom's plate," she chuckled, setting the flowers down on the table and collecting the items from him that he offered. "I'll put the yarn upstairs on her pillow as an extra surprise for her when she comes home."

After stowing the items away and placing the yarn on the table, she then reached up on tiptoes again to find a vase in the cabinets. Her long, lithe body stretched and gave him a full profile of her curves that made her appear to be a finely buffed sculpture. Dancer. Definitely. Then, she turned, gave him her back again, much to his chagrin, and bent over at the hips to look for a vase in the bottom cabinets. He leaned against the door frame to keep himself from passing out.

"If you keep this up, we're going to run out of vases." Her voice was bright and merry, and her motions smooth and graceful.

"I'll bring them already in water, next time," he heard his voice say. "And if they make you this happy, expect a regular delivery."

Then she looked up at him with those shy, big, brown eyes, and her lashes dusted her cheeks as she lowered them before staring at him dead on. He had to remember to breathe.

"I can't wait to get together again on Saturday. . . . Thank you so much, for everything, Forster."

She'd barely whispered his name, and she was simply

standing there taking in shallow sips of air. Had she any idea what she was doing to him?

"I can't wait to get together, either . . . and the thanks is all mine."

Silence slipped between them, and, as though trying to break the spell, she smiled, turned, and began putting the roses in water.

"Did you eat lunch, yet?"

How could he eat when his mouth had gone dry?

"No, I was gonna just grab a hot dog from one of the vendors on my way back in."

"Now, you know you've come to the home of Ida Graves, and if I told my mom I let you eat off of one of those dirty trucks when you had the option to sit down in her kitchen, she might not open the door the next time you ring the bell."

Her laughter and the offer was blackmail, extortion, unfair. She was a smooth criminal, and he had just been kidnapped from his job. He laughed, and the tension it released made him finally take off his sunglasses.

"Please don't rat on me, but I really have to get back . . . then again, we could eat, I could play hooky—I mean, stay connected by cell phone and pager without actually going back to the shop, and I could show you those photos? That is one advantage of the job—flexibility."

What was he saying! He had to go to work, had to get back to the paperwork on his desk. Had to catalog some prints. Had to stop thinking about how to get this woman into his basement lair. And, his mom was home, probably, and upstairs in her cups!

"Oh, that would be wonderful!" She paced toward the refrigerator and pulled out a honey-baked ham.

"Does your mother ever sleep, or does she just cook round the clock?"

Again she laughed, her voice rippling through his

bones and sending another wave of ache through his groin.

"No, and yes," Lynette giggled, grabbing the bread and rummaging for sandwich fixings. "How about if I make you a ham-and-cheese sandwich, some iced tea, then I'll run upstairs and throw on a sweater over this, and pull on some socks and sneakers, then we can jet? So, c'mon, sit down here in the kitchen, and take off your coat," she ordered.

"Aren't you going to eat with me?"

"I can't do a whole sandwich after yesterday, but I'll pack up a goodie bag for you to take home—actually, that's why Mom got up early this morning to make the ham before she left."

"I don't follow?"

"She said for me to bring you dinner for you, the girls, and your mom."

Now he had to take off his coat and sit down. "She didn't have to do that. Really."

"You know what it's like to argue with Ida Graves," she said with a chuckle, bringing out covered glass pans from the refrigerator. "I was given explicit instructions to dish out some macaroni and cheese, greens, corn-bread, and ham. That's what I was told—and I'm not getting into trouble with my mother when she comes in . . . especially since you came by with her plate, ice cream, and some roses, plus purple yarn. Now, how would that look?"

All he could do was chuckle as she made fast work of preparing a sandwich for him, and then she scampered away with the yarn and left him.

Lord help her! The man had brought her *roses* . . . Just came to the door, standing there all fine, with roses, ice cream, yarn, and a clean plate. She had to do some-thing. When all else fails, feed him, she had been told. Especially since he was standing there looking like he was about to eat her. And, if she had known a more exact approximation of when her mother was coming home, today, she might have let him. Have mercy, that man was fine.

Lynette pulled on her beige, bulky-knit mohair sweater and found a pair of thick scrunch socks, and then ran her fingers through her hair. Feverishly work-ing, she spritzed on a little fragrance, found her gold stud earrings, and her running shoes. Then, she looked in the mirror, added some eyeliner and a neutral shade of lipstick. She had to be presentable, just in case the man's mother was there and she met her. But, for sure, she had to get him out of her house—as there was no way to keep a ladylike demeanor with him in here, home alone. No, she wasn't hungry for a sandwich. Not when they were both playing hooky from work like two errant school kids.

"Okay," she announced as she barreled down the back staircase into the kitchen. "How you doing on that sandwich?"

"What sandwich," he replied with a chuckle, wiping his mouth with a napkin, and then polishing off his iced tea.

He looked at her as though she might be dessert. The quick transformation was icing on the cake. How did women do that?

She shook her head and laughed, clearing his plate and leaving it in the sink. "Let me put a note on the fridge for my mom, and let her know I'm doing a ham and macaroni and greens delivery."

"Don't forget to also mention the cornbread," he

added with an easy chuckle. "And, please, whatever you do, don't forget to put it in the bag."

"See, boy, I won't," she fussed good-naturedly. "You gonna get me in trouble with my mom."

"I promise I won't do that, but you might already be in hot water." He waited for effect until she turned around. "You allowed to have boy company in the house when your mother's not home?"

They both laughed hard.

"No, I didn't think so," he teased. "So, we'd better get going."

Sunshine only made her look prettier as it glistened in her hair and added golden highlights to her face. Parked in front of his garage door, they waited until it opened, and both got out in unison when his car came to a final halt inside.

"Oops," she chuckled. "Force of habit."

"I'll allow the transgression on account of you came here bearing gifts," he teased her, showing her through the door that adjoined the garage to the basement recreation room.

"Let me go upstairs and put this away—have a seat, make yourself comfortable, then I'll find those photos."

He needed a moment to do a reconnaissance pass through the house. He had to give his mother heads-up warning to put on a robe and to beg her to try to act halfway hospitable, if not simply civil. He had to check to be sure that Lynette could come up there to see where he lived without being totally offended.

She nodded, but a strange thought came to her mind. Why didn't he take her upstairs to meet his mom, if she was up there—and if she wasn't, why was she being told to wait in the basement? True, he'd said the woman drank, but that was still no reason to keep her sequestered from his family. It didn't feel right, and she would speak on it when he came back—maybe.

She let her line of vision scan the environment. So typically male—all leather and chrome and media center, a bar area, but no liquor in it. Deep. Sports equipment, bar bells . . . made sense. That had to be how he kept his fabulously hard body. But, the black and whites that he had framed and hung—wow.

"I uh, wanted to know if you want to come up for a minute and meet my mom?"

He looked so unsure, and so about to die, that she braced herself for what she was about to witness. And, at the same time, she projected as much confidence and lightness in her spirit as she could muster. The man had read her mind.

"Sure," she replied brightly. "Would love to."

He only nodded and turned, which she took as an offer to follow him. Upon coming up the steps, thick cigarette smoke surrounded her and her eyes focused upon a small, frail woman who wore a dirty blue bathrobe and a scowl.

"Mom, Lynette Graves—Lynette, Velda Hamilton."

"Pleased to meet you," Lynette murmured, extending her hand, which the older woman only stared at until she withdrew it.

"So, you're the one who's been sending food and trying to hook my son, steal my grandkids? Good luck. Forster don't go in for tricks and games."

"You know what, Mom," he said through his teeth, "I only came up here out of respect, and Lynette doesn't deserve that. Her mother sent the food for the kids, and they had enough for you, too. So, chill. They're our neighbors."

Lynette glanced at the floor, immobilized. Heaven help this man if this was whom he had to grow up under.

"So, now I'm supposed to be grateful? Oh, yes, where are my manners? Thank you, Suzette."

"Her name is Lynette," Forster growled, and then motioned for Lynette to go into the other room with him.

His gaze was cast down to the floor and in those few seconds her brain fought to recalibrate. Within moments her senses had taken in the kitchen with once light-blue curtains, now dingy from cigarette smoke—but clean. She now understood who mopped and shined and kept the home fires burning. The girls had been right: their gran was definitely sick.

The living room was devoid of drapes, hosting only miniblinds, Spartan malelike furniture, a wall unit with all things technologically modern, but also displaying beautiful photos on the walls. When she'd passed the dinning room, there was a table and chair, again photos, and no china closet or buffet—just one highly polished table in a room that looked unused. And in those seconds her heart broke for the man who she knew had such pride, cared so deeply for his children, and seemed to want a family so much.

"I am so sorry, Lynne," he whispered. "I just thought, that maybe . . ."

"You do not have to apologize. It's all right."

He could not look into her eyes now. Pity was the last thing he wanted to see in them.

"I can understand if you want to go back home and skip the photo tour. After this, photos seem pretty trivial."

"No," she said with resolution. "I've already seen some of your work, well, what I assume is your work on these walls. I'd like to see the stuff you're hiding down in the basement."

Her words, this time, made him glance up, and her steady, serene acceptance shone in her eyes. There was no judgment, no pity . . . and, unless he was mistaken, there seemed to be almost a fiery defiance in them.

"All right," he murmured in deep appreciation for her grace. "Then, we both had better get back to work."

"Nice to have met you," Lynette mouthed to the woman who had clicked on a small kitchen television and was blowing smoke at her. When the woman raised a glass in her direction, she simply turned and followed Forster down the basement steps.

"Never wanted you to see that," he said in a low tone when he'd returned from the darkroom he'd built just off the rec room. "I keep tenants on the third floor to help put something away for the kids' college fund, but might one day just move her up there . . . if I wasn't so worried she'd burn the house down at night, if nobody checked behind her."

He sat down heavily and began unzipping a large, dark brown portfolio.

She didn't speak, just waited, knowing that they were taking a major step forward—trust. All good friends had to have that first before a purge, before anything else could be built between them.

"Truth be told, I never wanted my kids to see that," he finally murmured, never looking up as he arranged the prints on the coffee table before them. "Thought I could go into the military to get away from her, then get married and have some kids—and make the kind of home my father's mother used to have, sorta like your house Sunday . . . But, I messed up and repeated history and married somebody just like that one upstairs. Go figure. Sorry you had to see that."

The wounds in his soul bled at her feet, and she had no idea how to staunch the hemorrhage in his dignity without causing him further pain.

"Every family has some drama," she whispered,

searching for a verbal tourniquet. "Mine, too. Life, sometimes, isn't all sweetness and light."

"Yeah," he sighed.

But she noticed that he hadn't really pulled out all his photos from the case, either.

"Look, your mom is not you—okay? I married a man just like my dad . . . a philanderer, a bar fly, even though he went to work everyday and tried to pay the bills and I loved him dearly, he hurt my mother to her core. And, okay, so on your first try, you married your mother. We live and learn."

This time he looked at her and held her in his gaze. "Thank you, baby . . . I needed that."

He'd called her baby, and his strained voice and tense countenance had relaxed a bit.

Lynette nodded and kept him from glancing away again by sheer force of telepathic will. "My mother would understand, too," she added, reading his apprehension, and knowing in that instant just how much, and why, her mother's opinion of him mattered so much. "Probably already does understand without your having to tell her . . . more than you know—more than I know. That's also why she was probably so adamant about helping with the children. She did this part alone . . . my father messed up money, hung out, did whatever came to his mind to do. Only difference was that he managed to make it to work everyday, and was in a perpetually good mood, a cheerful alcoholic. That's what made it bearable for me as a kid—for her, my mom, I cannot imagine . . . now that I'm grown. And, she stuck around and tended to him when liquor rotted out his liver and gave him a heart attack. She didn't have the options in her day like we have now . . ."

"Your husband drank, too?"

He had asked the question in a quiet voice, mercifully

allowing all that she had exposed about her own father to pass.

She shook her head no. "He snorted coke, a habit developed in the eighties when it was fashionable, that he never gave up—which I later learned after we were married, and when I couldn't seem to conceive, he couldn't bring himself to go to fertility specialists. His pride and his addiction wouldn't work under blood analysis, and so, he made himself a son somewhere else less problematic."

She'd stated her pain so plainly, so calmly, yet her eyes glittered with unspent rage. He knew that place well, where betrayal by the people you've loved and trusted simply implodes.

"They have no right, ya know?" She said with a forced chuckle.

"No, they don't," he whispered in return, so sorry that a visit to his home had dredged up demons instead of provided a small window of respite like hers had for him.

"I don't judge a person by what other adults do. I make my opinions by what that individual does. And, I know you didn't ask me but, I'm going to risk saying this to you anyway—don't let her rob you of the rest of your life, of happiness, or the children. Been there, seen it, done it, and trust me, it's not fun."

Her eyes held a level of conviction that he could not describe. She was simply enraged—not at him, but seemingly for him. The fine line of demarcation made all the difference in the world. Soul to soul.

"I won't," he murmured, staring back into those indignant brown eyes that glared in defense of his honor in a way that no one else's had. "I promise."

Thirteen

"These are positively beautiful," she whispered, now separating the photos on the table and arranging them in a way that he couldn't quite figure out.

"Just something I do to keep my perspective when the world closes in on me," he murmured, watching her as she looked at his work.

The awe on her face, and her sudden calm, even after what they'd just dealt with, made him want again to reach out to her. But not so much as a lover this time, just simply for the affection she so willingly shared.

"Don't you see the pattern in what you've shot?" Her question sounded so distanced as she continued to arrange the photos by some invisible order.

"No . . . I really hadn't thought about it."

"You have almost the same amount of shots in each category. Deep," she whispered, then sat back and beckoned him with her eyes to take note of the piles on the coffee table.

"See here," she pointed. "People toiling, looking as though they are at the end of their ropes, but aren't . . . they have a captured resilience. Perseverance. That's the word this set embodies."

He studied where she pointed, and then rubbed his palm across his chin. "They say sometimes it takes a

different set of eyes to see what's right in front of you
. . . deep."

"Very," she said with confidence. "Look at this next
set. Resignation—after grief. Then this pile: hope. Then
this one, with the fewest shots, Forster . . . joy."

"Wow," he whispered, taking that pile from her and
gazing at it intently. "I just never realized."

She took up the pile that she had labeled perseverance, and her voice became soft. "They said to keep my
eye on the sparrow, and that He'd always watch over me.
Some said fair exchange was no robbery, and others
told me that I'd understand it better by and by. But, how
do I hold on just for today, knowing that the stairs I
climb have rungs missing where I tread? This far by
faith, but I have so much further to go. Guess I'll understand it better, by and by."

She had spoken the words as she slowly put down
each photo like a slow-moving video, her voice music
beneath it. The compassion that she had, the depth of
knowing that she'd added to the photos, his work, his
soul, the very thoughts he'd frozen in stills, she spoke.
Then she took up another pile and put it down.

"Joy," she murmured, reaching for and accepting the
photos he held. "If wishes were fishes, I'd swim the
ocean round, or splash in the hydrant again like a child,
or I'd sit upon the stoops and let the breeze blow against
my face, and my breath would send dandelion seeds of
my hope for a better place . . . and I'd whisper to the
children that life is shades of gray, black and white
being too harsh for the beauty of this day."

"I know what my work has been missing," he murmured, accepting the photos from her and setting them
down. "You."

"Not me, Forster. You have captured life in its pure
essence," she whispered, "and what your lens sees is

what's in your heart. You see beauty where nobody else can, because it resides in your spirit—that much I'm sure of, now."

He wanted so very much to kiss the lids of her eyes, which held him in a state of wonder . . . and to lower his mouth to the one that had put into sonnet what he had no words to say.

"You did this on the fly, created poetry, right out of your head, just from seeing . . ."

"Because you gave me something to work with," she said in a shy, quiet voice. "These are just phenomenal . . . look at how you've found people of all races laughing together, or crying . . . surviving despite the odds, and so carefully preserved their personal dignity, so raw and real . . . just like you can see every pore in their skins and every line in their withered faces or gnarled hands."

"I used to watch my grandmother's hands, and the lines in her face and the depth of her wise, old eyes, Lynette, and I knew that beneath all the flesh and bone of every person, no matter how young or old, there was an essence, a soul inside. And, I wanted to take pictures to preserve that essence, that wisdom, that beauty, and that grace . . . and to pay homage to those who, no matter what, found laughter, joy, or struggled to rise above their circumstances. I suppose, I also wanted to leave my children something when I was gone—more than just a memory of me that could fade or be erased by other people's words. I needed to leave a part of me that was permanent, to help them know who I really was."

"Then," she whispered, "I'd say that you've succeeded, and should make this project a priority. However I can help, I will."

Quiet enveloped them for a moment, and he reached out and dared to cup her cheek.

"Then, would you put your beautiful words to the pages? If this ever goes into a book, I'd be honored to have your credits on it, but more importantly, you're the only person who has ever understood my shades of gray."

Her hand covered his, and the silken touch of it brought his mouth to hers. The kiss he placed on it was gentle, trembling, as though brushing against his might somehow damage the fragile petal of her lips. "I'll call it *Shades of Gray,*" he whispered against her mouth just as she found his again.

"I'd better go now," she murmured when he pulled back. "I don't trust myself to do the right thing."

He nodded, although her admission fractured his reason. "I don't trust myself, either . . . I've wanted to do that since the first time I met you."

"I wanted you to do that, too," she admitted.

Again her words sent a heat that was intolerable through him. Her admission, and her breathy proximity were too much on an afternoon alone in his basement. "If wishes were fishes . . ."

"I'd swim with you all afternoon . . ."

Her statement coursed through him, entering his veins in a rush that flooded his system.

"I'd better take you home now; I don't trust myself to do the right thing . . ."

"After more than three years, and getting to know you and your children, I'm not sure I can do the right thing unless you get up, immediately, Forster."

He closed his eyes and rested his forehead on her shoulder and allowed a sigh to escape against the side of her neck. "Lynette, I need a minute before I can stand. I just . . . but I don't want you to think this is all . . ."

A velvet hand stroked his close-cropped hair sending

an electric current through his scalp, his shoulders, then down his spine. With his eyes now tightly shut, he inhaled sharply, and then admitted the truth. "All my life I've waited for somebody like you to come along, and three years ago, I just stopped looking. . . . Woman, do you understand what I'm telling you?"

"Yes. I hear you," she whispered, nuzzling the crown of his head as his arms wound around her back. "It's been three years since you've felt this, or been held like this, and more than your body misses it—your soul does."

The soft mohair of her sweater filled his hands as he flattened her against him, and his nostrils drank in her intoxicating scent while his lips cherished the butter-smooth skin of her neck, and when a small moan that she tried to stifle worked its way up from her belly, and she shivered in his arms, he released her. No, he was beyond trust.

Leaning forward with his elbows on his knees, he allowed his head to drop into his palms and he shut his eyes. When her hand slid down his back and began to stroke it, he sucked in his breath and swallowed away the agony that had wanted to turn into a soft moan.

"Let me get my coat, and take you back home, okay? Right now. Or, this is going to escalate, and I can't promise . . ." Then, like a jack-in-the-box, he stood, paced over to a bar stool where he'd flung his coat, put it on, and pulled out his car keys.

Her nod, and the difficulty she had standing, and the way she adjusted her sweater, wore on him. The fact that she was there, willing, able, and obviously in as much heat as he, was maddening. Yeah, he had to take this woman home. His mother was upstairs. Uncool.

"I'm sorry," he murmured once they'd exited to the

garage and the sunshine and cold air had hit him. "I don't want you to think that I think . . . I mean—"

"I don't think that," she murmured, halting his stammering apology with her gentle tone. "We both got carried away . . ."

"I like you a lot, Lynette," his said suddenly, then pulled the car into an available space.

"I like you, too."

"I want to get to know you better, before . . . I want this to have a chance—do you know what I mean? I can't believe I'm saying this to a beautiful woman like you, but I do, I am, I mean. You know what I'm trying to say, don't you?"

"You want the package deal," she said with a smile and the barest whisper of a voice. "So do I."

He nodded and got out of the car. Cold air, yeah, he needed cold air to clear his head. Dear God, the woman read minds. Just open her door, walk her to it, go back to work, and work *real hard* for the rest of the day— then pick up the kids, heat up dinner, get back to the routine . . . just get back to the routine, man!

"So we take it slow," she said, quietly opening the front door.

"Yeah," he murmured, coming into the vestibule behind her and closing the front door. "Next Saturday, I'll pick you up."

"And, well take the kids bowling," she said as she turned around to face him, leaning against the wall.

"And, we'll stop at McDonald's," he added, his voice dropping an octave as he closed the space between them.

"And we won't allow the physical to get in the way of getting to know each other, right?"

"Not yet."

"And we won't allow the fact that we both haven't

been with anybody in years to make us rush ourselves, right? Since we want to give this a chance to be more than that . . ."

"No, we won't damage it like that," he murmured, watching the stained glass pour colors over her as his hands found her upper arms and he began rubbing them.

"And when the time is right, only when we both feel comfortable, we'll go somewhere private . . ."

"Where we won't have to be rushed," he breathed against her hairline. "Like it was the first time."

"And, even then, we'll take it slow, because we both have so much at stake," she panted into his ear. "We've both been burned before."

"Yes," he nearly moaned as his body blanketed hers and her softness molded perfectly to his.

"And, we'll give this our best effort by becoming friends before we become lovers," she breathed, her hips quivering as his hands slid down her arms, capturing them.

"Absolutely, baby . . . we'll take our time, and I promise to go slow," he told her hoarsely as he felt himself move against her.

"We have to," she squeaked as her hands found his shoulders and her mouth covered his, parting at the same time her thighs gave him entrance.

And he answered her with the deepened kiss he'd fantasized about, and she responded by clutching the back of his coat and arching hard against him, and his palms relished the shape of her bottom, until he had to pull his mouth away to gasp.

"Baby . . . it's been so long, I can't take it . . ."

"I know," she said on short, hard exhales.

"I'd better go," he pleaded, but his eyes searched her

face for a way to let him stay, and found a furtive expression held within hers.

"I don't want to go, though."

"I don't want you to."

"But your mom could come home at any minute."

"I know, but the car isn't back yet."

"I said I'd go slow . . ."

"Trust me, right now, you don't have to."

Why did she tell him that? It was like detonating a trigger on a grenade. In an instant, he'd pulled her back into a frantic embrace. Her mouth fought with his while her hands fought with the fastenings on his coat. His fingers found her skin beneath her sweater, and he allowed them to travel up her back, his hands made molten by the creamy soft skin against their roughness. He released a groan into the depths of her mouth, and she echoed it in a muffled cry. When her hand slid against his pants, his knees buckled, and he held on to her bottom with a tightened grip.

"If you open those, baby . . ."

"I know," she nearly whimpered against his neck. "It's over."

"Don't pull it out unless you plan to use it; it's loaded."

"I know, I know, I just can't stop touching you," she breathed as his hands rounded her back and slipped up her torso under her sweater.

"You so just feel so good I can't stop, either . . ." he said harshly against her cheek, finding the thin cotton T-shirt and sliding under it as well. "But, your mom . . ."

Tiny pebbles scorched the center of his palms, and she closed her eyes and allowed her head to fall against his shoulder with a whimper. The sound of pleasure that escaped her and the expression on her face when he'd touched her there . . . please, God, let Ida have gone to

Atlantic City like the other old ladies did . . . "Do you think there's time?" He had no more judgment, no more pride, the woman had reduced him to the insane—to begging.

"I don't know . . ." she wailed in a low, pained voice. "I'm not thinking clearly."

Then her hand slid against his length again, hard, and he responded to the rhythm of her palm with a deep, guttural groan. He fused his mouth to hers and found the waistband of her stretch pants, and ignored the distant tone in his ears until she wriggled and pulled back.

"The door bell!"

"Oh, shit!"

"The courier . . . my courier from work!"

"Okay, okay, be cool," he said in a panic, wresting himself away from her and quickly closing his coat.

She smoothed her rumpled sweater, raked her fingers through her hair twice, drew in a sharp breath, and then opened the door with a smile. How did women do that? His groin felt like an anvil had been loaded into it, and he could barely breathe it hurt so badly. Smiling and talking to somebody was way out of the question. A hard contraction seized him and he almost doubled over from the impact of it, but the cold air steadied him and became his friend.

"My package?" she said in a too-casual tone.

"Yeah, sign here," the courier replied, glancing between the couple in the doorway with a curious expression that immediately became a sheepish grin. He then handed Lynette the parcel and jogged down the steps. "Y'all have a great day!"

When Lynette shut the door, they both looked at each other for a moment and then burst out laughing.

"Close call," Forster said, wiping his face with his hands.

"Maybe we should back up and take this slow?"

Her giggle was infectious and it made him laugh harder—any kind of release was welcomed at this point. "See now, girl, talking about going slow is how we almost got to the point of no return in the first place."

"We did get close, didn't we?" She laughed a deep-down, hard chuckle of agreement—but in it was a sexy, teasing tone.

"Yeah," he murmured, the burn beginning to return with the way she'd reminded him of just how close the near miss had been. "And, on that note, I'll see you Saturday."

He brushed her mouth fast, then backed up, making her giggle again.

"All right, and I'm not coming near you on your way out. Just turn around," she ordered, "open the door, and keep your hands where I can see them."

Her laughter was more than infectious, it was a contagious, wondrous virus that took over his nervous system and stole his equilibrium, making him almost forget how to walk forward.

"You must be a cop, undercover division," he chuckled, opening the door and hovering in the frame of it for a moment.

"Stalling for time and letting me freeze to death in the vestibule—you're busted."

He laughed and shut the door behind him with much effort.

Lynette wrapped her arms around herself and swooned against the wall. Everything she'd imagined about Forster Hamilton had been true. The man's mouth, the way his hands felt against her skin, the sudden breaths of passion he sucked in . . . and help her . . . the way his voice sounded when it came up from Georgia within his chest. And his heart, his soul, what he shared with her—his wounds and his art. There was no anecdote to him. When the telephone rang she nearly jumped out of her skin.

Laughing at herself and her skittishness, she ran to get the telephone before it stopped ringing.

"Hello!" She had sing-songed into the receiver, not caring who was on the line. Joy was hers today.

"Well, hello, yourself," Dianne laughed. "Just checking on you, since they told me you were working at home today, and I was absent without leave all weekend . . . wanted to find out the scoop."

"The scoop?" Lynette laughed as she teased her friend. "We went to dinner, you were there."

"I know, girl, stop playing. So? What do you think— did he ask you out again?"

"Yes . . ." Lynette drawled. "He came by for Sunday dinner and—"

"He met Ida? Ida cooked for him?"

"Yup!"

"And?"

"She loved him," Lynette squealed, doing a little dance in the middle of the floor.

"He came over with the kids. . . . We'll I'll be . . ."

The pure awe in Dianne's voice erupted a round of giggles from within Lynette. Release, in any form, was critical now, or she'd burst.

"And?" Dianne pressed. "He just came over the next day, just like that?"

"No," Lynette corrected, flopping on the sofa with the cordless phone against her ear, dreamily gazing at the ceiling, and then proceeded to fill Dianne in on how her mother had made the connection.

"But, there's more . . . there has to be more. A man

just doesn't come to your mama's house, with his kids, dance with you, clean up the kitchen for you, and leave. Tell all now!"

"He just left," Lynette whispered, and then giggled again hard.

"What!"

"Oh, girl . . . what am I going to do? He brought me roses and—"

"What? Roses?"

"We're going bowling with the kids, and—"

"Where's Ida!"

"I don't know?" Lynette laughed. "Running errands, I suppose?"

"Lord have mercy . . . you didn't . . . not yet, I mean, I can understand if you just couldn't—"

"No . . . we went to his house to look at some photos, meet his mom—"

"He's already brought you home to meet his mom? Ooh, girl, this is serious—shut up!"

"Yup, then he brought me home and dropped me off . . ."

"And?"

"And, he dropped me off and I came in, and then the phone rang, and—"

"Stop lying, heifer," Dianne demanded, laughing hard into the receiver. "You are singing your words and your voice is two pitches too high, and—"

"Oh, girl, I don't know how this happened, but I'm crazy about him."

Dianne chuckled in earnest, and, judging by the pause, Lynette could tell that for once her friend was at a momentary loss for words.

"Well, knowing you, you probably hustled the poor man away from the door and put up a million barriers and didn't even let the man keep hope alive. Like Jessie says, you gotta let a brother keep hope alive," her girl-friend warned in good humor.

"Keeping hope alive almost got me into trouble," Lynette admitted on a sigh.

"Oh. My. God."

"Oh . . . my . . . God," Lynette repeated with emphasis.

"In Ida's house?"

"The vestibule, but not all the—"

"A taste, but no dinner . . ."

"But I am so hungry now, girl, that I can't stand it," Lynette confessed. "What am I going to do? I really like him and he likes me, but there's nowhere to take it anywhere, and Lord have mercy, the man blew me away, and his knees buckled, so did mine—but I'm not trying to tell his business—Forster, like me, is a private person, and I respect that, but we're both so afraid to get burned again, with good reason, and yet it's been so long . . . I thought I'd pass out when he kissed me. And, his hands, D . . . oh, man, I have a deadline to make by this afternoon at four, and I'm all messed up in the head, but that is insane—because I'm a grown woman. I'm thirty-five years old. But I'm sweating our date scheduled for Saturday like I'm in high school, but it's not really a date—he just asked me to tag along with his and Sharon's kids to the bowling thing, then to McDonald's. So, there won't be a chance—not that it's even appropriate at this juncture, 'cause we said we'd take it slow, get to know each other, build a friendship before taking it to the physical but—"

"The man absolutely wet your drawers, didn't he? Listen to yourself. You're babbling."

"Oh, girl!"

Both women hooted and fell into a chorus of laughter.

"Well, now I know for sure that you didn't play yourself, or your hand, or go all the way in Ida's house—you might pay the mortgage, but as long as she's alive, that is Ida's house," Dianne hiccuped though her laughter.

"How's that?" Lynette giggled out her question.

"Because the last time I heard my literarily adept girlfriend rattle off a string of non sequiturs like that, we were in high school . . . and, if I dare recall, you were trying to decide to give it up or not after getting dry pressed to a wall during a basement party. Flashbacks."

"Oh . . ." Lynette wailed with merriment in her tone. "How could I forget?"

"Brother's got you burnin' and yearnin' and just like in the old days, there's nowhere to get your swerve on proper."

Lynette sat up, wiping her eyes from the tears of hard giggles. "I know . . . but that's for the best. Right now, we both need chaperones."

"Yeah, but that's going to get old after a while," Dianne cautioned. "It could take months before the timing is right, the kids have a sitter, both your work schedules sync up, and you both feel comfortable, Ida leaves, his mom goes somewhere, you can count on the privacy— that could even take years."

"I know," Lynette whispered, sobering a little at the thought. Months . . . of waiting for a chance to feel Forster against her again? "I know," she repeated, groaning as she flopped backward on the sofa. "Well, if it's meant to be, and if we really want to be sure . . . and I know I want to be sure, this will pass and simmer down, and we'll be rational about—"

"Be rational about being as horny as this man makes you? Chile, pulleeeaaaase! The man has you stuttering and babbling and sighing and singing. This is a real 9-1-1. . . . And if you're feeling this way, then y'all need to be practical, a little less romantic, and go to a hotel. Just get over the whole phobia you have with that, and plan it out—"

"You can't plan a first encounter. Are you serious? I mean it's too—"

"That's the explanation the young girls give their mothers when they come home pregnant . . . I didn't know it was going to go there. I didn't want to take a condom with me to give him the wrong impression. I didn't want him to think I was like that. Be serious, Lynette."

"Oh . . . Dianne . . . you are making so much sense and right now I'm not."

"That's because you've lost critical blood flow to your brain. That's how us older sisters wind up in trouble, too." Her friend laughed, but the tone of it was patient and kind.

"Well, I can't be the one to plan something like—"

"Let him do it. Just go to a hotel with—"

"What, are you crazy? We can't do that on, just like that, I mean with no prior foundation—without getting—"

"Okay," Dianne sighed with a mischievous chuckle lacing it. "Suit yourself. But, after you guys do all your talking, and tiptoeing around your personal baggage, and excavating your deepest, darkest fears . . . and once you two finally dredge up the courage to go out on a real date, alone, sans children, and he looks into your eyes and is tired of taking a cold shower . . . and when you cannot bear to hug your pillow at night while you dream about him anymore, before you two snap—let the brother know you'll follow him to a safe house, if he asks. Just do that for me, will you? If he's a good man, and becomes your true buddy, and you trust each other, then, what's the harm?"

"I can't think about that right now," Lynette hedged. "That's too far in the future, and I'm not sure how I'd actually feel about it, you know?"

"The only reason you can't think about it is because if you think too hard, you'll call him tonight, get me to watch his kids, and you'll finish what was started this afternoon."

"I can't go there right now—don't even start, D," Lynette groaned, flopping over on her stomach.

"That bad . . . wow." Her friend laughed with her on the telephone.

"Good-bye. You bad influence—you. Get thee behind me, Satan."

"I love you, too, lady," Dianne giggled. "See you Saturday."

"Are you and Rick going?" Lynette perked up and rolled over to sit up, and then stood.

"Yeah, yeah, yeah," Dianne sighed. "We missed the event on Sunday, and we were too bogus. . . . Plus, y'all obviously need a chaperone. Can't have the kids all in your business while you two make googly-eyes at each other and sit in the lanes breathing hard. So, me and Rick will be there to pick up the slack."

"Thanks, girl," Lynette said on a hard exhale.

"Your deadline is looming, and it's two o'clock. Go splash your face with cold water, and get back to work."

Fourteen

There was no reason to argue with her editor, who had been telling her all week that her submissions were beginning to sound more literary than journalistic, and that they had too much emotion, were too editorial in nature. So, what was there to say when the man told her to rework every piece from a more objective point of view, and to stop singing in prose on the pages? It was true; her perspective was off. He'd told her that her work sounded like she was trying to repeatedly capture some kind of we-are-the-world theme, and she worked a crime beat. Was she crazy?

Fastidious cleaning of the house made sense, just like her now-daily exercise routine did. Stay busy, keep moving. Ida's catch phrase, *just in case,* had gained new relevance. Keep the place presentable, just in case. Always have on a small dab of lipstick and eyeliner, just in case. Always cook a little extra, just in case. Always have on pretty underwear, just in case . . . and a little perfume.

Now she understood why the old dolls wore lipstick even to the supermarket. They were veterans of decorum and took preparedness to a new level like an art form. They were also the champions of diplomacy—at least Ida Graves had been all week. The woman hadn't even said a peep about her new cleaning and

cooking regime, nor did she even look up the one time
the doorbell rang and Lynette knocked over her chair,
only to find out that it was the paperboy coming with
his father to collect the weekly receipts. She just wore
a perpetually amused expression on her face, and from
time to time seemed like the Cheshire cat as she swallowed a grin.

But as the week had slowly drizzled by, and she'd absorbed herself in enough productive activity to actually
make her stop running for the telephone or jumping
when the doorbell chimed, Saturday morning seemed to
reset the clock on her case of the jitters.

Dusting feverishly with the radio on to help her keep
a fast tempo, she hadn't realized her mother had come
down the steps until the last one creaked.

"Hey, Mom—wow!" Lynette exclaimed as she gazed
at her mother. "Look at you all dolled up on a Saturday
morning."

"You like it?" Ida Graves smoothed the front of a
classic, winter-white Chanel-style suit and toyed with
the gold buttons, then went to fish in the closet for
her hat.

"You look maaaarvelous, darling," Lynette teased,
following her mother toward the closet. "Wow. Where'd
you get that suit . . . and when did you get your hair
done at the beauty parlor? Where are *you* going today?"

"Oh, this old thing? I've had it in the back of the
closet under plastic for years. Took it to the cleaner's
this week, and if you must know, I got my hair done yesterday and tied it up to keep it nice for today."

"Oh . . . makes sense," Lynette said with a chuckle.
"But, you never answered the other part of what I asked
you."

"I'm going to Virginia with the choir for the interstate
Gospelrama, and will be back Sunday night. If you

came to church, or ever read the bulletin, you'd know this was the big event for the fall—but I'm not in your business these days, you might have noticed. In any event, our church bus stops in Williamsburg, and we'll have dinner there at a nice buffet, and stay over, go have fellowship with our sister church, sing, and come home. I think they stop in Baltimore along the way for lunch. I would have asked you, but you have plans to go bowling with your friends."

Lynette stifled a wry smile as her mother found her best hat, brown velvet coat, *and gloves*. Not protect-your-hands-from-the-elements type of gloves, but, coy dressed-to-the-nines-accessory-to-my-outfit kind of gloves that women wore in her mother's heyday.

"The gloves pull it all together, Mom," she said with a grin, inspecting the new, smartly dressed woman who discretely pulled a fine leather suitcase out of the bottom closet.

"I just can't seem to place my good scarf and broach," her mother argued off-handedly. "Things just are never where you need them when you need them."

"Here, let me help," Lynette offered, reaching up to grab down another hat box that stored the balance of her mother's most finely milled collection. "Knowing you, you probably put the scarf with the broach in the box with the other hat—just in case."

Both women smiled but neither said a word, as Lynette's suspicions were proved correct.

"I'd say you'll be the most stunning woman on that bus," Lynette said in earnest as she allowed her gaze to rove over her mother, drawing a shy smile from her. She handed her mother her scarf and helped her pin on her broach, then stood back, sampling a whiff of the good-smelling fragrance her mother wore. "You smell as pretty as you look, too. Very nice, Mom. Very nice, indeed."

"You think so, Lynne?"

"Oh, Mom, you are positively gorgeous. A knockout."

Her mother giggled, then tried in vain to summon a serious, casual demeanor.

"Well, if you approve, then I guess I'm ready," Ida Graves said in a too-calm tone. "And, I left two little vests up on the bed for my girls," she added in a singsong voice, "and I'll put the address and bus itinerary on the refrigerator under a magnet—I know people are still so nervous about traveling these days, but we're going on a church mission, and I know we'll be under God's wing. . . . So, expect me back around eight or nine on Sunday."

"No problem," Lynette cooed, chuckling at her mother's melodic ending to her statement and the obvious evasion about who else worth all this trouble might be going on the trip. "I'll just get my keys and take you—"

"No bother, suga'. I have a ride."

"Oh . . ." Lynette opened her mouth and then closed it.

"Didn't need to trouble you, as I know you have things to do, and your work, and all."

"It wouldn't have been any trouble, Mom—but if you have a sure ride, then it's all good."

"Yup," her mother said with a smile, and then dusted Lynette's cheek with a kiss—the kind of kiss that doesn't mess up a woman's makeup.

Deep.

When the doorbell sounded, Lynette was sure to pace herself and to allow her mother to open it. She heard a male voice from where she stood in the kitchen, and after a few moments she wiped her hands on a dish towel and slowly sauntered into the living room.

"Deacon Charles, what a pleasure."

The elderly gentleman held an exquisite gray felt hat in his hands that hosted a tasteful pheasant feather on the side under its black ribbon. His gunmetal gray Chesterfield coat matched his thin gray hair and its velvet collar matched his highly polished black lace-up shoes. On his handsome face he wore a wide smile. No wonder her mother couldn't look her in the eyes.

"The pleasure is all mine . . . my, how you've grown up so."

Lynette leaned in and gave the old man an embrace, more for her mother's sake than anything else, and she watched her mother's tense smile relax. Yes, Mom, it's all right, she said in her head, hoping that her mother's ability to read minds still worked. "Thanks, Deacon Charles. Well, listen, don't let me make you all late for your bus. Have a good time, and tell everyone I said hello."

"We will," he murmured, his eyes filled with appreciation, and then he glanced at the radiant Ida Graves and sighed.

"Now you have everything you need, Lynne?" Her mother, flustered, began rearranging her scarf as she spoke. "I left plenty of food in the refrigerator, and there's the vests upstairs for the children—don't forget. And you have the numbers to where I'll be, and—"

"Have fun, Mom. I'm fine." She brushed her mother's cheek with a delicate kiss and stood back from her again. "You are the prettiest woman I have ever seen. Take care of my favorite girl," she told him with a smile, offering Deacon Charles a wink of approval to go with it.

"That I will," he added bashfully. "She is indeed the prettiest woman I've ever seen."

Lynette turned the locks behind them and watched the graying couple make their way down the steps. Spying out of the window, she saw how he helped her into his big, black sedan, and the way her mother smiled at him once the door closed. A deep sense of joy swept through her, and she left the window to sit on the sofa. Wow . . . this was the way it was supposed to be. Love, evergreen, always in reach for everyone to cherish. Now she knew how her mother felt, being happy for someone else's good fortune, hoping for her happiness, wanting so much in your heart for things to work out for her— simply because you loved her.

"Let them have the time of their lives," she whispered out loud in a short prayer to God. As soon as the words escaped her mouth, she also realized that today the roles had again changed. She was becoming more and more like Ida, and Ida was becoming more and more like her. She was talking out loud to God on behalf of another soul in a room alone . . . oh yeah, Lynette giggled, that was definitely Ida's DNA coming through.

Then, as she stood, it dawned on her. She was home alone.

What, exactly, did one wear to a bowling party with kids? She hadn't a clue. As she hunted and pecked through her closet for the third time, she settled on a casual sweater, a long jean skirt with a short, appropriately modest split in the back, some royal-blue tights to match the sweater, and a pair of flat loafers.

Looking at the selection, she went to her underwear drawer and hesitated. Her mind was on overdrive, and she wasn't making sense. What difference would it make if she matched her royal-blue sweater with silk beneath it? They were just going out with a bunch of children, and then they'd still have chaperones. Besides, Forster hadn't called her all week, apparently disciplined enough to stay the course on taking things slow and building their friendship first. She oughta be ashamed of herself. And it had been just ridiculous to go to CVS to buy a product that she hadn't had in her possession in years—latex. Just in case. But, crazy.

And, why in the heck had she changed her sheets, selecting the best ones, then cleaned every bathroom in the house, and ensured that all the towels were freshly laundered, when she'd just cleaned on Friday night? Not to mention, why had she bothered to layer on fragrance, matching the soap to the lotion to the perfume she now sprayed. They were only going bowling—as friends.

So, what was the big fuss about sweeping her hair up, and putting on a nice pair of small teardrop silver earrings, and why was she so frantic to find her thin silver necklace, the one with the tiny balls on it that sat perfectly in the center of her throat? Under heavy stockings, and with her hands about to get banged up by a bowling ball, why had she spent an hour doing a pedicure, and why had she wasted all that time on the nonsense of doing her nails in a subtle silver shade? The theory of just-in-case was crazy, ludicrous, and all it did was make women act simple—as though they'd lost their minds!

"Why you puttin' on cologne, Dad? Specially just to go bowling?"

Forster tried to ignore his seven-year-old, who sat in the center of his bed and grilled him while he hunted for his good, light beige knit sweater.

"Huh, Dad?" The child persisted. "Why you got on your good black jeans, instead of your sweats? You ain't gonna be able to bend down good in those, specially with your nice belt on. An' you never shave in the middle of the afternoon."

"How many times have I told you there's no such word as ain't? And why can't your father just get dressed without a lot of questions? Do I question what you decide to wear?"

"All the time. You be telling us what to wear all the time, Dad."

"All right, all right," he conceded with a chuckle. "Go help Rachel put on her coat. And make sure your sister doesn't spill something on herself before we get out of the house."

Forster tried to steady his nerves as he found his good watch. How was he supposed to do this—court and baby-sit at the same time? If the kids were in his business about what he was wearing, then they'd really get suspicious when he made a run to go pick up some more flowers. Maybe flowers would be overkill? Then again, he could tell them they were for Mrs. Graves. . . . Then again, maybe he'd just say that the flowers were for the privilege of Miss Lynette coming along? No, no, no . . . that didn't even make sense to his own ears. Going to a Saturday afternoon event with the police athletic league group had *never* been this much trouble.

Finally dressed, he went to the kitchen to find his mother. She was sitting in her usual spot, sipping from a glass and watching the small portable TV.

"I'm going to take the kids bowling, the party is over at like six—then me and Rick are taking them all out to eat at McDonald's . . . should be home around eight. You need anything while I'm out in the street? Dinner is under foil in the fridge, if you get hungry, and a new pack of smokes are on the dining room table with the paper."

His mother looked him up and down and then shook her head. "So, you and Rick are dating each other these days? Humph. Seen that mess on Jerry Springer," she said sarcastically.

"Do you need anything while we're out?" Forster repeated. He'd let the remark pass, refusing to be baited before he left.

"No," she snapped, taking a deep sip from her glass. "You seem to have me all set. You got the paper, some smokes for me, even cooked. This way, whether you come home or not tonight, you won't have to be bothered by me."

"I will be coming home—I have the girls with me, and will have Rick's friend's sister's brood," he said, summoning patience. "Plus, if I'm not at work, when do I ever stay out?"

She didn't immediately answer, just glared at him. "So, you shave, put on cologne, and start talking a mile a minute to just take a bunch of kids bowling? I wasn't born yesterday."

He let his breath out hard and counted to ten. "I'll see you around eight, and try to be careful . . . for real, for real—no smoking in bed. I've got my cell on, so if you need me for a real emergency, you know how to reach me."

"Whatever," his mother grunted with a wave of her hand. "Tell Suzette I said hello."

After the first few awkward moments when she'd opened the door and again accepted a stunning floral arrangement from Forster—this time wildflowers, they seemed to pick up a natural rhythm of companionship.

Albeit they both seemed to appreciate the obvious care that the other had taken in putting just a little subtle polish on their supposed casual attire, the children broke the ice.

The girls had squealed in delight at the crocheted vests Ida had made and left for them, and insisted on taking off their coats to wear them to the party. Oblivious to their father and Lynette's glimpses of each other, the posse had made it to Dianne's house and then to the bowling alley, for increasingly more chaos at each stop, without a hitch.

Laughter, selling wolf-tickets in old-school male-bragging form about who could best who in the lanes was the order of the day. Kids yelled, formed, and dispersed themselves in little cliques, chaperones scolded and equally cajoled children, and everybody ate. The amount of food consumed by the group would have cowed even the great volume chef, Ida.

"Girl, I haven't had this much fun in years," Lynette confessed as they stood in line with the other adults, while the McDonald's cashiers looked as if they wanted to run for the hills.

"I don't know how my mom dealt with this madness," Dianne laughed. "They're heathens. Just uncivilized little banshees!"

"Yeah," Rick chuckled, shaking his head. "But your mom only had girls, though, and half as many kids. You know what my house had to be like."

"No, I'm not even trying to fathom that," Dianne said, laughing harder. "Forster, tell your boy not to even get the thought into his brain."

"My name is Bennett, and I ain't in-it!" Forster said, waving his hand. "Nope. I do not get in between grown folk's business."

"Lynette, tell your man—"

"Uh-uh," Lynette jumped in, cutting off Dianne's words, and not addressing the fact that Forster had been referred to as *her man.* "I'm with him," she fussed, beginning to chuckle hard. "I stay out of it. That's between you and Rick."

"Aw, c'mon, baby . . ." Rick crooned, making them all laugh. "Why don't we keep all the kids, Forster's too, at your place tonight, just to see what it's like?"

Lynette and Forster stopped laughing as the couple ahead of them in line passed sheepish glances. They were being set up. Deep.

"No, boy," Dianne argued with a wink, and speaking loud enough for the girls at the adjacent table to overhear. "Are you out'chure mind? Donell, the twins, and both little girls all under the same roof—all night, till like late afternoon in a movie fest?"

"Oh, pleeease, Aunt Dianne," the twins yelled from the nearby table.

"Ooh, Daddy, can we?" Rachel and Rebecca begged.

"No way. See what you done started in here, Rick—with your big mouth. I want to go have a real dinner, and maybe go listen to some jazz, and you got me up in McDonald's talking some rhetoric about—"

"Please, Aunt D—you and Uncle Rick go out all the time. Dag!" One of the twins fussed, while the other just shook her head.

"She ain't gonna let us, told you," the other said in defeat.

"Good," Donell piped in, "'cause I don't need to be around all you yucky girls, anyway."

"Aw, baby . . . do it for me?" Rick was making Dianne laugh as he pulled her into his arms. "It'll be fun."

Lynette and Forster could only stare at the elaborate scam unfolding.

Did she say something to her girlfriend?

He had to have said something to Rick?

He would die of embarrassment if Dianne ever knew what happened between them in that vestibule. God, women told everything!

Dag, men just couldn't keep a secret. Now she couldn't even look at Rick!

But, how would Lynette explain it to Miz Ida if he kept her out all night?

What would his mom think of her, if her grandchildren didn't come home and her son was AWOL? The woman already clearly disliked her. This was not good.

"Aw, Miss Dianne," Rachel and Rebecca pleaded. "Before, we had so much fun, and—"

"All right, all right," Dianne fussed with a wide grin, addressing the table of children. "Y'all twisted my arm, and he's no help—so, if you'll promise to behave . . ."

"We promise!" a chorus of little girls boomed, then the four-part harmony broke off into rapid-fire pleas, drowning out the minority voice at the table, Donell.

"Dad, we'll be real good."

"I won't pee the bed," Rachel promised. "I won't!"

"We'll be good for Mom!"

"We won't wake up the baby!"

"I'll help Miss Carol with the baby."

"I can clean up the toys I play wif!"

"Daaaad . . ." Forster's girls harmonized. "Just this once. Miss Lynette, Uncle Rick, get him to say yes!"

"Well," Forster stammered, ignoring Rick's droll expression and not dignifying the wink. "I, er, uh . . . suppose . . . if it's not—"

"Oh, it's no trouble," Dianne immediately shot, not allowing him to finish his sentence.

Lynette looked at her shoes, wondering if there was some way she could disappear into the toes of them.

A moment of weighted silence gave way to an

avalanche of squeals of delight that boomed out in the fast-food establishment when Forster finally nodded his assent to Dianne, then glanced away. This was the most contrived, embarrassing, totally humiliating *blessing* he'd ever had. If the women and children weren't looking, he'd have given his boy a high five.

"It's cool, man," Rick said in a low murmur, the unspoken message passing between the two stone-faced brothers in well-rehearsed male Morse code.

"Cool," Forster said without looking at his friend— his tone distant, relaxed sounding, and totally belying his anticipation. "You got my cell number, if there's a problem."

"Yeah. Turn it off, though. It's all good. We got dis."

"We got it," Dianne repeated, her voice markedly discrete. "We both are used to watching kids."

Lynette couldn't look up or add a word to this parental discussion. It wasn't her place; besides, her vocal chords had taken a leave of absence. Conspiracy theory swirled in her brain. Had Dianne called her mother, or something? Collusion was afoot. How much did Rick know? What would Forster think about her, if he thought she'd plotted on the removal of his children? She hadn't! She was innocent. The circumstantial evidence looked so bad!

Now what? Forster jammed his hands into his pockets. He'd promised the woman he was gonna take it slow. She probably thought he'd talked to his boy, they'd schemed on her, and gotten her best friend to blend in as an accessory to the crime. He was innocent! He had no idea what they were cooking up behind his back. And just look at Lynette's face—the woman appeared practically mortified, and hadn't said a word since the sting began. Now how was he going to explain it to her

without it seeming like a total scam? He sighed and
tried to focus on the menu board in front of him.

Five Happy Meals, with toys. Right.

Fifteen

Awkward moments punctuated more awkward moments as they worked through the logistics of delivering all the children to Dianne's house, leaving in the two separate cars they'd driven in, and coming to Lynette's home to park it in order to continue with the evening.

Forster rubbed his palms over his face as Lynette pulled into an available spot on the block. An evening out shouldn't require all of this, he thought, and no carefree beautiful woman in her right mind would put up with the nonsense for long. This was why all of these mundane details were supposed to be done once married and everyone was in place . . . the romancing done BC—before children, and before privacy and spontaneity became extinct.

But there she was, nonetheless, putting up with all of this chaos, and smiling through the process. If she lasted through tonight, would she be able to hang through the chicken pox, flu season, and other stuff that came with parenting? Then again, she was Ida's child. The thought relaxed him; the apple doesn't fall far from the tree that bears it. However, if that was true, then what was she in store for given his roots? He just hoped that nothing from his dysfunctional upbringing would ever erase that beautiful smile from her face.

As he watched her vehicle taillights go out, he

hopped from his car to escort her to his. But he had to make her understand there had been no collusion between him and his boy.

When they both started talking at once, they laughed.

"You first," she chuckled.

"Look," he said with a wry smile, "I know you're not going to believe me, but I didn't say a word to Rick other than I liked you and had a good time at the movies last week. If you don't want to go out I'll under—"

"No, trust me, this is a Dianne setup. I know you didn't mastermind this. Only Miss D could have gone to such lengths; I know my girl. But I didn't say anything about anything, other than well, that we'd be going bowl—"

"I believe you, I believe you . . . I just know Rick, too. He's always gotten me into trouble—not that you're trouble, what I'm saying is—"

"We have a window of opportunity here, you wanna use it and go somewhere? I trust you. Deal?"

They both fell into companionable laughter, knowing that they'd been set up by the best of friends, and loving every minute of it.

"Okay," he chuckled. "Deal. So, what would you like to do? Go listen to some jazz, go have a glass of wine? Maybe go get some real dessert somewhere?"

"It's your rare baby-sitting coupon . . . whatever you'd like to do, I'm with it."

"Wow, er, okay . . ." He hadn't thought of what to do if he had an evening to himself. At least not anything he could voice so soon. It had been so long since he was on a real date, he wasn't sure where to go, what places might require reservations, and then he looked down at his clothes. That limited the options at eight o'clock at night in Philly, and he really didn't want to take her to a club. They'd already gone to the movies. Dilemma.

Cold night air surrounded and hugged them as he struggled to decide.

"Why don't we get in my car and figure it out? I mean, the sky is the limit," he hedged, trying to cast the decision back to her. He really didn't know the full range of her tastes. If it were during the day, he could have suggested a gallery or the Art Museum, since he'd recalled her love of art. But where could they go that would work out on the spur of the moment, especially since he was so out of practice with nimble, carefree moves?

"Why don't you park, come into the house, I'll put on a pot of coffee and some dessert, and then we'll look in the paper and see what we can figure out from there?"

"Cool."

The woman was brilliant, but he had to admit that he wasn't exactly looking forward to a long conversation with her mother. Tonight he'd gotten a furlough pass to have her all to himself. But he'd relented out of sheer lack of knowing what else to say or do, and he didn't have a better idea at the moment.

He watched her safely into the house, and moved his car, noting that she stood in the doorway until he came up the steps. Maybe she wasn't ready for Ida yet either, but that was probably just a hopeful thought.

"I think we both need a minute to decompress from the bowling alley, and definitely from McDonald's," she chuckled, turning the lock on the vestibule door and motioning for him to follow her in.

As he shut the outer door and bolted it, the brief enclosure in the vestibule sent a shock wave of memory through him. Please God let Ida be on her way upstairs.

"I'll just be a second," she said brightly, tossing off her coat onto an armchair as she paced across the room. "I need to listen to the answering machine to be sure

Mom arrived in Virginia safely with her church group. Call me a worrywart, but she doesn't travel much."

Ida was not home? Ida was in Virginia? This woman had the house to herself with her mother three states away? His kids were with their uncle, a man he trusted with his life. And Ida Graves had gone away with the church—overnight? He bowed his head in reverence and patched up any remaining argument he had with God.

While Lynette went to check the machine, he even called his own mother—just in case, and just to keep the Good Father on his side.

"Yeah, Mom . . . I know you predicted—yeah, okay, okay, okay. The girls are at Rick's friend's with Rick, and I'll be out for a while. I was just calling to check on you to be sure you were okay, not to argue. I guess you're okay, then? All right . . . that's why I called, because I said eight, and I'll be later than that. Look, I gotta go."

When he hung up, Rick's words came to his mind, and he turned off the cell and sat it in front of him on the coffee table. Not tonight. Voice mail could pick up.

"Is everything all right?" Lynette's eyes held a note of worry as she walked back into the room.

"Yeah, just checking on Mom to let her know where the girls were—and that I'd be out for a while. Told her I'd be in by eight, before Rick and Dianne ambushed us. Didn't want her to worry . . . your checking on Ida made me think of it."

His voice had come out flatter and less cheerful then he'd intended, but his mother always got under his skin. It would take a few moments to recalibrate, and the fact that Lynette's expression still held a hint of alarm worried him.

"Listen . . . I don't want her to think. . . . Hey, I know

you got ambushed, and if you need to go home, or would feel more comfortable, then it's all right with—"

"No, for real . . . my mother, as you know, has issues, but she's still my mom, and she loves her grandchildren, although it's hard for her to show it, but she does . . . and she'd worry about them if I didn't bring them home. So, I do check on her, respect her, and worry about her, but she can be a pure pain in the behind when she's in her cups, which is often. And she starts in on these winding paths of reason, which are totally illogical, from time to time, and then she picks a fight. That's what you heard the tail end of; I'm sorry about that. You didn't have a thing to do with it, and the ambush was frankly a gift."

For the second time, this man had given her an honest glimpse of himself, and his plain-speaking manner, and his ability to always let her know where she stood in the middle of whatever fray was going on in his life, reassured her. He'd called Dianne's ambush a gift . . . while babbling. He was nervous, and obviously wanted to stay—real bad. Hmmm . . . the awareness of just how much he wanted to be alone, too, made her smile. She'd also noticed that he'd turned off his cell phone, which was now dark and silent and dead, right in the middle of her coffee table.

Again, they started into the conversation, bumping into each other's words, and then laughing.

"Okay, then let's find out what there is to do with this time gift we acquired by nefarious means."

"Yeah, this night literally fell off the back of the truck in a heist."

"Well, Officer Hamilton, the choice is yours. You call it if you see it in here . . . I'll do the same."

He chuckled as she opened the paper and they perused the options. The weekend, however, was as dead as a doornail. Without planning, there wasn't much to do in their age and taste bracket, other than eat or go to the movies. It appeared that all the really eclectic activities had been scheduled during the day, or required advanced tickets at night, and certainly would require a change of clothes. Atlantic City was too far to go on the short time frame they had, and would lop off a full three hours round-trip in the commute. Everything in between those options were for kids.

"Looks bleak, doesn't it?" Lynette sighed, handing him the paper and going to put on some music.

"Al Jarreau, yeah . . . that's nice," he murmured, allowing the music to apply topical balm to the nerves that his mother had frayed.

"You know what?" Lynette said with cheerful resignation, flopping down beside him on the sofa. "We could just sit and talk, boring as that might sound . . . I mean, we could have a chance to talk about anything we'd want, without eavesdroppers, without fighting to get a word in edgewise past Rick and D—"

"Or, without kids . . ."

"Or, mothers."

They both laughed.

"Yeah, I could get to know my new friend better," he said in a quiet tone. "In a comfortable environment, where we can hear ourselves think . . . no, I don't find that boring at all."

She glanced at her hands in her lap. He set down the paper and leaned back and smiled when she glimpsed him from the corner of her eye. Then she smiled.

"This is so crazy," she chuckled. "It's not supposed to be this hard, I mean, it used to be . . . I don't know . . ."

He chuckled, feeling more at ease. Her simple brand of honesty had been all the balm he'd needed.

"It used to be that boy met girl, boy asked girl out, they went to several places, they got to know each other and each other's friends, then they hooked up. Then, somewhere in the eighties, or maybe it was the nineties, girl met boy, they hooked up, maybe if they were lucky they got to know each other, and friends heard about it after it was on the rocks. Then, in the new millennium, girl or boy drag in children, baggage, and all sorts of drama around with them, have to wrangle for a little time alone, and either boy or girl or both have to try to hook up, get to know that person, and deal with their sideshow all at the same time."

Lynette stared at him for a moment and then burst out laughing. "I thought evolution was supposed to stream-line the species and make it faster, leaner, better?"

"Yeah, and because humans are constantly tampering with the natural order of things, we've managed to re-verse engineer everything."

His laughter blended into hers, and they sat back looking at each other, now more relaxed, more open.

"All right then, where do we begin? I know I'm a journalist, but I don't want to just sit here asking you stuff that'll make you feel like you're playing twenty questions. And, I know there's stuff you probably want to know about me . . ."

Again he laughed. "Ask me whatever you want to know. My life is not that interesting, trust me, but take your best shot. I don't have any hard questions for you right now, and I won't be shy about asking, if and when I do."

"Okay," she began with a sly grin. "What's your fa-vorite color?"

The smile on his face softened and his gaze slowly considered her form. The latent desire in his expression almost made her look away.

"You're wearing it," he murmured.

"Oh . . ." She toyed with her necklace and his eyes

followed the trail her fingers made at her throat. "Then, what's your favorite music?"

"You're playing it on the stereo now . . . the ballads from that era."

"All right, all right," she said after a moment, forcing the volume of her voice up a notch. "Then, what's your favorite pastime, and you cannot tell me photography, because I already know that. Pick the second thing, then."

"You wanna dance? That's it, you know. You did it with me before."

He stood and held out his hand as Al Jarreau's slow-moving ballad "After All" came on, and she accepted it to stand. Rounding the coffee table, she found herself in an easy embrace, swaying to the words that made her heart feel tight in her chest. Yes, there was a time she knew that whatever come what may, love would prevail . . .

"When's your birthday?" He murmured to the woman looking up at him, trying so hard to fight how good this woman made him feel. It was too soon. The vestibule had been a circumstantial fluke. And they were supposed to be taking things slow.

"July eleventh," she whispered, her sway perfectly complimenting him in the lazy rhythm. "When's yours?"

"Same month . . . but the seventh, and an earlier year, for sure . . . fifty-nine."

"That is so deep . . ."

"That we were born in the same month?"

"No, the combination. Seven-eleven."

"Lucky number, huh?"

Her lids had gone half-mast but when the next cut came on, his desire to hold her gave way to the promise—to get to know her, to build something special first. But God she felt so good and smelled so good, and those beautiful, sexy, half-closed eyes . . .

"What do you like to eat?"

Her question came from out of left field, and her voice seemed flustered as the spell broke with the change in the music. It was as though she'd caught herself, like a person falling, then quickly grabbing on to anything, regardless of how fragile. He had to give her room, maybe even let the opportunity that the night held pass, if he wanted her to fall on her own and not feel pushed.

The intellectual side of his brain knew that—the difficulty at the moment was, getting it to cooperate with the more primal side of his mind that had awakened when she slid into his arms again. But also he noticed that she hadn't left their embrace when she'd asked the question. He thought about how to answer her, first from the primal side of him that vied to offer her a visceral response, and then it struggled with the gentlemanly code of conduct stored within the more reasonable side of him.

"What do I like to eat?"

Her question had messed with his primal side, which was now giving the rational side an old-fashioned beatdown. He had to clean up the repeated question. Relaxing his hold on her, he stepped back a bit.

"I mean your favorite food!" She shook her head and then giggled.

Too late. She'd obviously read and processed what was on his mind. Her smile and the teasing tone that came with it confirmed his hunch.

"I'm a basic kind of guy," he said pleasantly, using distance as an ally as he walked over to the stereo to find a different album and selected something a little more romance neutral than a heady ballad—instrumental. "I'm easy. I like the kinda food that sticks to your ribs all day like I had here before."

There. He'd told the truth, vanquished the thoughts declaring war on his promise to take things slow, had gotten them back on a platonic track, and he had paid the woman a well-deserved compliment.

"That's cool," she said, suddenly and irrationally feeling dejected. She had to get her mind straight and stop taking everything he said with two meanings. The man had changed the music and had let her go to play with the stereo. All that he'd said before about her wearing his favorite color was just a fact, and she'd been the one mentally interloping into areas they'd agreed to by-pass. "You like fried fish?"

"Yeah," he murmured, now looking at her and holding her with a heated gaze, "with grits and biscuits for breakfast."

"Oh . . ." Maybe she wasn't wrong? Breakfast . . . oh boy . . .

Why did he say that? "But, you'll have to let me bring by the groceries, like your mom said, if you are planning on cooking," he added, trying to clean up his comment. "I was holding back before, but I can put away good cooking, if it's done right—like it was done here. Will practically eat myself into a stupor if you let me." The smooth instrumental sound of Grover was not a good choice. It wasn't feeling very romance neutral at the moment. Breakfast? Was he mad?

Again they were inches apart, and she could almost feel the electricity in the stereo crackle and pop within the small space between them. If he was talking in read-between-the-lines code, yes she was sure he could put it away . . . if it was done right . . . like it had been done here, started and not finished in the vestibule, before.

"You hungry?" she found herself asking in a whisper.

"Yeah, a little," he replied, moving to close off the inches between them but without touching her.

"Want that dessert now?" she asked, hoping he'd read between her lines.

"Yes," he murmured, sealing the gap and lowering his mouth to hers.

"Okay."

His hands gently held her upper arms and he neither pulled her to him nor backed away. The kiss he'd landed on her lips was so brief and so light that it felt like he'd whispered near her mouth.

"I'd better go get that dessert."

"I'm already holding it."

"Oh . . ."

This time when he kept her gaze within his, he didn't move to kiss her. The repressed intensity from him made the tiny hairs on her arms stand up with goose-flesh. And the hunger that she witnessed in the depths of his eyes made her need to close her own. She had to, briefly, in order to block out the shudder of anticipation it caused within her.

"But I promised to take it slow, remember . . . even though that's the last thing I want to do tonight."

"I remember . . . and then I told you that you didn't have to."

"I remember . . . how could I forget?"

The honesty in his words and the way he'd breathed out the truth . . . the pained look of patience in his expression, and the way the static charge sent a current through the small sliver of atmosphere again separating them . . . the way his Adam's apple bobbed as he swallowed hard and waited for her reply. No, not tonight, he didn't have to.

When she sealed off the open space this time, his grip on her arms tightened, and her body melted into his, allowing the intensity to pass back and forth between them like alternating current and causing her hands to seek his back. Ignited, he enfolded her, and sought her mouth hard.

"You have to be sure," he whispered, finding her neck and pulling the lobe of her ear into his mouth. "I can't go home again like I did this week," he told her, breathing fire against the wetness of it, causing a steam burn on it.

The sensation he'd sent through her made her fingers pull his sweater into them and she held it tightly in what slowly became fists.

"You want to go upstairs?" she asked in a quiet tone that she was beyond shame to censure. "I can't stand it another day, let alone a week."

His response was nonverbal, and he explained his need for her with his body, hard hands traveling down the length of her, cupping her bottom then raking her back, and the moan he released when she nipped his neck said it all. She answered him by finding his palm, clasping his hand in her own, and leading him to follow her up the stairs.

No more awkward moments stood between them as she shut the bedroom door behind them. Moonlight and streetlamps became their lantern, and she dropped his hand to step back and pull her sweater over her head. The look of unburdened desire on his face changed her once-frantic movements to a slow, sensual removing of her clothes, and he stood immobile, watching her as though she were indeed good enough to eat.

No man had ever made her feel the way his eyes did now . . . cherished, adored, and so badly wanted all at the same time. And she reveled in the way his gaze paid homage to every inch of her skin as she shared it, drawn even more by the way his stare penetrated her outer being and connected to her spirit.

The sight of her drenched in moonlight, her fragile necklace occasionally catching shards of light that glinted and spilled over her perfectly formed breasts, was paralyzing. Nile-blue silk cupped them, and his line of vision followed her hands as they pulled away more fabric and her stockings, revealing a delicate navel, and the lush curve of her hips.

He could barely breathe as she took her time, finally giving his gaze full access to the wisp of royal-blue silk hiding her swollen mound. For a moment he was transfixed as she reached up and pulled the pins out of her hair, and velvet tresses fell to her shoulders. His gaze scanned the oasis called woman . . . Lynette. The pressure within his veins traveled through his body until it caused a dull ringing in his ears. And there she stood, in all but a hint of obstruction to her natural wonder.

His hands shook as he tore off his sweater, and when his gaze again locked with hers, the passion in her eyes haunted him. Half closed, they made an unashamed survey of him, and her nostrils flared ever so slightly as he unfastened his pants with unsteady hands, stepped out of his shoes, and removed all that was in her vision's way.

There in the dark in her bedroom as her mind had so vividly imagined, he stood. A tall ebony statue carved in stone. The sight of him and the way the light hit him, beautiful, dark, cut and polished . . . trembling in need of her . . . drew her to him like a slow magnet, and her hands reached out, fingertips running up a granite torso, six hard hills until they reached the continental shelf of his chest and fanned out to cover tiny chocolate rocks that made her mouth moisten and open to accept them. Then he quaked as a sudden convulsion rippled through him. Massive hands cradled her face, and brought it to his mouth to sear hers.

And she felt her bra straps give way first, and then the clasp, and soon her panties were gone, and his hands splayed her backside, and rock-hard arms seemed to try to pull her inside of the mountain she clung to. Then a low rumble formed and she felt it before she heard it. It came from deep within a cavern in his chest. The force of the vibration traveled up his throat, made his neck bend to bring his lips to her shoulder, where a hot whisper blanched her skin.

"Baby, come to bed."

When he separated from her to take her there, the cold rush of air felt like it had cut her. And she stood before him when he sat down on the side of the bed, waiting for his thighs to part, knowing that they would, feeling his pull, feeling her fall halted by the roughness of his cheek against her belly. The infraction was kissed away, the scrape of his new beard stubble made bearable by the unbearable heat of his tongue. As her legs began to give out, his mouth continued to torture her, making her almost lose her ability to stand when his lips clamped down on a nipple—his fingers offering restitution to the other that had been denied.

Her moan betrayed her, bringing not mercy but more agony instead. He must have misunderstood the cry for relief to be a cry for renewed punishment. . . . That had to be it, because his lips doled out patient justice to both stinging pebbles, his tongue followed suit, and then gently pushing her breasts together he suckled them as one.

Searing pleasure arched her back, and again cold air cut into the distended, burning flesh his mouth had abandoned. The mountain she leaned against for support sought her mouth and pulled her to blanket him. Friction from the skin-to-skin contact made her body catch fire before he rolled her onto her back. Cool air only fed the inferno when he slid away from her torso. She could not speak, but only point to the drawer of the nightstand. He simply nodded, but covered her again nonetheless.

His eyes told her not to panic, he'd not forgotten about what was real, nor had he lost control . . . but rather he was intent on holding to his promise. She knew that when he moved down the length of her, placing kisses on her eyelids, the bridge of her nose, her chin, the center of her throat, until his kisses became long, agonizing strokes of his tongue, intermittently distracted by a slow, wet kiss, then a long-burning trail of pleasure. It was impossible to guess what sensation she would feel next. All her body could do was quiver with hope as his mouth neared her valley, but hope was tricked by false hope when his mouth found her inner thighs and didn't go to the heart of her wishes.

Too weak with desire to reach the crown of his head, her fingers took out their frustration on the sheets, turning her knuckles white as she clutched them. She was beyond shame as his response to her wishes became more elusive, teasing.

"Please," she whispered, tears finding the corners of her eyes and running from them, flowing like her flooded valley, making her squeeze them shut because his hands kept her from squeezing together her thighs.

His answer to her plea was to send a hot shaft of breath against what was now almost too engorged to touch, and the burn anchored itself from the point of contact to thread white heat up her spine, drawing her head back to dig into the pillow, making her pant, suck in air through her mouth and cry out as his tongue sliced open her lips. When he found the hidden diamond amongst the pyramid he'd plundered, she whimpered from the devastation. His tender pulls to excavate it with his kiss, and the darting tip of his tongue, began the fall of her empire.

The spasm began so deep inside her that it had to come up from her soul, and the wail of pleasure was released from within every pore of her skin. Her voice sent into the night upon staccato chants as his mouth convulsed her in jerks until she could no longer move.

What had this woman done to his mind, his body, and dear God, his spirit . . . ?

It was as though every sensation he'd sent through her had been visited upon him threefold. Beyond reason or promise, he crouched over her on all fours, looking down at her, no longer a rational man. Succulent, ripe fruit lay beneath him. . . . The drawer was only an arm's length away. But below him lie the Nile. The temptation to just enter her and quench his thirst made him shut his eyes for a moment. Wet, rushing heat would meet him if he just lowered himself to her. And he'd been traveling so long in the desert . . . and had waited so long to drink his fill of her. But her sweet, pungent nectar only tore at the other part of him, making it fill and weep on its own with need.

And she now peered up at him with such trust on her face, and he couldn't move—he was so close. The drawer seemed farther away, as though it were moving on a pulley, away from his reach, as her arms encircled his neck and he could still smell the sweetness of her pool on his mouth. Her perfume became one with it, branding him by her scent. Her hips tilted up, her legs opening wider beckoning him to enter by siren invitation.

"I have to . . ." His words trailed off as reason abandoned his voice, and he could only motion toward the nightstand. He was drowning in desire and desperately needed her lifeline to keep them from both going under. "Baby, please . . ."

She'd mercifully retained her ability to read minds, and when she reached beneath him to open the drawer her thigh brushed him. His sharp gasp answered the contact, completing without words what he'd needed to tell her. It ached so good; hurt now so bad; breathing was painful; her touch was the cure. Deliver him. If only for a moment. Her hand slid against the taut skin, his own essence slicked her palm's embrace. "Get the package."

Agony made him grimace as she temporarily ignored him. When her body slipped lower and he felt her kiss on his chest, then a kiss planted on his stomach, his fists gathered the sheets as he braced himself for her impact. The anticipation made his hips move against air. Then a soft, slow-moving, exquisite wetness covered him, dredged him, summoning tears to his eyes. As it retreated and returned with force, he could feel the muscles in his jaw lock, setting off a chain reaction that sent muscular constriction across his chest, down his abdomen, making his hamstrings tense and pull at the last vertebrae in his back. "Lyn . . . nette . . . baby . . . please . . . don't . . . I . . . can't . . . hold . . ."

Cool air replaced the oven that had once surrounded him, stinging him, making his stomach muscles clench and release on their own volition in phantom memory. Her impassioned gaze searched his face, yet he couldn't risk even touching her cheek again.

"Fair exchange," she whispered against his stomach, "but I'll hurry, baby . . ."

He groaned as the words hissed through his skin and entered his system.

He closed his eyes, feeling his weight make his arms tremble as he waited for the sound of paper. Then her smooth hand slid against him, wrenching a shudder from his depths, and the sound of rustling beneath him created a Pavlovian response that made him swallow hard twice. He took in shallow inhales, and his chest rose and fell to the rhythm he needed to exact upon her. Hurry, baby . . . his mind tried to bore the thought into hers. Please.

"I just need a second to get this on," he whispered harshly, waiting for her to give him the key to completion.

But she just smiled and slowly opened the foil, staggering his agony as she sheathed him in increments until he groaned. And the knowledge that he was now a free man dropped him from his knees and allowed him to take the weight off his arms, and it made him find her flooded passageway without guidance or sight . . . and like the exiled welcomed home, he sank against the memory of it, the sudden warmth fused to the heat of his dreams, and enfolded him, then held him tight. The acute pleasure of being siphoned into her drew a sound of painful relief from deep within his chest . . . and as that sound exited him, it embraced her own cry of recognition as he in turn released her from an exile of her own—touch drawing them both to the core, the same conclusion.

Her hips lifted to meet him, and the ever-tightening wreath she drew around him heralded his wishes. Going so slow at first to be sure that this was no dream, no mirage, he let her rhythm break his promise.

And his promise shattered as her legs wrapped around his waist and her hands clung to his shoulders, and his palm flattened against her spine while the other gripped the mattress for leverage. His mind could no longer define the meaning of slow. Then his voice splintered once again into a hyphenated use of her name—calling her baby no longer brought her deep enough into his soul . . . no matter how many times he'd uttered it to her before when he was able to pace himself to the promise.

And when she began to tremble for him again, this time her voice broken by a sob, there was no way to stop, pull back, or prolong what had driven his thrusts. Every sense was overloaded by the blinding pleasure that began as a hard contraction that fused the touch of her with the feel of her with the taste of her with the smell of her with the sight of her that was now locked in his memory in a black void behind his shut lids.

His head fell back and his mouth sucked in a huge gulp of air—the gasp of the drowning. And then wave after wave of explosive sensations crippled him, knocked the wind out of him, and seized and released him in epileptic completion.

Trying not to crush her with his weight, he shifted slightly but could not yet break his connection to her warmth. Soft hands petted his shoulders, then found the way to the nape of his neck. A gentle kiss drew the shuddering sensations in his groin up his spine like a lightning rod. She'd brought him back from the dead, and had given him new life through her touch. The release gave way to the pent-up emotions that had been roiling within him for too long.

All he could do was bow his head before the gift beneath him and sob with her.

Sixteen

His finger traced the delicate line of her jaw as she slept and his gaze drank in the wonder of how something so fragile, yet resilient, had so quickly become a part of his life. The hours she'd spent in his arms didn't compare to the place she'd now taken up residence within—his heart. And the completeness in which she'd opened to him had begun within those wide, honest brown eyes the first day he'd met her.

She'd given him so many gifts that his chest tightened with heavy emotion as he considered the exquisite simplicity of them all. Laughter, excitement, admiration, passion, caring, friendship . . . when he'd married the first time he'd been searching so hard he didn't know what to look for.

Instead of following his heart, he'd allowed his exterior sight to be his guide. Eva had laughed with his mother, had fed into her addictions, and he'd mistaken their dysfunctional camaraderie and her surface beauty for the real thing. It had masqueraded as acceptance when it happened to be just a sad pattern that he'd come to believe was normalcy. And her exterior hid such dark passageways.

But as he watched the innocent sleep, he saw Lynette from a new and clearer perspective. Her inner light had shone bright enough to light a path for him, even before touch had led him to sanctuary. It was in her eyes. The joy and peace contained within them. And she bestowed that light upon him without games, and she'd shared her hurts without visiting bitterness upon him. She didn't judge him or sentence him because of his affiliation with the male species, nor did she exact revenge on him because of what another had stolen from her.

Yet, he wanted to make restitution to her, for any violation her soul had endured. This woman who lay beside him sleeping deserved to be honored and cherished and adored and cared for . . . if wishes were fishes he'd give her the world, just to see her smile. And if he could move mountains he'd gladly bring her one and fashion a castle out of it for her. If she wanted love, he'd shower it upon her and devote the remainder of his life making up for all the wasted moments that foolish men had allowed to pass. And he'd revere always the one who had brought such light into the world: Ida Graves, who had shared her most prized possession with him.

But with so few ways to demonstrate the feelings that caught his breath within his chest, how did words and deeds communicate all he needed for her to understand?

How did a man with so many other responsibilities show a woman how much a priority she had become? How could he make her know that he'd never leave her like the others had? How could he provide for her the way she truly deserved?

"Good morning," she murmured sleepily, opening her eyes with a sated smile.

"Good morning, princess," he whispered, brushing her mouth and continuing to trace her cheek with his finger.

"You look so sad," she murmured, her gaze searching his. "What's wrong?"

"Were I a knight in shining armor," he whispered, "I'd lay the world at your feet."

Her hand gently cradled his face. "You already have, in so many ways."

He watched tears rise and sparkle within her eyes, making them shine, and he kissed them away feeling the need to hide the sudden moisture that had now filled his.

"No," he murmured, "you deserve so much more than I can probably ever give you . . . Lynne." The words *marry me* traveled up his throat and caught within his Adam's apple. He had no right to ask her like this . . . so soon, with so little to offer her with that request.

He dropped his head and rolled over onto his bed, gathering her in his arms to lie against his chest. And her gentle touch soothed the wounds that he now understood her soul could detect, applying balm to his internal injuries by the simple stroke of her hand.

"Do you have any idea of what you've given me in this brief time we've had together?"

He closed his eyes to the question, too overwhelmed with the feelings that she stirred as she peered up at him. A warm breath found the still-sensitive side of his throat and her soft lips tugged at his ear.

"You made me feel wanted, and respected, and cared about. You honored my mother, and me, and you loved me with your whole heart last night."

As the words escaped on a throaty confession, he realized in that moment that she'd again given form to the images he'd captured in his mind but couldn't describe. He did love her—beyond the physical. And it had happened so quickly . . . at a Sunday dinner, he'd fallen, and had perished in his basement, and had again dropped five-hundred feet in the vestibule, then began free-falling when he'd watched her interact with his children, and when she'd calmly accepted his circumstances, he'd nearly hit bottom . . . and when she'd opened herself to him last night, he'd splattered.

Yes, he'd fallen and was falling all over again as she whispered her tender words, and he reached out to slow his rapid descent, grabbing on to her delicate shoulders, helping her to straddle him, pulling her against him.

"Lynette . . ."

The heat of her seal so dangerously near . . . His hands roved over the soft flesh of her buttocks and his mouth sought sanctuary in hers. When her back dipped low it drew his hands up it to her shoulders, and to the small orbs topped with pink, hardened pebbles that match the color of her mouth.

"I don't want this to ever end," he breathed against them, bringing his lips around them and nursing away the doubts in his mind.

"It doesn't have to," she moaned, moving against him as her hands found his shoulders. "Oh, Forster . . . just once more, before you have to leave me today."

Her request had trembled out of her on a shudder, and her oozing warmth slid against him to summon a deep shudder from him.

"I can't go back to being alone, after you," he confessed, her rhythm vacating time and space and reason from his brain. "I can't."

"I can't either," she murmured, her words trapped halfway between a sigh and a moan. "It could be weeks . . . if not months before we can be together like this again."

Delirium had him in its grip, nearly returning him to semiconsciousness. "I'll make a way, baby . . . somehow, I'll make a way, I promise you." Her butter-soft warmth, the exterior of her haven moving in excruciating friction robbed him of speech and hijacked his mind. "Just once, I want to feel you . . ." he heard himself murmur.

But she shook her head no. The expression of her face became pained as her tempo increased, her control of the situation unsteady.

"We can't," she whispered harshly, lowering her mouth to his and clamping her knees tightly, then releasing them in a maddening rhythm—her hips negating her words as they made deep, round plunges against him.

His resolve to heed her warning was near fracture, and on each pass he could feel his length graze the desired point of entry, dangerously close and yet so far away, it collided with soft kisses from her nest, the bud of her licking at him like a tiny tongue. "Then . . . baby . . . you can't . . . because I can't . . . please . . . don't keep . . . oh, God . . ."

And he stared up at her, with fragile hopes that she would relent, just for a moment, but all hope was dashed as her pace quickened, and she lifted just enough to gently stroke him with motion, just enough to drive him out of his mind.

"I can't stop right now," she breathed out hard, her lids closed in full as her head dropped low enough for her forehead to rest on his, and her arms trembled under her weight.

The sight of her unrestrained pleasure arched him, and all he could do was lie there beneath her hungering without a will. And when she deepened her thrust against him, hurrying the licks that now lacerated his mind, he reached for the box with one hand and took her waist with the other. Rolling on top of her for a moment, her stunned expression mixed with so much want that he could barely do so, in a deft motion he sheathed himself and entered her hard, the force of entry wrenching a wail of completion from her.

Her shudders became his and he cemented himself to her in deep, harsh returns. His hands no longer controlled or gentle, he pulled her to him by her hips, feeling the vertebrae of her spine as they made their way up her back to cradle her head. His mouth punished hers for not listening to him, and his tongue found hers in a frenzied dance. Her legs entangled his as she broke from his mouth, biting her release into his shoulder, and then calling his name.

And the sound of her voice sending his name in staccato burned the shaft of his ear, releasing him with her, breaking him down, making his motions finally ebb.

They both lay together drenched, catching their breaths, as though they'd run a mile to get in from a sudden storm.

"Close call," she finally uttered, her eyes still closed as her fingers trailed his shoulder blades. "I'm sorry, baby . . ."

"Don't be," he huffed on a short pant. "I'll go to the edge with you anytime."

"But, we nearly jumped without a bungee cord," she chuckled.

"I know," he murmured, kissing her lids.

"This is dangerous," she whispered.

"I know," he breathed.

"What if we had, though . . . ? We almost hit bottom."

"I don't know," he confessed. "But I believe in life after death."

Total, satisfying fatigue made him weave where he stood at Dianne's front door. He braced himself with his hand against the wall to stop the vertigo caused from exertion without sleep. No ribbing could rob him of the extreme joy in his bones, and no matter what he faced when he got home, all he was going to do was sleep. His heart had been filled, his body was fulfilled, and his stomach was laden with fried fish, eggs, and grits . . . and he'd left an oasis that was no longer a mirage in the vestibule, breathless, with his lasting imprint marking that territorial space.

Just the thought of their last encounter in the tight confines sent a mild shiver through him. Now, every time he crossed the threshold, he'd have the vivid memory of Lynette's half-robed form, clinging to him, stained-glass colors defining her flushed complexion, her heated gasps answering his thrusts, and the sound of her whimper when he withdrew. God he had to find a way . . .

Again he rang the bell, his head now resting on his forearm as it held his body up and kept it from passing out. The bright sun had at first made him squint, despite the dark shades he wore. Now the sun felt too bright as his bones, jellied, threatened to collapse under their rays, so he closed his eyes, claiming sleep as he stood and waited.

"Yo, man," Rick said with a chuckle as he opened the door for him. "Daaaamn, brother. You all right?"

"Yeah," Forster breathed, and slowly pushed himself away from the wall.

"You look like you could use a few hours? To sleep, that is," Rick teased.

"Just hook up an IV of coffee," Forster chuckled. "I'll be all right. I'm cool."

"Cool? Sheeeit, your butt is liquefied. You okay to drive the kids?"

"I'm cool, I'm cool," he chuckled. "I just need a minute to sit down."

"Naw, dude. Been there. Go home and lie down for real, for real. I'll bring the girls home later. They're upstairs playing and it's all good."

Forster nodded and yawned. It was indeed all good. "Thanks, man . . . you have no idea how much I appreciate—"

"Oh, yes I do, my brother," Rick teased. "That's why me and Dianne did it. Her girl was actin' all crazy, your evil butt was too hard to work with, *we* needed a break from the tension."

"I'm going home, man," Forster replied, chuckling with another yawn.

Dianne seemed to come from out of nowhere as she marched up the front steps carrying bags from the corner store.

"Oh. My. God."

"D, don't start," Rick laughed, trying to defend his friend.

"Oh. My. God," she laughed hard, waving her free hand and walking in a circle inspecting Forster.

His face burned. It was bad enough that Rick had prescribed medical treatment, but seeing the amusement in Dianne's expression was just too much for a man who at the moment needed an ambulance.

"Daaaaag! Is my girlfriend still breathing over there? Call paramedics—get some help into her mama's house quick. What'd you two—"

"D, stop," Rick chuckled, "can't you see this man is injured and needs a gurney? Y'all females don't understand."

"Well at least feed the man, then, boy."

"I already ate," Forster protested. "I just came to—"

"I bet you did, and I bet you did," Dianne teased. "Now stop fussing and come on in and get something *else* to eat."

Forster's gaze pled for backup. "She fried some fish and made grits and eggs, I'm not hungry, for real, for real. But thanks."

"My girl made you fried fish and grits and eggs? Whew . . ." Dianne whistled. "Ya know what, Rick—we gonna have to baby-sit more often, 'cause this is bad. Real bad. This has to run its course."

"Don't listen to her, man," Rick jumped in. "Go get some sleep. I'll bring the kids by for dinner . . . you think four hours is gonna do it?"

"Yeah," he murmured, trying hard to ignore the knowing expression on Dianne's face as he addressed Rick. "Thanks, man. I owe you."

The telephone rang, bringing her out of her dazed repetitive motion. She'd had to wash each plate twice to be sure she'd done so. A shower with peppermint soap hadn't revitalized her; only eight hours of comatose rest would have done that. But she'd had to pull the house back together before Ida whisked in. Her mother had said not to put it in her face, and had been gracious enough to give her a little room . . . and Lord what a gift that had been.

She hadn't reached the telephone by the fourth ring, and she was having difficulty coordinating the intent to dry her hands, turn around, walk, and reach for the receiver. Her legs were wet spaghetti.

"Hello," she said in a hoarse whisper, her own voice too loud for the serenity that the kitchen held.

"Oh. My. God!"

A familiar female voice had shattered the calm, and the effect of its force made her seek a kitchen chair.

"D. . . . Many blessings upon you and your generations as the saints crown you and enrobe you with

gold. . . . I am not worthy, oh master of romance. . . . I
am humbled by your scheming, crazy, off-the-wall wisdom. I love you to death, girlfriend . . . but I am so beat
I can't talk to you right now. You just got my last breath
before I pass out."

They both laughed hard, and Lynette put her head
down on the table and sighed, cradling the telephone by
her ear.

"Girl . . . give up the tapes."

"Not on this one, D," Lynette said half laughing, but
was very serious. What Forster had given her was private and special and his privacy deserved protection.

"Oh. My. God. . . . In all these years I've never heard
you say that to me. I mean, sure, you were always close
mouthed, but . . . daaaag. . . . This is deep."

"Oh, Dianne. . . . Dianne . . . Di-anne . . ."

"Girl . . ."

"Yeah . . ."

"Gi-irl!"

"I know . . ."

"That serious?"

"Oh, yeah . . ."

"That fast?"

"Oh, yesss . . ."

"You sure?"

"Absolutely . . ."

"Deeeep . . ."

"Uh-huh . . ."

"He came by for the kids, and couldn't pick them
up."

"What?"

"Stood at the front door, a broken man, leaning on the
wall, trying to breathe. Rick and I told him to go lie
down before he fell down, and he just nodded, told Rick

he owed him, and zigzagged down the steps to his car like he'd been shot in a drive-by."

Lynette laughed from deep within her chest. "Poor baby . . ."

"Is he coming by again soon?"

"I hope so . . ."

"How y'all gonna go back to abstinence now, and work around these little kids and mama drama?"

"Oh, Dianne . . . I don't know."

"Listen to you; you're Jonesin' for the man and he just left."

"I know . . ."

"Gi-irrrl . . ."

"I know . . ."

"We gotta figure out—"

"No, please, D . . . no more getting involved. Ida will be home soon, the man has his dignity to preserve, and I can't wrap my brain around the next minute, let alone the next hour or day."

"You got it bad, though."

"I know," Lynette whispered. "So does he."

"So, work it out, go to a hotel . . ."

"Yeah . . ."

"Oh. My. God!"

"What?"

"You agreed with me?"

"I can't keep my hands off the man, D, for real, for real, I'm like a damned junkie that fell off the wagon, I almost didn't let him leave, I mean, I know he has kids, has responsibilities, has a house, has things to do, the man's gotta go to work, so do I, hell, yeah, so do I, but Lord. . . . Oh, D . . . D . . . Oh, Dianne . . . Girrrl." Spent from the sudden confession, she let her breath out hard; the sound of it reverberating off the linoleum sent a quiver through her belly as it reminded her of him.

"Listen to you . . ." Dianne whispered with awe. "I am so jealous . . . Rick never . . . I mean, I love my baby and all, but daaaamn, listen to you."

Their laughter released the tension as it climaxed, and Lynette wiped her eyes and she pushed herself up.

"Get off the phone without another mumbling word. I have to clean up and get myself together before my mama comes home."

"I remember those days, but they were never like this."

"Yeah . . ." Lynette breathed into the receiver. "They were never like this."

Seventeen

"Well just look at what the cat dragged in," Velda Hamilton stated flatly as Forster entered the kitchen from the basement staircase.

"Mom, don't start. I'm tired."

"Bet you are—"

"Cut it," he warned, and then tried to pass her.

"Don't you raise your voice at me just 'cause you been out all night with some floozy so hard you can't even take care of your own kids!"

He stopped his progression toward the living room and spun on her. As the last shred of his resolve snapped, he leveled his gaze at her and fired. "Don't you *ever* refer to her like that!"

"Sorry. Whew! Suzette must—"

"*Lynette,* Mom. Her name is Lynette!"

"I don't care what her name is; I got a name for her all right—"

"Things gotta change around here—*today*. Right now. And don't tell me squat about my responsibility to my children. Not coming from you. Ever."

Bitter hurt glittered in her eyes and she thrust her chin up at him defiantly as she dragged hard on her cigarette. "Well, I know you don't think I'm going to just—"

"All my life, Mom . . . all my life you've been like

this," he raged, turning his palms up and motioning in her direction. He could feel his voice tremble in his throat as she stared at him, seeming shocked, and the sight of her oblivion to his reference made him want to simply walk out the door, but he didn't. Today, something had to give.

"And after waiting all my life, I've finally found someone who makes me happy, who has some integrity, some honor, and who comes from something I never had—a home . . . and I can't even bring her here, or make one with her because of your nasty, sarcastic attitude, and the drinking and smoking. I don't, and didn't, want her to see that—in fact, I never wanted my children to see that. You talk about responsibility? My children, *your grandchildren,* are at risk every night because you can't even remember to put out a damned cigarette—not because they spent the night with their godfather and a bunch of other kids their age!"

"So why don't you tell me how you really feel, Scottie?"

She'd crossed her arms and folded them over her chest, and the cigarette now dangling from her lips smoldered into her squinted eyes.

He paced away from her into the dining room and she followed him. The newspaper on the table drew him to it and he picked it up and held it out to her.

"You have two choices before I start making some choices: either go to rehab or find somewhere else to live. I'm not going to live like this any longer," he warned in a low tone, using the paper as a pointer and sweeping it past all of the areas of indignity he surveyed. "I'm not going to work like a madman all day, come home tired to a drunk mother who has watched television and messed up the house. I have little girls who ask me every day, what's wrong with Gran."

He ignored the tears that filled her eyes and the way she'd swallowed hard. He'd seen the look of contrition before, but it had not changed anything in her ever-worsening condition or behavior.

"I've had a lot of problems . . . things have happened to me that you can't imagine," she warbled, finally allowing the tears she'd fought to control to fall.

Undaunted, he pressed on. "I'm not going to do security checks after they go to bed, then pray to God you don't get up in the middle of the night, light up, and burn the place down. I'm not going to come in here and find these children haven't had their homework done, or eaten anymore—unless I live alone as a single parent. Because, if their own grandmother doesn't care enough about them to even see that they eat, then I am, in truth, living in here with a ghost of a person, and not another adult."

"I'm not your maid," she spat. "I didn't make them babies—"

"No," he boomed, "you didn't. But, you are a part of this household. And as a part of the household, we've all got ways we can pitch in to help."

"I've done my household stint," she said in a flippant tone, now taking another drag. "You want a maid: Hire one."

"You did your household stint, you say?" Forster began circling the table walking and talking to the floor. "Let me see, could that have been when I was eleven? No. Because from that point on, I can remember being the one to learn how to cook for a mother who was always laid out. Could it have been to pay the bills? No."

He stopped walking and looked at her square when she covered her mouth with one hand and let an ash drop. "I seem to recall Dad sending the money back from the bar for us, your peeling off a knot of cash, and sending me to the electric company, the gas company, to whomever we were supposed to pay—*and I was eleven,* fighting in the streets to protect a wad that would keep our lights on! I stood in those lines. I went to buy the groceries so you wouldn't drink up our food allotment. I was the one who had to peep over the counters and look into eyes that held nothing but pity. I did, not you."

"Was it that bad?" His mother's voice was but a whisper.

Her pained expression and the question she'd asked drove hot pokers into his temples.

"I need *peace,* my children need peace. I demand it in here now—as a permanent part of our lives!"

When she opened her mouth to speak, he jumped in, casting the paper onto the table and then pointing hard at the center of his chest.

"The maid? *I have been the maid.* Responsible for children? I have been responsible for myself as a child, for you as my mother, and became the man of our house at eleven. My kids? I had them since they were in diapers and couldn't walk. I take them to school, I do their homework, I braid their hair, I clean up their messes, I kiss their boo-boos, I feed and clothe them and teach them right from wrong and keep them out of harm's way—me, *their father.* The maid? Because I ask for respect as the man of this house? Because I am grown, and have been a responsible, respectful son? Because I ask another grown human being to clean up after themselves, and to keep the environment safe for the children that live here—that is too much to ask?"

He closed his eyes briefly and dragged in a huge inhale and let it out hard. Pinpoints of light formed behind his lids when he did so. Pure frustration had formed knots of muscles in his neck, shoulders, and back. Oh, yes, today something had to give.

"You had choices," his mother lamented in a defensive tone. "You—"

"You have choices, too, and I'm giving them to you now. Either you seek help, or you take this toxic slop out of my home and away from my kids. Are we clear?" His voice had been steady, even, and his gaze held hers in a deadly serious threat. "When I was eleven, I didn't have a choice. And all the years growing up until I left to go into the service, my choices were very slim—either gang war and sell drugs and possibly get shot or sent to jail, or not. We all have choices. I made mine, just like I made these kids. But, at their ages, they don't have a choice. So as the only responsible adult in their lives, I'm making one for them."

He paused and looked at her hard to be sure she got it. "I saw how children are supposed to live. . . . I finally saw it, Mom. And whether or not it is done here alone, or with another person, I am going to give my children, and myself, a fighting chance. They deserve that. I deserve that."

Her bottom lip trembled and she damped out her cigarette after taking the last, long drag, and then fished in her robe pocket to find a new one. She lit it with care, studied the tip of it, and took a drag on it. "If your father hadn't left us, things would have been different."

"No they wouldn't have," he immediately spat back. "Eva left me. She died. But my behavior and responsibility level didn't change. Whatever was going on with me and her had nothing to do with them, and they shouldn't have had to suffer through adult addictions or drama while I got my head together—that was the choice I made. To not let them suffer because of adult issues was a choice, Mom. How many people do you know have gotten a bad break, but keep going nonetheless? Dig it, accept it . . . these reasons are excuses and you need to deal with your own issues."

"Easy for you to say," she spat, blowing out smoke hard.

"What about any of what I've told you sounds easy, Mom?" He was incredulous. "That is addiction talking. Like I said, you need to dig it. But whether you do or not, I told you what my choice is—the girls, who cannot make choices on their own yet, versus a full-grown woman who has been wallowing in self-pity all her life, and who has been wasting her life . . . the choice is real clear. My daughters win. So make a choice about where and how you want to live. Today."

"My son goes out for the night, gets his brain twisted and his pipes cleaned, and then comes home with delusions of a perfect—"

"Enough!" He'd held up his hand to stop the ugly trajectory of her words. "Crazy is doing the same things over and over again and expecting different results. I'm no longer feeding into your insanity, and I'm not going to argue with an alcoholic on a Sunday morning. Not today."

Her stunned expression seemed as though he'd slapped her, and her gaze narrowed as she pointed her trembling fingers at him using the cigarette like a wand.

"An alcoholic?"

"For thirty-some-odd years."

"Is that what that whore—"

"Not another word." He'd whispered the threat through his teeth and it had stopped her cold and froze her animated retaliation. "Peace in my house from this point forward. I am going to lie down, and then bring my children home, and all that you have messed up in

here by your own hand better be back in place before
they get here."

"How dare you—"

"This is my house!"

The sonic boom of his voice made her draw back,
and for the first time in his life, he saw fear reflected in
her eyes. The sight of that coming from his mother's
gaze haunted him, and he paced away from her, and
began tearing though the cabinets, finding bottles of her
stash and smashing them in the kitchen sink. She rushed
behind him screeching out her complaints, but his ears
were deaf to them. Tears of hysteria, pleas for him to
stop, he ignored, until he'd found every vessel of poison
and eliminated it.

He turned to face her as he grabbed the broom and
dustpan, brandishing them like a sword and shield. "Not
in my house, ever again." His chest heaved with the
emotional weight that was upon him. "If one single bottle comes in here, if I find another ash, I will take you
out of here with your bags packed to a church or a shelter . . . but I *will not* have it in here. Period. Make a
choice, Velda Hamilton. And make it a wise one."

"My own son . . . my own son," she wept, her eyes
searching his face. "My own son would do this, go off
like this, threaten and hurt me so."

"My own mother," he repeated with emphasis to let
her know that even tears of manipulation would not
work this morning. "You can pull out all the stops,
Mother. Guilt, long stories of woe, tears, I don't care
what—but my decision is very final. Make a choice.
Clean up your life. Clean up what you've messed up in
this house. I am cleaning up the glass I just broke—but
nothing else. Then, I'm going to lie down for a few
hours—and demand peace for the duration. Are we
clear?"

She didn't answer but simply paced away from him and left the room. He began carefully removing the broken bottles and sweeping up any splinters of glass. When he heard the vacuum cleaner, his shoulders relaxed.

The sound of banging at his door awakened his from a deep slumber. He sat up quickly, his motion making his head pound as though he had a hangover. Still groggy, he paced through the house, yelling that he would be there to stop whomever it was from knocking so loudly. A slip of paper on the clean, polished coffee table made him hesitate and grab it up as he made his way to the door.

The scrawl on it was familiar; its manipulative intent crystal clear.

> *I cleaned up, and I have left. I have choices too. I'm grown too. When my real son comes back into his right mind, I'll be back.*
>
> —*Velda.*

"Whatever . . ." he grumbled, snatching up her door keys that she'd obviously pushed into the house through the mail slot after she'd locked the front door. Seeing Rick on the steps with the girls, he opened the door.

"Sorry, man," Forster intoned flatly. "Didn't hear the bell. Was in a coma." He hugged his girls as they barreled through the door; the sound of their voices too high-pitched to deal with, he squinted at the sensory intrusion, then stood and gave his friend a quick embrace. "Thanks again, man."

"Uh, can I talk to you in the kitchen for a minute?"

Rick's worried expression immediately got Forster's attention.

"Yeah," he said fast. "Look, girls, go on in the living room and watch some cartoons. I need to talk to Uncle Rick for a minute."

"Where's Gran?" Rebecca asked, ignoring Forster's command.

"It smells good in here, Dad," Rachel added in, looking around the room and seeming confused.

"Gran went out to run an errand, so go get your coats off and chill. Me and Uncle Rick are going in the kitchen."

He exchanged a tense glance with Rick, who followed him when he began walking.

"Where's Velda?" Rick said in a quiet voice, leaning against the sink.

Forster rubbed his palms over his face and then raked his fingers through his short hair. Then he handed Rick the note.

"What happened?"

"I got tired, man." Forster motioned for Rick to have a seat at the table as he took one and sat down. "I gave her a choice—get clean or get out."

Rick sat down slowly, turning the chair around backward to straddle it. "Yo, that's your mom, dude . . ."

"You know how this goes," Forster murmured, "better than anybody."

Rick nodded. "You know what we went through with my brother, right?"

"Yeah. Addiction is a demon, and you can never appease the beast."

Rick rubbed his face and sighed. "True dat. It's just a shame, man . . . it being your mom, and all."

"Been coming for a lot of years, you know that."

"Yeah, bro, but damn . . . your mom . . ."

"I hear you. But it was her or them," Forster said calmly, motioning toward the other room where the children laughed at cartoons. "Her or them, and that's just how I told her."

"My mom told my brother the same thing. Us younger kids in the house, or the pipe."

"Same difference."

Both men nodded.

"But, it broke her up bad . . . don't know if she ever really got over having to go there."

"Well," Forster said, shaking it off and summoning macho to shut out the hurt, "what's done is done. She made a choice. I'm changing the locks."

Rick shook his head and kept his gaze focused on the frame of the chair. "You don't think that's a bit extreme, dude? So soon?"

"Nah," Forster replied on a long exhale. "That note," he added, nodding toward where Rick had left it in the middle of the table, "Was a ploy."

When Rick only gazed at him, the question in his friend's eyes, he elaborated.

"No different than a tantrum. I've seen my mother run every game in the book—the runaway scene is not new to me. I tell her to stop drinking and take her stash, she goes to a bar and gets totaled, and comes home with a whole litany about seeing the light because of what some barfly told her in conversation. I become afraid for her safety, so I let her bring her bottles back in—as long as she promises to cut back, and then we start the same old dance over and over again. It's a guilt, enabler cycle. But not today."

Rick nodded. "And when she comes home banging on the door?"

"I'm going to take her and her suitcases to a good shelter or group home and put the rest of her possessions in storage and hand her the key to it," Forster said without reservation. "She is my mother, so I will see that she has food and medical care, and will ensure that she has her necessities covered in a safe place—but she will not be allowed to conduct her drama here in front of my kids. I won't allow it, bro. That's an old dance, and I'm through with it. I'm done enabling . . . it doesn't help, and it doesn't make the person get better—just prolongs the inevitable until they make the commitment to themselves to change."

Both men sat in silence for a moment, and memories flooded Forster, each vivid, in color, with no shades of gray.

"Went through this same process with Eva," he murmured. "She ran from place to place, bar to bar, man to man, always with promises of improvement each time she came back home with a long story."

"Let it go, man," Rick whispered. "You don't have to explain . . . don't guilt trip over this."

"She has to get her head together," Forster went on, pointing at his temple, then looking away as his throat tightened.

"I know you love her, man. Loved Eva, too, and tried your best. Ain't nobody gonna fault you for doing what you had to do."

"Yeah," Forster agreed through a thick swallow. "I had to, man. This was a long time coming."

"Sho' you right. It hurts like hell, but it's for the best."

Forster could only nod.

"Want me to cruise with you to see if we can find her . . . so at least you know where she is? That way, you can drop her off and get her signed up somewhere safe, then be able to sleep at night. It's the waiting part that's the hardest."

"No. Not this time. I'm not going to posse up and go looking for her. There's nobody to watch my kids, and . . . No. Not this time."

"As long as you're cool with that," Rick said in a quiet voice. "You have to get to the place where you're cool with the choice you gave her, too. Ask me how I know—after me and my brothers would go out time after time looking for Jose when my mom would put him out, change the locks, and cry herself to sleep at night. *You* gotta get cool with it and stand firm on the line you've drawn. Dig?"

Forster nodded and fought against the moisture that had filled his eyes. "I'm cool with it, man," he murmured. "I'm cool."

"Look," Rick said on a heavy breath. "It kicks my ass to have to tell you this, now, in light of all the rest of the madness going on. But, the reason I came by, other than to drop the girls off . . . Oh, man. Timing of this sucks."

"Just spit it out," Forster said, having gained his composure. "Tell me now, tell me later, either way, if it's bad news, I'ma have to deal with it."

Rick pushed himself up from his chair and began pacing. "All right. Listen. That set of shots you got on the DeCicci case . . . it's not a slip and fall. It's now over at homicide."

"Yeah. Okay?" Forster sat back in his chair and studied his friend's expression. "I just take the film. Homicide's got it from there. The prints are over in Forensics."

"I know, man, but listen." Rick walked in a tight circle and then stopped, leaned against the sink, and studied his sneakers. "The hcad wound didn't have brick or wall in it like it should have. On the scene, the blood and the state of decomposition of the body, just made it look black and ugly at first glance. But when they analyzed the cut, it had traces of gunmetal in it. So the old dude was hit and probably pushed facedown in the water . . . and whoever did it, had to have a key to his house. That's why it looked like there were no intruders, and that he was in there all alone when the so-called accident happened."

"Okay," Forster repeated, waiting until Rick looked up at him before pressing on. "So, what's that got to do with me?"

"We swept the house after that for a family, friends list . . . you know the drill. Pictures on the mantle, photo albums, letters, bills, anything that could give us a read on who might have a key. Then we ran a battery on any of the names and faces . . . trying to see if anyone might have a motive. Funny thing was, we found your father's will in DeCicci's possession—in a waterproof strongbox hidden under a false floorboard panel in the basement closet. After the storm, and the water receded, the floor had buckled—that's the only way we would have spotted it, truth be told, when we went back over the crime scene and reopened the investigation."

Rick held Forster's gaze and his voice became gentle. "Listen, I work Vice, and this isn't even my case . . . but the guys in Homicide called me, 'cause they know you're my boy . . . and being one of us . . . they wanted me to talk to you personally before the press gets involved and we have to amp this thing up to the next level."

"My father's will?" Forster stood and began walking back and forth the length of the kitchen. "That's been settled for years. My stepbrother and stepsister got everything, me and my mom didn't get a dime. The house in Cherry Hill, the bar—which Reginald parlayed into several bars . . . Regina got his bankroll and military and private pension . . . He'd even left his new wife, their mom, a fat monthly allowance from his business receipts, which kept her living nice until the day she died." Forster stopped walking and flattened his hand against his chest. "I was there at the reading of the will. I was there, dude. The executor was his new wife's brother—a judge. My halfsister, Regina, an attorney, doled out the little memorabilia and then gave us her ass to kiss. It was cut and dried, end of story. No contest."

"Not according to the will we have in the evidence room," Rick murmured. "And the date postdates the one on file that was used to distribute assets."

Forster let his breath out hard, absorbing the magnitude of what his friend had just told him.

"Your father was shot, man," Rick said in a too calm voice. "In a bar incident, a regulation holdup after hours. Right? And they took some young boy in and threw away the key. But now . . . that leaves a lot of questions. . . ."

"You don't think . . . Rick, man, c'mon!"

"You're talking to me, brother." Rick's voice had become urgent and firm. "I know you, man. That's what I'm trying to tell you. The thing points a lot of fingers in a lot of directions. Homicide has got to do their job, and ask questions to find anybody who might have an ax to grind. You and your mom woulda had a big ax, by rights. But I'm trying to get them to go down another path, and look at the beneficiaries . . . especially since the judge that heard the case on your father's murder is real tight, like best friends with, your old stepmother's brother—who just so happens to be a judge."

"Damn!" Forster walked away and then slammed his fist on a cabinet. The sound brought two worried little faces into the room, but he kept his back to them as he told them that everything was all right.

"Go on, y'all," Rick urged. "Your dad just accidentally shut his hand in the drawer. He's gonna be fine. Go watch your cartoons."

Forster closed his eyes as he heard his children shuf-

fle silently into the next room. How many more lies
would he have to tell them on the behalf of adults?

"Listen," Rick nearly whispered once the children
had left the room and Forster had turned around, "do
you know why Thomas DeCicci would have your father's will and why the old man might have hidden it?
Do you know anything about him?"

"No," Forster replied, his brain searching, scram-
bling, and trying to cling to any branch of the foggy
memory he had of his father.

"Look hard at these photos, Forster," Rick warned
as he offered an envelope to him from his bomber-
jacket breast pocket. "Do you remember even seeing
this guy around? That's what he looked like before he
got waterlogged."

A slow dawning awareness made his pulse quicken.
"Jesus Christ . . ."

"What, man? Tell me. You know him?"

"I don't know him," Forster explained. "But I have a
lot of shots of him."

"This is not good," Rick murmured, following
Forster's fast pace out of the kitchen and down into the
basement.

Both men stared at the photos still in piles on the coffee table, and Rick reached for them gingerly as though
they might burn him.

"Has anybody else seen these?" Rick's voice was a
hoarse whisper when he'd spoken and his gaze held fear
when he held Foster's in his own.

"No," Forster lied, immediately protecting Lynette
from any possible implication.

"You know this is bad evidence?"

"Yeah . . . but on my life, I swear, I just shot people in
the neighborhood, folks milling around in the park . . .
I mean, you know me, Rick. I swear on my life . . ."

"It might be that serious, brother . . . it could mean your life. This looks like you'd been stalking the old man, if somebody didn't know better. And, when the press starts unraveling this story . . . I mean, you know how stuff leaks—the department can never keep a lid on . . . Jesus, man."

Rick dropped the pictures onto the table and walked away. "You've gotta come down to the station with me, on the down low, and read that will. You've gotta help find out who DeCicci was to your father, and we've gotta build a link bridge back to whoever did him. And, we don't have much time—like, we gotta go now, before Monday morning and the joint starts jumping."

"But, the girls . . . I can't, I don't have anybody to—"

"What about Lynette? D and her sisters hit the streets to go to some mall when I left them to bring the kids here."

"I can't take them to Lynette, like this, under these circumstances . . ." Forster walked in a circle, trapped, and his heart slammed against his breastbone.

"Make the call, Forster," Rick commanded. "Like your life depended on it."

Eighteen

"You must be living right, kiddo," her assignment editor boomed into the telephone. "That story we had to
chuck because an old man slipped and fell, and wasn't
a crime—is."

"The Thomas DeCicci piece?"

"Yeah, kiddo, that's what I'm telling you—and it'll be
a headliner."

A rush of excitement pulled Lynette to her feet from
the edge of the sofa. "Wow! That's great, Dan. Can you
fax me any details from your little birdie over at the
precinct?"

"Yeah, doll, and it's a barn burner. Seems as though
the old man was bagging some young attorney chick
from Cherry Hill, New Jersey, who was apparently at
the house the night of the storm . . . got that from our
friendly secretary down at the round house, though.
Wonder how long it'll take the boys in blue to figure it
out? Something about she and her brother own a bar
DeCicci frequented—whatever. If you snoop around
there, you might be able to get a name on her, because
our source only picked up snippets of the conversations
about that. But, DeCicci had a colorful past, and held a
will—a different will than the one that was filed. Our
inside girl saw them put it in the evidence room."

"Get, out of here, Dan! This thing is sounding more and more like a soap opera."

"Well, since you've been so literary here of late, figured you'd have a great time writing this juicy tidbit. But the real inside story is, the will names a cop and his mother in it—that's the part I want you to wrap the details around. We'll break this before the TV news guys get it for film at eleven, because my birdie also said that they're not going to haul him in for questioning until Monday or Tuesday . . . guess he gets a little special treatment as professional courtesy, since he's a local one of their own."

It was something in Dan's combination of words that froze her, and she slowly stood. "Do you have the cop's name . . . know anything about him, or the other person named in the will?"

"Nope. Source only knows it's within the station, because the fellas were all hush-hush and talking in little clusters about it. She can't get it out of evidence unless an officer or one of the detectives requests it. So, you'll have to do that part of the digging on your own."

Her pulse had quickened as she paced back into the kitchen with the phone pressed to her ear. "You got a photo of DeCicci, then? A rough bio, anything that I can pick up the thread with?"

"Turn on your fax," Dan chuckled. "It just so happens that they brought in a couple of photo albums from the DeCicci house, and had our source tag 'em . . . and she slipped one for us, copied it, and got it back into the album before she got herself in trouble. It's dark, not a good, clear image, and it'll be worse when I fax it to ya . . . but, it's a recent one of the old man at a summer gathering of some sort—looks like Jersey, but who knows? Regardless, the chick and her brother are in a group shot that somebody must have snapped and given to the old man. When I send it, look for a stunning African-American woman."

"Done," she murmured in a tone that belied her panic. Her mind dredged her memory for the things Forster had told him about his life, his family, and about Rick's. "Give me five minutes to turn on my fax upstairs in my office, and I'll get on it."

"You love me, darlin'?"

"Yeah, Dan, I love ya," she replied in a forced chuckle.

"Then get off the telephone and get that story in before the presses roll. You're wasting time. Bye!"

Lynette clicked off the talk button on the receiver and numbly peered in the oven at her baked chicken. She moved very slowly, filling a pot with water using only one hand, and put a box of rice in the center of the kitchen table next to the beans she'd broken. Then like a zombie, she walked up the back staircase and switched on her fax machine. She would not panic. Dinner would be prepared for her mother's homecoming, and they'd eat together first, before she went work.

This would not touch any of the people she loved. Forster and Rick would understand if it was a bad cop—and they would not hate her if she did her job as a reporter, and told people the facts. If this was indeed foul play, it didn't matter that the person might have been on the force or one of their brothers . . .

When the phone rang in her palm the sound gave her a start. The vibration sent chills up her arm, and it was difficult to breath as the laboriously slow process of the image coming through made her want to snatch the paper from the feed wheels.

But as the dark, slightly blurry image of the happy gathering fell into her palms, she gasped and dropped it. She'd seen this man before!

Standing in the middle of the floor she covered her mouth with her hand, looking down at the dead man's photo at her feet. Nausea and bile churned in her stomach. It couldn't be . . .

No. It was just a bad picture in the first place, made worse by the faxed image of it. She shook off her uneasiness and bent to pick it up. Her gaze narrowed as she studied the details of the old man's handsome face . . . that was soon made indistinguishable by the hot tears that immediately rose within her eyes.

"Oh, God no . . ."

This time when the telephone rang, she accidentally dropped it. The sound had sent an electric shock into her nervous system, and she had the jitters so badly that it took three attempts to retrieve the annoyingly persistent instrument from the floor.

"Yes, I mean, hello," she stammered in a pant to the caller.

"Baby . . . listen, I know you were probably dozing and relaxing, and I didn't mean to startle you like that, but, I need to ask you a huge favor . . ."

The familiar male voice that she'd come to adore was now the last voice she wanted to hear.

"Startle?" She said quickly. "Startle? Why would I be startled? I'm fine. Just fine."

"Oh . . . wow . . . I guess Ida came home early—judging from the sound of your voice. You sound tense, but I really need to—"

"I'm not tense. No stress here. What's up?"

"Good," he sighed. "'Cause I need to run down to the station with Rick, and Dianne and her sisters are out—and I really need someone to watch the girls . . . if I bring them by . . . do you think, just for a few. But there's a really serious situation going down at headquarters right now—and by Monday or Tuesday, it could get worse . . . I'll try to explain everything to you later, baby, and I'm not trying to take anything for granted, but I really need your help, Lynne. For real, for real."

Under any other circumstances, she would have cut off his flow of words and brightly jumped in to help. But if the terrible things rumbling in her gut were anywhere near true . . . and, as a matter of simple practicality, the multiple layers of conflict of interest— not to mention her heart's conflict. Children possibly could be caught in the crossfire, just like her heart, but as an adult, she could become a material witness, an accessory . . . if her eyes and memory didn't fail her . . . if the photos in his basement meant what she thought they might . . .

"Lynette?"

For the first time since he'd been in her company an uneasy instinct coiled within him. He'd practically begged her for help, and there was nothing on the other end of the line but silence. And he'd asked her to help with his children. . . . What was going on? Was everything she'd said about adoring them a female game? Was the whole home-sweet-home vibe a put-on, especially when she claimed that she was not doing anything for the rest of the day but puttering, and cooking for Ida's return. And she'd dropped the phone like a thief, answered it out of breath . . .

He stopped the jaded path his mind was going down—the blind alley of old demons killed but still rising with another head like a Hydra within his psyche.

"No problem," he murmured to her silent answer. "It's cool. Some other time." He couldn't focus on relationship bull right now.

The hurt in his voice threaded through her ear. What if she had been wrong? What if he'd collected the pictures because he was out pursuing this undercover or something? What if he hadn't been able to come out and tell her that, but had wanted to show her some of his deeper work all the same. And what if he and Rick were going down there to pull together the final elements of the case? She had to let go of her bitter memories of a man who lived a double life, and not allow it to ruin the new one she was starting.

"No, if it's just for a couple of hours, that's cool. I was cooking anyway, and when Ida gets in, I know she'll be happy to see them. I only hesitated because my editor gave me a punk assignment to do with a heavy deadline . . . which I can tell you more about later, anyway."

Relief swept through him and made him close his eyes as he spoke.

"Thank you, baby," he breathed. "I promise I'll make this up to you."

She took her time getting to the door, and when she actually saw Rick's expression and the ashen look on Forster's face, she knew it was not good. Herding the children inside amid their hugs and kisses, she sent them deeper into the house to hunt for the cookies she'd left on the kitchen counter as a diversion.

Something was definitely not right. He brushed Lynette's cheek with a kiss and she stiffened just ever so slightly, and the singsong in her voice had sounded brittle and forced when she'd pasted on a smile for the children and then shooed them away.

"You sure this is no imposition?" His question had been issued from a low, flat register when he'd said it, and all his instincts and police training made him survey the environment quickly with an alert glance.

"None whatsoever," she said with tension filtering

every word. She monitored him carefully with trust abandoning her as his eyes roved the interior of her home.

"This might take a little longer than a few hours, Lynette," Rick said in a very formal policelike tone. "I asked Forster to bring over the kids' books and some clothes . . . just in case we have to do some legwork, and I thought you should be prepared, if it got late."

Stunned into numb silence, she accepted the two backpacks and a small piece of luggage Rick held out to her. Dear God in Heaven . . .

"If I can get back for them tonight, I will," Forster said too quietly for her liking, and the double entendre it contained made her blood run cold.

"If that's a problem, I'll raise D by cell phone, and maybe she can come get them and keep them at her place . . . Forster mentioned you were working on a special project tonight, and we respect that. But, we need some latitude, if you can give it to us, now."

Lynette simply nodded and then found her voice. "That won't be necessary. If you're late, I'll put them to bed. Eight-thirty, right?"

"Yeah," Forster murmured with a nod. "But, let me hug them before I go."

Silence rode in the SUV with them like a third passenger, and Forster braced himself for their unavoidable entry into what once felt like a second home. Now it was a place he dreaded, because it could be the place that might hold him on the wrong side of justice.

"You ready?" Rick asked as he parked and turned off the ignition.

"As I'll ever be," Forster replied, hopping out of the

vehicle, looking straight ahead of him, and walking to take whatever faced him like a man.

"Okay, Detective Sanchez, this is on the down low—professional courtesy only."

Rick nodded as he accepted the will from his brethren officers Mifflin and Conners. "Much appreciated."

Forster's jaw had locked as the muscle in it ground out his frustration. Humiliation tore at his entrails, and at the same time, a cold scythe of fear hacked at his nerves. He'd seen how investigations go. They could take months, years . . . and time would never heal the scar left on his children's minds if they brought him in, his face was flashed on television, whispers began within the school, or anything worse went down before he was cleared. And, Lynette . . . dear God. She might have been tired, preoccupied with her job stuff, or even worried about her mother's return, but if she found this out . . . Why was fate conspiring against him? Was he being punished for putting an end to enabling his mother, or was this just chickens coming home to roost—and he happened to get crapped on while just being in the wrong place at the wrong time?

"How are we going to do this, fellas?" Forster finally muttered with disgust. "What's the party line—so we can get this done did with the quickness?"

"We've allowed a fellow officer to peruse the documents, you, not Hamilton, and if you read aloud, we didn't hear you. You have a learning disability, or something, and can't read in your head. And you will have handed the document back to us, because a suspect cannot have access to tamper with material evidence once it's in our possession. We are all clear on the procedures, right?"

Detective Mifflin riffled his fingers through his thinning gray hair and let his breath out hard when all four men in the small circle nodded.

"This bull could cost us all our badges."

"And Mifflin went to get a cup of coffee, while I went to take a whiz," Detective Conners added. "Which only took a moment—which shouldn't have mattered, since Sanchez was assisting to see if there was a vice angle driven by the bar aspects of the case—given the will ties to bars in Camden, not our jurisdiction, but does to the original one owned by one of the suspects."

"Right," Mifflin concluded. "And Sanchez was trying to ascertain some of the shady dealing that might have gone down in the original North Philadelphia establishment mentioned in the will . . . with a suspect."

All eyes landed on Forster, and Rick's grip tightened on the document.

"About that coffee?" Mifflin asked in a sad tone.

"Yeah," Conners stated flatly. "Meet you there, I gotta go take a whiz."

Nineteen

Forster slid the copy of the will across the table toward his friend and allowed his gaze to cross the room to settle on nothing in particular. The eerie void within him kept expanding, until it suddenly flooded with emotion that threatened to drown him.

"What am I supposed to do with this information, man? Tell me," he said through his teeth, now standing in the interrogation room and pacing over to the far wall. All of his life he'd filled in the missing pieces, beginning that process as a child. His parents constantly argued, his father had split, he'd hooked up with a new woman, and had thrown away him and his mom. Money came in, guilt payments of child support and what he imagined had to be alimony. His father owned a bar—and had given it to his second, preferred set of children. That's all he knew, and all he'd wanted to know . . . and his mother had refused to talk about it beyond that.

Rick took his time responding, and had ignored Mifflin's orders to read the will to Forster aloud. He couldn't voice the words that would cut his friend to the bone. But witnessing his friend's quiet pain still made moving forward to do what had to be done difficult.

"He loved you, man," Rick began in a tentative manner. "The way he worded his will, saying that you were his only real son . . . and that the others were pretenders to all that he'd built . . . man, the apology . . . it ain't good, from a legal perspective."

"You don't have to string it together for me," Forster replied hoarsely. "I got that. It gives me motive, now more than ever, to have been the one to kill to reclaim all that was mine by birthright—and by my father's final wishes."

"Yeah," Rick murmured, pushing himself up from his backward-turned chair at the table. "I wish he would have been more specific when he put in all those murky references to *those who plotted against me*. It's too vague, and would never hold up in court, even if we brought in his other kids for questioning. Who plotted, what did they steal from him, what specifics do we have to hold on to, other than the ramblings of a possibly guilt-ridden old man?"

Forster nodded and leaned against the wall, now looking at Rick square in the eyes. "We can start with the young boy that shot him. By now, if he was paid to do the hit, he's probably ready to tell somebody something, anything to get out of the joint. They might have double-crossed him, too, giving him some cash, telling him to cool his heels in the joint for a few, and with a judge on their side, they'd get him out on parole to enjoy his money. Some such bull."

"That would have been a good idea, if the kid hadn't gotten whacked within six months of being on the inside," Rick said carefully. "Fight in the laundry room, no witnesses of course. Slit his throat. Happens all the time, so nobody gave it two thoughts—then."

"Yeah, but a paid-off man with a scam and a lot of game to him had to run his mouth to somebody."

"We're working on that, trust me."

Again Forster nodded. "The other businesses my father owned—we need to see if he had any other business associates in the limited-liability corporations set up. More importantly, we need to see who the original participants were, and if any of them changed subsequent to his death. That's the beginning of the paper trail."

"Yeah, we're working that, but at some point, you might have to go in and have a chat with Reginald or Regina or both while you're hot."

"You want me to wear a wire to talk to people I haven't spoken more than three sentences to in my life? C'mon, Rick, you know the deal. The most I ever interfaced with them was at the funeral, and then when they read the will. It was hello, thank you for allowing us to come, good-bye. I wasn't even listed in the funeral program as a surviving son. And, I really don't care what he decided to leave me and mom at the last minute. Money can't buy what his absence cost."

"I know you're upset, but if you cooperate and look like you're doing everything to help do a sting, it could bode well . . . a cooperating witness versus a recalcitrant suspect. Take your pick. Your choice."

God most assuredly had to be getting him back. Choices. Hadn't he just told his mother that?

Forster shook his head and wiped his face with his palms. "All right, all right, all right!"

"Good." Rick picked up the will and held it in Forster's direction. "Nothing in there rings a bell?"

"No," he replied in a sullen tone. "And get that out of my face. I just wish I had some pictures, something to jog—"

"There's the photo albums from the house, mantle pictures . . . Wait, let me go work on Mifflin and Conners and take the will back to Evidence."

Forster walked in a circle, punched the wall, and circled the table again. The situation was damnable. Who the hell was DeCicci to his father, a predator or a protector, or both?

Soon Rick returned to the room, toting a box of silver-framed photographs and two large scrapbook-sized albums. "This is going to take a few," he sighed and sat down hard.

Forster joined him, shaking his head no at each of the mantle shots when Rick slid them before him.

"Forensics already dusted for prints—nothing out of the ordinary," Rick mentioned as they continued the laborious process of going through the photos.

"Amateur camera work," Forster said sarcastically, becoming so impatient to leave that he could barely sit. This was ridiculous. He didn't know this man, and poring through an old album like it was . . .

"Wait a minute," Forster whispered, stopping on a black and white under yellowing plastic.

"You see somebody?" Rick questioned anxiously, leaning in so he could peer at it, too.

"Yeah," Forster whispered. "It's my mom."

Tense silence brought both men's eyes to the photo that contained a young Velda Hamilton in a nightclub on the stage. Her head was thrown back, eyes closed, and the microphone was inches from her darkly painted mouth. Her hands clutched the mike and her expression was frozen in a soulful wail. Her shape unmistakably bombshell, and her beautiful dark skin contrasted with the beaded white satin that clung to every curve. Black, white, and many shades of gray.

"Whew, man . . ." Rick whispered in return. "That's Velda?"

Still stunned, Forster pointed to the other men in the shot. "There's my father, and next to him, clapping, is DeCicci—check the profile from some earlier shots. And, now, the one time I really need to talk to my mother, the possible one person who could put faces and context to these people, she's gone—at my request. Ain't life a bitch?" God was definitely mocking him.

"Deep," Rick murmured. "I wonder where this was taken?"

"North Philly, in my father's first club. After the nightclub era cooled, I hear, he just turned the stage area into more bar space—but all the old fixtures, everything, are still in there. Went by there once or twice when I was a teenager, hoping to catch him. But the old brothers working around there told me he was over in his Camden spots, or Cherry Hill—you know the three-card monte when someone is trying to blow you off. Left my number, all that, but never heard from him. So, I stopped trying."

"We should go by there," Rick said carefully. "See who or what we can dig up. If any of the old brothers from that era are still around, maybe they'd be able to put a finger on who DeCicci was in this picture?"

"Might be worth a try," Forster conceded. "And bring a copy of the photo—if they're that old, they're gonna need a memory boost."

Velda Hamilton closed her eyes as the dark bronze liquid slid down her throat. The burning sensation lit her insides with a satisfying fire, and she swayed as she hummed the old Billie Holiday ballad that had become her personal gospel. "Your mama may have . . . your papa may have . . . but God bless the child . . . that's got his own . . ."

"You sing that real nice, sweetie," the bartender said. "But after this one, I think we'd better switch you to coffee."

Velda smiled and waved her hand. "I had a real voice,

once. This ain't nothin'. But I ain't ready for no coffee. I'm celebratin' my birthday."

"That's real nice. Happy birthday, suga'. But shouldn't you be celebrating with your family? It's getting late, and wouldn't want you to get hurt out here walking around in a very cheerful frame of mind. Okay, sis? Coffee for the next round, on the house."

"That's awful sweet of you," she laughed and took another swig. "But tonight, I'm celebratin' wit' my best friend, Jack. Me and Jack Daniels go a *long* way back. That rhymes," she tittered, and polished off her drink. "C'mon. I ain't got no family, and if I get hit over the head or killed, won't nobody care, no how. Just one more, then I'ma go find somewhere to rest my weary bones."

The look of pity on the bartender's face cut her like a razor. There was a time when she owned this bar by proxy, and every man that came to it brought her drinks and jealously coveted what Forster Hamilton, Sr. had acquired—her. And there was a time when she commanded the stage, her form lithe, beautiful, graceful, and awe-inspiring, just like her voice. Tears filled her eyes, adding to the blur that they already saw. What had happened to the gorgeous mural, the elegant chandelier, the big-band stage, and the throng of upscale, well-dressed notables that had once frequented her palace? And what had happened to her?

When the bartender brought her a cup of coffee rather than what she'd asked for, belligerence tore through her body. But instead of a string of nasty expletives issuing forth, a sob came out, and she lowered her head to the bar on her folded arms. God was the meanest person on earth! Today was her self-determined birthday, not her God-given one, and yet she couldn't even celebrate her decision to change her life.

Where was her son, the only man in her life that had ever done right by her, when she needed him?

"What's happening?" Forster said in a casual voice in the bartender's direction, taking a stool at the far end of the bar as Rick also filled one. They had business to get down to, and he didn't need what they were about to ask the man to be studied by the stragglers and the old woman crying at the other end. But there was something in the quiet way that her shoulders shook, and her body curved . . .

"Life," the bartender replied, putting two clean glasses in front of them. "Name your poison."

"A Miller," Rick said, "and give my brother a shot of Jack. Tonight he needs one."

"Everybody's celebrating with Jack tonight," the bartender said with a smile. "Comin' up." He removed the short glass from in front of Rick and put down a beer in its place, and then filled Forster's glass with a shot.

"Got a question for you," Forster said, taking time to toss down his drink. "More like a picture that we need to fill in the blanks on." The shot hit the back of his throat and warmed his insides as it slid down his esophagus into his stomach. There, it created an ember.

The bartender sighed. "Five-O, shoulda figured. Look, I don't know nobody, I don't see nothin', all I do is take care of my customers. If y'all want to help solve some crimes, why don't you help that poor old sister down the other end of the bar, who's crying 'cause it's her birthday and she ain't got no family," he fussed. "She's tore up, and I can't serve her no more licka in here—and she's about ready to sob herself into a heart attack. So, don't even pull it out your pocket. Talk to the owner, I just work here."

Rick and Forster exchanged a glance as they peered

down the other end of the bar for a moment, then returned their focus on the bartender.

"All right," Rick shrugged. "Then, how about if you give us an idea of when we can do that?"

"Reg don't come into any of his places he got down the way. North-side, Camden, nah. You want to peg him, check him out in the plush zone, Cherry Hill."

Forster nodded and gave Rick the sign that it was time to roll. Placing a bill on the bar to cover their drinks, he noticed that the bartender had given him his back to consider. "Yeah, this is the cash-cow side of their business, and where anything else they want to run can get washed."

"Right," Rick said letting his breath out in frustration, then downed his beer. "Look around at the options. Nobody in here really, and nobody that isn't already too tore down to be of much help, or too young to recall the era. We could sample the tables—but we're probably wasting time with these folks. Maybe we can shoot on over to Jersey?"

"Yeah . . . and thanks for the drink, man. Tonight, I definitely needed something to steady my nerves for the long haul in front of us."

Again both men nodded and headed for the door, but listening to the bartender's pleas to his distressed patron, and her throaty responses made Forster stop.

"What's up, man?"

"Give me the photo," Forster said slowly, accepting it from Rick. "Stay by the door."

An eerie sense of knowing came over him as he heard the off-key tune being sung. The thick voice quickened his pace, and when he slid beside her there was an inaudible understanding that passed between the bartender and Forster. Withdrawing with a nod, the bar-

tender left him beside the woman who sang a sad, muffled ballad against the sleeves of her coat.

"Mom?" Forster whispered, rubbing her back to
make her look up.

She smiled and chuckled, rifling in her pockets for a
cigarette. When she found one, he lit it for her.

"I knew my son would come for me and take me
home. God is good."

"All the time, Mom," Forster whispered. "But
tonight, I need your help."

"You need my help?" She giggled and motioned for
the bartender.

When he came over he cast a glance at Forster as
though waiting on his approval before pouring her
choice.

"Would you have a cup of coffee with me, at a table,
so we can talk?" His voice had been gentle, and per-
suasive, and he'd tried to interject as much respect into
the request as possible. "It's your choice . . . and I am
only asking you."

"I'd like to have a cup of coffee with my son," she
murmured, looking at him with deep appreciation and
accepting the bartender's nod. "My son is going to take
me to a table like a lady," she said proudly, holding on
to Forster's arm as he led her to a quiet place near an intimate cluster of empty seats.

"Mom, look," he began haltingly, "I'm sorry I went
off to the degree that I did—but something has got to
change."

"Yeah," she sighed, dragging on her cigarette and allowing her eyes to scan the room. "That it does.
Everything does. That's why I had to just come here one
last time to see for myself . . . never could walk in here
for the last thirty years."

"I never expected to see you here," he said in earnest,

his voice just above a whisper. "This would have been the last place I looked."

"This was the scene of the original crime," she said shaking her head as their coffee arrived.

He remained perfectly still and focused his full attention on her.

"I used to be so beautiful . . . so full of life," she said in a faraway voice, casting her gaze to the second bar, which used to be a stage. "Me and your dad had so much fun running this place, and making you." She laughed and covered her mouth, coughed, and then took a drag on her cigarette.

His eyes filled as he watched her go down memory lane, and his mind adhered to the picture of the gorgeous young woman with her head thrown back and wearing white satin.

"You can't imagine how alive this place was—how alive I was, but that's all changed, all gone, just like your father."

"What happened here, between you and Dad, Mom?" His whisper cracked but his line of vision on her remained steady.

"I was young, ambitious, headstrong, and so was your father. He wanted to have a string of nightclubs like they had in Harlem, or in Atlantic City—but he was a black man trapped in an era that made that hard. Hell, it's hard to do it today." She took a careful sip of her coffee and then set it down and looked back toward the long-gone stage.

"I didn't make it easy, either," she admitted. "I wanted what I wanted, and would throw tantrums to get it, and he'd indulge my fiery, artistic nature and I'd indulge his grand visions, and we'd make up after . . . it was good between him and me for a long time." Her voice trailed off with a sad chuckle. "Then, he brought a stage in here, just for me, and he earned enough money to buy the adjoining property, go through the wall to expand . . . and he built me my club . . . just so his baby could sing. And," she whispered, tears now streaming down her face, " I sang my heart out in here for that man who adored me. All ballads—he loved the ballads."

Hot moisture threatened his eyes, and he looked down at the table, her truth too powerful, and about to consume him. He sipped his coffee and swallowed away the tears that required private sobbing to release. The ballads, the music, the dancing . . . the artistic vision; he now had a piece of his genetic code.

"Did you all ever have a friend in here named Thomas DeCicci?" His voice was a mere whisper as he asked the question, knowing she had an answer.

His hands covered his mother's as new tears rose in her eyes. In that moment, looking at her and the depth of pain in her expression, anything negative he'd harbored against his parents began to crack and peel away like the paint on the ancient walls of the club. They were human, had lived, and loved, and made many mistakes in their youth . . . but it had nothing to do with him, even though it had trapped him. They loved him, and had tried. It was simply their dance.

"Thomas," she whispered, the hurt in her expression giving way to a softness in her he rarely saw. "God rest his soul in peace."

"Who was he?"

Forster waited and watched his mother's face transform until she seemed to be a girl of twenty.

"He was a knight in shining armor," she finally whispered and let the ash fall from her abandoned cigarette, then took a long drag, allowing the smoke to exit her body through her nose as her eyes closed on her sadness. "He saved your father's life—the first time . . . but broke his heart. So, he decided to save yours to make up for it."

"Please, Mom," he gently urged, "I have to know."

"Your father," she said in the most clear, direct voice he'd heard from her in a long while, "was ambitious, and had gone to the wrong people for money . . . do you understand?"

He nodded, and she played with his hand with her fingers as she talked, her voice steady, gentle, patient, as though explaining something complex to a child.

"And, those people want to own you for the loan, which you can never, *ever* pay off. So, when your father wouldn't allow hookers and heroin in here, they sent some of their people to *reason* with me and your dad. And they walked into the club while I was singing . . . and they sat at a table over there," she said, here voice dropping as she removed her hand from his and pointed with an unsteady finger.

"And, Thomas . . . dear, sweet Thomas was the youngest in his family, but the smartest, and the kindest soul . . . and he heard me sing, and never took his eyes off of me."

He watched his mother's eyes glisten in the low bar lights as her gaze stayed on the invisible table that had faded away into a place so far away.

"The camera jockey took a picture of us . . . they did that then in clubs in those days, and they'd come around to the tables and hawk them—Thomas bought it because it got me and him in the shot . . . your father was at the very edge of it, but all Thomas cared about was that it had me. And when the set broke, me, your dad, and the men that had come in with Thomas, went into the back . . . and we were made to understand by the leader in the group that cooperation would be in our best interest. But Thomas told them to leave us alone—he'd front the debt for the short term, and this club was off-limits, it wasn't to burn down, and the lady wasn't to be hurt . . . nor was her man. And, they made a call to somebody from that office, and Thomas's word made it all right. And the club and us got a reprieve. But, time and circumstance is a funny thing."

Forster nodded, understanding what his mother implied. "No judgment, Mom. I just needed to know."

"He was a good man, Forster," she whispered, "was a complete gentleman and became your father's best friend. They expanded together, over in Camden, and then little by little as the times changed and the crowds thinned, your father's ambition, and his fear of failing, made him make some decisions that even Thomas couldn't help him out of. Thomas kept trying to get him to put his money into other types of ventures—clean ventures. But your father only knew the bar trade, and wasn't comfortable about that. And they fought about it, we fought about it, it was a horrible time, and you were so little, and I was so afraid, and the only person in the world I could talk to was Thomas . . . who'd been there all along. Time and circumstance is a funny thing . . ."

"Oh, Mom . . . I'm so sorry . . ."

"Don't be. Like you told me, choices, right? Those weren't the times when two different colors could make a family, not easily, and Thomas had a family he couldn't divorce . . . and I had a son to raise. So, time and circumstance can make a person make hidden choices." She looked at him square and held another cigarette to her lips for him to light. "In all seriousness, son, if I'm going to tell this story, I need some liquid painkiller."

He nodded and motioned for the bartender, no longer judging his mother's demons.

"Bring the lady what she wants," he said firmly. "I'll be responsible for seeing her home safely." When the man paced away, Forster returned his gaze to his mother's face, and she wiped at her tears, sniffed, and tipped her chin up just a notch with an air of dignity.

"I had stopped singing when I got pregnant, had stopped drinking because it made me sick when you were in me," she chuckled sadly. "I would sing around the house, and sing my ballads to you all the time, and you used to just beam at me like I was the only woman in the world that could make you happy. But when I was ready to come back, things had started changing in the place . . . it just wasn't safe, your father didn't want me down there with a baby at home, and he'd started taking up company with other women. So, I'd be home giving you your bottle and I had mine . . . and my best friend would come to see about me. Always the gentleman, always made me laugh, always a shoulder when I needed to cry."

Her voice fractured and cracked, and she accepted the drink the bartender brought. She sipped it slowly, looking at the dark liquid in the glass, swirling it around as though answers and absolution might come to its surface.

"Then, one day you were asleep, and your father had stayed out all night . . . and Thomas came by, and you woke up crying, so I sang for you in front of him, right in the middle of the kitchen, a cappella . . . and he followed me upstairs to help tuck you into your crib, and somewhere along the way we came to no longer be just friends. And it was our dark secret, a stolen moment frozen in time, and one day, drunk and angry as I could be, your father and I fought about his goings-on . . . and I threw the unthinkable in his face. And, your father walked out the door and never came back home."

"Mom . . . you can't blame yourself for . . . I mean, there was so much on both sides," he heard his voice tell her. He'd remembered, witnessed, saw his old marriage to Eva, and knew that it took two wrongs to tear a house down.

"I took your father away from you, I broke up a friendship between two men that were like brothers, I lost my best friend, and two men that I deeply loved for different reasons . . . and then I lost my voice, my figure, my son to the streets, then one day the service . . . my mother and family shunned me for destroying my marriage for a man with different skin, and I eventually lost my mind . . . women had so few choices in those days, Forster, especially once branded as a whore."

His hands reached out to hers to draw them away from her mouth, and he clasped them in his own and forced her to look at him. "I had no idea . . . and no right to judge you so hard . . . I didn't know . . . I didn't understand—and you didn't do this all by yourself . . . he'd run on you, and left you before that thing with DeCicci ever went down. Forgive me."

She caught a sob and swallowed it down and let tears roll down her cheeks uncensored. "No . . . forgive me . . . all the pain I caused one poor little boy caught in the middle of grown folk's business . . . Father God, help me."

"I'll be there for you, Mom," he whispered. "Together, we'll get you some help, if you want it."

"I do," she whispered back. "And that dear man, Thomas, walked away to keep you and I safe, put his seal on us and hovered at the edges of our lives . . . He wouldn't let them go after us, Forster. We were off-limits; he'd spoken on that from a long time ago. And, times when your father was so angry at me that he wouldn't acknowledge us, Thomas sent money for me and his best friend's child. He did that, which was why I couldn't even look at it to pay the bills. I replaced him with my next best friend—Jack Daniels. Least this one was colored," she added with a sad chuckle, and then finished her drink. "But that man didn't deserve to die in his house alone, falling down the steps in an old basement and hitting his head."

"What happened to him, Mom . . . after everything passed between you and Dad?" The question was beyond the investigation: It was personal.

"He pulled back and turned things over to his son. He'd married, like his family wanted him to, had a boy, and did what his fate had planned. But he always contacted me a couple of times a year, to see how I was faring, and to check on the boy that made his best friend sing in the kitchen." Her eyes shone with quiet resolution. "He checked on you out of a sense of honor, Forster. Sounds crazy, and I don't expect you to understand—but your father was his dear friend, once, and he had breached the trust. . . . So he gave to you what your father would no longer accept from him, security."

"Let's get you home and tucked into bed, Mom . . . you look tired."

"I am," she whispered. "I just want to lie down."

"The girls are at Lynette's, and me and Rick have to work tonight . . . but come home, Mom. We'll face whatever we have to in the morning."

Twenty

Multiple cable stations and Disney had been a blessing, because it had allowed her to keep the telephone pressed to her ear after dinner as she walked around the house and contacted all her sources in a low murmur without the children hearing her. But the more she dug, the uneasier she became.

After she'd tucked the girls in with a bedtime story, her leads and a search of the society pages on the Internet had given her a positive ID for Regina Hamilton—recently seen draped over the arm of the son of the late Thomas DeCicci at a black-tie event. The problem was that this prominent society chick was Forster's halfsister, unless there were two Forster Scott Hamilton seniors, who were also African American, owned a string of nightclubs and bars, and who had a junior named for him that was his spitting image, and who lived in the Delaware Valley area. This was beyond bad: It was horrible.

The only mild comfort she was able to glean from the whole nightmare was the fact that it had been rumored the Philly and Camden establishments, run by Reginald Hamilton by a long-handled spoon, were notorious for their under-the-table activities—the cash-flow engine that kept the dollars flowing, big time. Therefore, it brought a secondary character more visibly to the fore.

The swank, upscale Cherry Hill establishment was where the beautiful people were, albeit funded and supported by the toxic elements of the inner city.

That also meant Reginald had some filthy ties—the kind of ties that got people killed . . . and through his sister's relationship with DeCicci's son, there was access to the old man's house. But what could have been in the will that would have made somebody with everything go after the old man?

The tips of Lynette's fingers tingled as she studied her notepad and began drawing lines to link the players and what they might have at stake. She was not going to allow an innocent man to go down on a hummer—not her man, at that!

The sounds of the door opening made her stand up fast enough to knock over the dining-room chair she'd occupied.

"Mom," she said in a rush. "How was your trip? I'm so glad you're home. I left dinner on a plate in the fridge, if you're hungry. How was your trip? Where's Deacon Charles?"

Ida Graves surveyed her daughter carefully with a smile. "Did I come back too soon, or something? You seem awfully jumpy . . ."

"No, no, no, I hope you all had a good time. I'm not jumpy, just working on four cups of coffee and pushing to a deadline."

"Four cups of coffee? Have mercy, child, you're gonna give yourself a heart attack," the older woman said with a chuckle as she set down her suitcase, and then removed her hat and coat. "Deacon saw me safely to the front door, but had to go home—everybody is tired and—"

"Excellent, excellent, that's a good thing, tired, good-kinda tired, which means you had a good time, good,

Mom, real good. It's all good. Forster's kids are asleep upstairs, and—"

"Child of mine, what is going on? You look like you're running from the law? The man's children are here?"

"Oh, Mom, Jesus . . . I'm working against a deadline, and Dianne is coming over here at any moment to help me. He had to work late, so I offered to sit for him. Now you just go on upstairs, and rest yourself, if you hear the door, it's just us girls, everything is fine, and I'm glad your trip was good—you did eat, right?"

"I did," Ida said with a stern look of suspicion that slowly eased into a smile. "We had dinner at one of the return stops as a group . . . and I am indeed exhausted, so I suppose I shouldn't be coming down the stairs tonight for any unnecessary reason. And, if the doorbell rings, I will just ignore it, since you're up with four cups of coffee pumping through your veins—but, if you need to go out and to know that another adult is home with the children, I will be in earshot of any trouble . . . tired though I may be. But it sounds as though things between you two are progressing very fast, his children are here and—"

"I love you, Mom," she said quickly, kissing her mother's cheek hard and hugging her tight, then pacing away. "I promise, I'll explain all of it to you soon—it's just that, right now, I don't have all the facts."

Her mother gave her a puzzled look, then shook her head and hung up her coat. "I guess I'll understand it better by and by."

"Your Mom all right?"

"Yeah," Forster said, deep in thought. "She's tucked in good, and safe."

"Anything in that long discussion you feel like might help the case?"

Rick had taken his time with the question as his SUV pulled away from the curb. It was as though his friend understood that there was a delicate balancing act going on, where the fine line between friendship, police work, and private family matters was getting more blurry by the moment.

"DeCicci and my mother had a relationship," Forster said in a quiet voice, looking out the window as he spoke. "The reason the man was always in my neighborhood and around for the shots I took, even though his house was in Darby, was because he was watching over me . . . it's very deep. Him and my father were boys at one point. I never even had to show Mom the picture . . . but I'd like to make a copy and give it to her one day." He didn't glance at Rick; didn't want to see the shock register on his face. Not now, not while the wound of the unveiling old scars was still raw. Later, he'd explain further . . . and he'd never leave his mother's behavior open to public scrutiny, not even Rick's, without a defense.

"Okay," Rick said in a matter-of-fact tone that Forster appreciated, "where to now, Jersey?"

"First stop by Lynette's. I just want to let her know this is going to definitely be an all-nighter. From there, let's do Jersey."

"Bet."

Again the sound of the bell made her run for the door. But when she swung it open, it took a moment for her mind to process Rick and Forster's images.

"Listen, Lynette, I know you're working, and we really appreciate all you've done—I appreciate it more than you know . . . but, we have to make a run to Jersey, and in truth, it could take a while."

"That's cool," she said fast with a nod, her eyes darting between the two men at her door. "Well, you all have things to do, and—"

"Wait . . . something's wrong, Lynne. Talk to me."

Lynette shrugged, and when she spied Dianne's car over Forster's shoulder, she cringed. "We need to talk. We got a problem. I—"

"Hey!" Dianne boomed, rushing up the steps with a folder in her hand. "Babe, I didn't expect you to be here!" She brushed Rick's mouth with a kiss. "Yo, Forster, look, we're gonna get this all resolved."

The two men looked at each other and then glanced at Lynette and Dianne.

"I think we need to step inside on this, man, don't you?"

"Yeah, Rick, this doesn't sound right."

"You mean to tell me they sent you in on this case already, you of all people, and the info isn't even twenty-four-hours old?" Forster walked in a circle in the middle of the kitchen floor.

"We gotta do something about the leaks in the department, man," Rick spat out in disgust. "This is bull."

"Damn right this is—"

"Keep your voice down," Dianne fussed. "Ida is home, you don't want to freak her out, be in here with that language, and the kids are asleep. Stop panicking!"

"Yeah, and what do you mean, me of all people? You're lucky it is me of all people, because I'm going to dig to get the facts, right, and tell it humanely, and not fry your ass in the paper!"

"Why didn't you just tell me this was your headline

when I came by earlier?" He hated games, dishonesty, and yet, couldn't blame Lynette for not being wary.

"Because," she spat, "I didn't know if you hadn't killed the man, and truth be told, I wasn't trying to deal with that."

"Straight without a chaser, brother," Rick fussed. "The woman is being honest, and you can't—"

"After last night . . . after . . . you think you might have slept with a person who would off an old man? Is that what you are telling me straight without a chaser?"

"Why not just tell all our business?" Lynette fumed, crossing her arms over her bosom. "I swear; men are so . . . so . . . exasperating!"

The room went still for a moment and Dianne wrung her hands, then quickly jumped in. Lynette thrust her chin up and her eyes glittered with indignation.

"Look, emotions are high, y'all just met each other, girlfriend is stressed, you're stressed, people do strange things when—"

"Yes, I wasn't sure, and that stressed me!" Lynette cut in, blowing a mental gasket over the fact that Dianne was put in the position of defending the logical. "I had only known you for a week, and all this stuff just looked so bad, and I was dealing with my own demons for about an hour . . . so sue me!"

"Then why did you sleep with me, if you didn't trust me?" Sudden fury at the concept made him draw in and release hard inhales as he spoke.

"At the time, I did, and at the time, I couldn't help myself . . . Jesus, I can't believe we are even having this conversation with everybody else in the room!"

"Well, honesty would have been—"

"Honesty? What! You're the pot calling the kettle black, if ever I heard it—now that's honest!"

"Ooh, wow . . . Okay, honesty is not always the best

policy—but, we're in the media, and we see a lot of deep stuff . . . serial killers, ax murderers, you know, the whack kind of—"

"Don't go there, D," Rick warned. "Stay out of it. We see a lot of unspeakable things, too, up close and real personal, but—"

"No, no, no . . . it's a woman thing, and you wouldn't understand. Y'all can be dangerous—men, that is. Security issues, okay, girlfriend has baggage, we all do, but I assure you that she only thought that he might have offed the old man for a very short window, then she learned differently—you two are being counterproductive. We have solid info to share! So, chill."

"Save it for later, man," Rick warned. "Stay focused. You and I are not going to logic it out with two of them in the room tag teaming us."

"Your best bet," Lynette seethed, "is to work this as a foursome. Any way you slice it, either I write the story or somebody less friendly does. I want to get to the bottom of this to clear you, protect your family, and to keep any speculation from your door. Make a decision, brother—me or the pit bulls in the press?"

"Can't argue with that," Rick sighed. "The girl took your kids in through the door, no questions asked, when she was still half scared of your butt . . . so, let's just save the who-shot-John for later . . ."

"All right, all right, thanks," Forster huffed, his pride still stinging from the fact that Lynette had even for a moment considered the unthinkable about him.

"You're welcome." Lynette crossed the room still undone. What did he think she was supposed to think? Basic survival instinct always kicks in way before anything else with a city girl. She didn't play damsel in distress, and her mind was like a razor, sharp, analytical, and definitely her own.

He stood on one side of the room glaring at Lynette, who stood on the other side of it glaring back—with Rick and Dianne caught in the middle.

"Okay, Rick," Dianne finally grumbled, shooting daggers at Forster, who had paced to lean against the sink, "here's what we got on the girl, Regina."

"At first we thought she was seeing the older DeCicci, but it seems that she was seeing the son, junior," Lynette said with triumph, then weighed her words. "I know this is your halfsister, and maybe we should be more—"

Forster shook his head and held up his hand. "It's not like that," he murmured. "These are not very nice people, Lynne . . . and I have barely ever interacted with them on a speaking basis. They, and their mother, did some really foul things along the way that helped make my mother's life a living hell—will fill you in one day—things I saw, tricks and games they played at Velda's expense."

"Okay, then," Dianne sighed with relief. "Then, we can take the gloves off when we're talking about these people, right?"

"Seems so," Rick replied, casting his gaze to Forster, who nodded.

"All right," Lynette began, "so we have a person who has an issue—a will problem, who now has a key, or access to a key . . . via a man she's sleeping with, dear old Mr. DeCicci's son. I'm just brainstorming here, but Dianne and I were approaching this from a lot of angles based on who had the most to gain or lose."

"From the grapevine, we hear that the inner-city bars have a double set of books, and there's some significant off-the-record activities going down there—but we have a hunch that the Jersey shop, where the brother stays most of the time, will be squeaky clean," Dianne chimed in, brandishing her folder to Rick, who accepted it.

"Now, we checked on what DeCicci junior does for a

living, and he's quite the man-about-town . . . a very good-looking, successful, playboy attorney, and seems to be living large and in charge—but his father lived in a small home in Darby . . . and Dad was the one who built the DeCicci legitimate family businesses, so where's the extra cash, above even a fairly successful attorney's salary, coming from?" Lynette folded her arms over her chest again and leaned against the refrigerator.

"They say like attracts like . . . Regina ain't no slouch herself," Rick added, and then glanced at Dianne, then Forster. "Don't y'all get mad at me, but she *is* a good-looking woman, vampire that she may be. Both are attorneys, make fat dough, can see the connection."

"Right," Lynette sighed, "but more importantly, the paper trail. Young DeCicci was the lead attorney for his family's books . . . just like DeCicci senior had been the family attorney for his father's unsavory business endeavors—but old man DeCicci cleaned it up and legitimized that branch of the empire."

"We've been fact-finding, y'all. The women got the scoop," Dianne giggled, pleased at the shocked expressions on Rick and Forster's faces. "All sources are under the secret-source seal, but it's accurate—will give you a trail later, so you gentlemen can make your case."

"That's a whole 'nother issue," Lynette sighed, "but just go with what we've got for now. We've been on the phone for hours."

"Internet, office buildings . . . secretaries have keys to everything, and know who's sleeping with who, trust us," Dianne chuckled. "Women can get the lowdown."

"All right, all right," Rick urged. "So, keep rolling."

Lynette drew in a deep breath and reorganized the facts in her mind. "Regina is probably the one handling things for her brother—which means you've got two people, attorneys on both sides of the equation, either of whom could draft up a legal documents and know how to keep it real quiet . . . see a pattern?"

"I see an intersection," Forster muttered, rubbing his chin. "I heard through my own grapevine that the father was trying to move his holdings into legitimate enterprises since the forties. What father would try to move out of the old way of doing business, and then drop his son right back into it? Doesn't make sense. You'd want to keep your kid as far away from that as possible— you'd take the risk, but you'd want better for your kid."

"But, what if your kid wants to empire-build on his own, and tries to go find some of your old stomping grounds?"

Rick's proposal wasn't lost on the group.

"DeCicci and my father fell out years ago, over an irreversible issue. They'd been the best of friends, then something serious came between them, and they didn't speak for years—so how'd he come to be the legitimate executor of my father's estate?"

Silence engulfed the room as Forster's statement hung in the air.

"In the will, your father went on and on about people who had tried to scam him, betrayed him, and how they'd hurt him by going against his wishes after he'd tried to build a better life for them . . . so he cut them out, completely, and cut you and your mom in, Forster," Rick leaned against the door frame and rubbed his chin.

"Deep . . . Then, we have two sons and two fathers— and possibly two young Turks, who wanted more than what pure, old-fashioned hard work would pay," Lynette offered. "DeCicci had a son who would be heir to all his legit holdings—I assume . . . we ought to see if the old man has a will of record?"

"Yeah, we can do that," Rick said with confidence. "Monday morning, we'll run a check."

Lynette nodded. "Plus, we have Forster's dad's will, which I understand would have given you all of his business assets, from what you're saying—the clean part of it. But that would totally estrange and piss off his second set of kids. And, the only thing that could make two sworn enemies become allies again is if the common enemy is greater than the strength of each ally standing alone."

"The whole is always greater than the sum of the parts; synergy of common effort," Forster murmured. "Yeah. The art of war."

"Yup," Lynette said, her ire gone and renewed respect for Forster's intellect replacing it. "The kids close to them offered some very real and present danger—to their hearts, if nothing else . . . but possibly to their lives, too."

Her soul hurt for Forster, as she really thought about how ugly this whole transaction between the fractured families had become. She only hoped that if they ever got past this to exonerate him, then they could talk, alone, so that he could know once and for all how deeply he made her feel about him . . . and how much she ached inside for the pain he was now going through. What must he have seen as a child?

Again the room fell silent, and he glimpsed her sad expression, which had trust and hope as its foundation. It was so clear; he'd been crazy to doubt what he saw flickering in her irises. Sure, she had doubted him, with just cause. But she had also fought that fear her own way to get to the bottom of those doubts. She'd pushed past the panic and had clung to hope. This woman was in his corner, and had raised a posse for him in his defense . . . and it was about more than her deadline, and her career . . . that he could tell from the warmth she sent to him from those big, brown eyes.

"That could have been enough to make the two old men talk," Forster finally said, collecting his thoughts and gathering the linear facts. "Especially if the female in the equation, the daughter, had brought the warring sides to the bargaining table. They used to send a bride to bring old kingdoms together to ensure peace, and I'll bet that Regina used the oldest method in the book—after all, she was daddy's little girl."

"Yo, man . . . we have that picture of DeCicci at some gathering in Jersey, right? He's there with your halfsiblings. So, somewhere, there was a reconnect, and your father's daughter was dating his son . . . You're right. It's sorta like an arranged marriage from the old country type of vibe."

"I have a copy of it," Lynette said in a quiet voice. "Don't ask. Media sources."

She paced out of the room, leaving both Rick and Forster hang-jawed, returning with it and giving it to them to inspect. "This looks like a happy little reunion, doesn't it?"

"It looks like two old friends who have buried the hatchet," Forster said, his tone distant as he gazed at the shot. "But, DeCicci's expression is strained." He offered the photo to Rick to inspect, who returned it after a moment. "If the old men got wind that something foul was going on, then they were also longtime players enough to play along like nothing was wrong. What's that saying, keep your friends close, but your enemies closer?"

"They were OGs—*original gangsters,*" Rick chimed in, agreeing. "If they thought they were being set up and fleeced by their greedy kids, they would have tried to act like they were down with the program and oblivious, until they could get a plan in place to strengthen their position."

"I'm going to brainstorm a theory based upon human

nature," Lynette announced. "For my child, I believe, I would do anything, suffer any indignity to make sure that they were all right. And there can be no greater hurt for a parent than a selfish, ungrateful child—who turns away after you've literally given them life."

All heads nodded in unison and audible sighs released in staggered intervals within the small confines of the kitchen.

"And, if you'd found out that, after all these years, a person who had wronged you had still taken care of the child you left behind . . . as a matter of principle, of honor, would you not at least hear that person out if they came to you with a proposal?" Forster had begun pacing.

"You thinking what I'm thinking?" Rick said quietly.

"Yeah," Forster murmured. "I am."

"Well, will somebody tell us what y'all are thinking?" Dianne demanded, folding her arms over her chest.

"Old man DeCicci was a wise old business hack. Probably began transferring assets to his son so that he wouldn't have to pay inheritance taxes when he died— a lot of wealthy people circumvent the system like that in a wise move—co-ownership, or a complete transfer. Would bet my paycheck that his son, against his father's wishes, began coinvesting in the bar business, and other businesses his father didn't like, with my halfbrother. Since these guys are from the old school, I would also guess that DeCicci went to my father with the word, and told him—and used his dedication to me to prove that he still had some honor, despite what had gone down thirty years ago."

Lynette covered her mouth with her hand and wrapped an arm about her waist.

"Yeah . . . kid's will make you do that," Forster murmured. "Will make you unafraid to face whatever you have to in order to see that they're safe. And, I would figure that, in turn, my father started delving into what was going on with my halfbrother's holdings—the legacy he'd started allowing my halfbrother to manage early."

Lynette sucked her breath in hard. "And when the two old men found out that their kids had betrayed them, they tried to close the hole with their wills."

"And, those vipers probably set their fathers up," Dianne rushed in, her expression one of total shock. "Just like some old Roman drama, or Greek tragedy stuff . . . deep. And the woman, Regina, is all about the Benjamins . . . so, why not hook up with young Caesar, who's about to do his dad?"

"Especially if you know you're cut out of the will because you've been secretly investing in your brother's deals, initially unbeknownst to your father, and now your brother doesn't have a dime—why not hedge your bets? She's a smart woman . . . probably had the ear of old man Hamilton initially, as a daughter and confidant and an attorney, and he more than likely told her what he was going to do—but that would have jacked her finances, which were all heavily loaded into the LLC—my guess, that would ultimately become worthless overnight." Lynette gave the group a triumphant glance, her line of vision scanning their expressions for input.

"But, check it out, y'all," Rick chimed in. "Her grandfather was a judge, and his best friend put away the guy who shot Forster's father. Then brotherman has a fatal accident in the joint after being there for only six months? Uh-uh. Too fishy."

"This definitely sounds like the work of a skilled female," Dianne admitted.

"Deep . . . man, oh, man, the mastermind behind this mess had to be a woman—brothers can't think up or pull off something this treacherous. It takes a real smooth criminal," Rick said, shaking his head and pushing away from the door frame to pace.

"Let's not get carried away," Forster warned. "This is only conjecture, wild speculation, at the moment—without hard facts. We could be off by a long shot—but either way, we're gonna have to have evidence . . . without it, what you print is slander, and no judge will hear it."

"D, baby . . . is there any way for you to find out who owns the limited liability corporations on both DeCicci's estate and old man Hamilton's?"

Dianne shrugged and pecked Rick's cheek with a kiss. "Sure, hon. Information is power."

Twenty-one

She didn't like it one bit, especially not the part about Forster wearing a wire while Rick played backup. It was too dangerous—for both of them. Plus, there was the not-so-small issue of Forster's state of mind. Emotion made people take risks. Emotion made people lose focus. Lack of emotional distance made people hesitate, and that's when people could lose their lives. She could not imagine what the emotional roller coaster that had to be screaming out of control within him was doing to his concentration—especially at a time when he needed to think fast on his feet. Her man was in trouble. She did not like it one bit.

Lynette turned around in a circle as the group talked, then she finally interjected, her own emotion cresting and breaking her surface calm. "You two are talking about dangling Forster out there to baby sharks like human bait. Small time wanna-be gangsters though they may be, they've shown that they have teeth and will bite. Plus, they're desperate."

"I know," Dianne warned. "God forbid if anything ever happened to either of you . . ."

"We'll be all right," Forster said calmly, "if we stick to the plan." He nodded toward Rick, who nodded in return.

"Yeah, we just want to make sure you ladies stay somewhere safe while this all goes down."

"It's a tight schedule," Forster added in, moving to Lynette and placing his hands on her shoulders. "Trust me, we'll be fine."

When she didn't speak, but simply looked up at him, fear for his safety glittering in her eyes, he pulled her against his chest, not caring what his friends saw.

"I promise," he murmured against her hair, then kissed her forehead. "Up to this point, haven't I been a man of my word?"

"You better come back in one piece," Lynette said in a shaky voice. "You just better."

"Listen," Rick soothed, gathering Dianne in his arms where they stood, "all you have to do is place the calls at the intervals we discussed. First Forster's call goes in to Hamilton at his home, and he tells him that he's got the will because a dirty cop wants a cut—but that he'll make the will go away if they can come up with a mutually beneficial arrangement. That should draw Hamilton out to meet at the spot in Cherry Hill. My boys are working on coordinating with Jersey's squad, finding cell-phone numbers, and pager numbers—that way all the calls can connect."

"I still don't like it," Dianne said in a hoarse whisper. "Why can't you just let Homicide know where the leads are, and let them run them down? There's enough here to create doubt about Forster's involvement to clear him . . . why can't you all just turn it over and leave it alone?"

"Because it's personal, and the fellas in Homicide won't be able to get inside of their heads like I can, like we can—at least not fast enough to catch them off guard before they can destroy any evidence." Forster rubbed Lynette's back as he spoke, and he and Rick exchanged a glance.

"If you all don't want to place the calls, then that's okay," Rick reassured Dianne and Lynette.

"Absolutely. You have to be able to sleep at night with this," Forster agreed.

"They killed an old man . . . your father did your mother wrong, hurt you, God only knows what else. I'm down," Lynette protested.

"Me, too," Dianne said, reaching out her hand to high-five Lynette's from where she stood. "We got this. From a phone booth I'll call DeCicci and tell him to tell his woman to stay away from my man, and no matter how much money his girlfriend, Regina, is supposed to be coming in to from some old will she found at her father's house, she was not taking my man. Then, I'll tell him I'm going up to the club to kick her ass, because I did some snooping, got my man's voice-mail code, and knew they were going to meet at the spot in Cherry Hill with her brother to split up the money—and that would make De-Cicci think Reginald was also in on it."

"That part is the risky bluff," Rick said, sounding concerned. "First of all, we have to bank on DeCicci barging in there in such a state of jealousy, all jacked up with a testosterone rush, that he'll just launch into a verbal exchange with Forster—without describing it all the way in front of the woman's brother."

"That is a gamble, but all of this is just that—a gamble," Forster admitted, "because Reginald will smell a rat, and find it hard to believe that his sister would do me, no matter how much money is at stake."

"But let's bank on the playboy's overblown ego," Rick offered. "Most guys don't want even their best friend to know their woman has been running . . . so, maybe he'll just come in and start raving about the will aspects, trying to act like that's all there is at stake—and keep the personal, personal . . . especially in front of her brother. He wouldn't be crazy enough to go there and risk having her and her brother team up against him."

"All right," Dianne sighed, her voice sounding less sure. "They know old man Hamilton left a will, and are still hunting for it, but who's to say that they haven't gotten old man DeCicci's yet?"

"If there's one out there," Forster murmured, "I have a hunch where it is and who might have it. And, they haven't got it . . . let's play this out."

"Play it to the bone, bro," Rick said, exchanging a fist pound with Forster. "Play this to the natural bone."

"Right," Lynette quipped, pulling back a ways from Forster's embrace. "When DeCicci calls the club, his insiders will probably tell him that some unknown tall, fine, brother none of them has seen before just went into the back with Hamilton—which will be Forster. DeCicci will freak."

"Then," Dianne pressed on, leaving Rick's embrace to walk around and think aloud as she talked, "Lynette places the bombshell call."

"Right, right, right," Lynette said slowly, giving Dianne another high five. "Been there, girlfriend."

"Yup," Dianne said with another hard slap of agreement. "I don't care how much money is involved, how much education she has, if another woman calls your cell phone with some yang about your man, you're going to go address him about it."

"Truth," Lynette said, folding her arms. "So, I tell her that she'd better stay away from my man, Thomas—since we have plans, nice plans, courtesy of the will his father gave me to hold for a rainy day. I will put on my best non-African-American-girl voice, and tinge it with some Cherry Hill nasal twang, and say some very disparaging things about how the old man never really thought of her as wife material, given she was black."

"Oh, girl . . . she will definitely flip."

"Right . . . So, the story is, the older DeCicci drafted up a little persuasion to help his son come into his right mind and to keep the DeCicci bloodline unaffected by his son's momentary wanderlust . . . while he sowed wild oats with some black wench. I'll tell her to meet me at the bar so she can see the authentic doc, if she doesn't believe me, and I'll close by saying, now or later, water seeks it's own level. When I'm not there, and she gets word that Thomas is in the back talking with her brother, the girl is going to hunt Thomas down for a confrontation—that you can take to the bank."

"That will make girlfriend go back to her roots," Dianne chuckled. "Brothers, trust me, she will come to the bar."

"Damn . . . women are cold," Rick said, scratching his head. "Treacherous."

"Ain't no match for 'em," Forster sighed and rubbed his palms over his face. "Hell hath no fury, man."

"Well, it's two-to-one on this side. I feel better," Rick said nervously. "Y'all, just promise to stay on our side, though."

Lynette smiled for the first time since they'd begun talking and both she and Dianne chuckled.

"That should get them imploding on each other, trying to figure out where the double cross is. We'll just use their tactic—and deploy the closest weapon on them that they've been using on others—betrayal." Triumphant, Lynette paced over to Forster again and pecked his cheek.

"Everybody knows what they've gotta do," Rick said with a nod in Forster's direction. "D . . . I just need a minute to talk to you, in the other room, baby. Okay? C'mon in here with me while I call in to headquarters to give the squad the heads-up. But remember, no calls from the house to Jersey during this operation—we don't want anybody doubling back in the future tracking this to your door from caller ID."

Forster nodded and leaned against the sink, watching Rick and Dianne as they left the room. Then he looked at Lynette.

"How's your head?"

"How's yours?" she whispered, coming nearer to him and touching his face.

"I'm all right," he murmured. "I'm sorry about all of this—all of it." His finger traced her jaw and he brushed her mouth and pulled away.

"You didn't start this chain reaction that built into a storm, honey," she whispered. "And, I would have gotten this assignment and would've had to dig for the truth at the bottom of it, whether I knew you or not."

"I know that, but the level of involvement at this point," he said with a sigh of disgust, "and I'm also sorry for the things I said, and thought—"

"Don't," she whispered, placing a finger over his lips. "I am, too."

Again he nodded, and he filled his arms with her and petted the delicate curls at the nape of her neck. "I feel like a man who has been through outer space, all in one day." He held her back from him and gazed deeply into her eyes.

"I'm still wearing the same clothes from twenty-four hours ago, I spent the most wondrous night with the woman of my dreams, I came home and had the most bitter, long overdue fight with my mother, who ran away from home . . ."

"Oh, Forster . . ."

"But it was all good, because I found her again, the real Velda Hamilton, and I came to understand her as a person, and she came to understand me. Then I find out all this stuff, and wind up defending the honor of my father, who I find out really cared for me . . . and defending the honor of the man who wanted me to be his son, and who was my mother's lover . . . and I found out that I really had two fathers, not one—a fairy godfather, and a biological father, after thirty years of thinking I had none. God is good," he whispered.

"All the time," she murmured back.

"And I found out that I didn't want any legacy—the money didn't matter, and yet, both fathers left an embarrassment of riches at my feet. And I put myself in their shoes, and my mother's shoes, remembering that I had played each role." He kissed her forehead when her brow creased in puzzlement.

"Lynette, I cannot imagine what old man DeCicci went through, carrying a torch for a woman he wanted as badly as he wanted my mother . . . but couldn't have with all the obstacles in their way. I know what one week of hungering for you was like—but to be held at bay for years?"

"I know what seeing someone and experiencing an instant recognition is like . . . and now, because of you, what finding a soul mate is like . . . and while none of it makes sense, time isn't a factor, and as a woman you keep telling yourself, this can't be, it's too soon, pace yourself, but you can't."

"Yeah," he whispered near her mouth. "And finally, one day the fragile line between them snapped . . . and if it was anything like what we experienced last night, how can I stand in judgment? I can't dare cast the first stone against something as powerful as that."

Their kiss deepened and he pulled away slowly to look again at those beautiful, soulful eyes. "I also found out what anger will do for you . . . it tore my father apart. If he could have forgiven either one of them, and accepted some of the blame that rightfully belonged at his feet, who knows? He had treated my mother well in the beginning, then what they had eroded until he treated her so poorly that someone else filled in the empty space within the woman who had so much love to give. I have been on that side of the coin, too . . . me and Eva went through that, and I stood in Velda's shoes, just like her, hoping for change and needing someone to fill that inner vacancy."

"So have I," she whispered, "and I also learned so much from and about my mother, her and my father's marriage and sacrifices, my own failed marriage . . . all because our worlds collided. There is a master plan."

"All I know," he whispered, sealing the space between them, "is that time waits for no man . . . and if we all get out of this unscathed, I'm not waiting, Lynette. I want to be with you, whatever come what may."

"Then, taking a page out of Ida's book, let's pray on that, right now."

"Yeah."

"You cool?" Rick's eyes scanned Forster's face, and his expression held unconcealed worry.

"I'm cool," Forster said, trying to reassure his friend and patting him on the shoulder as he prepared to exit Rick's SUV.

"You strapped?"

"Locked and loaded, but you know they're gonna shake me down to take my weapon when I go into the back room. That's why I made it visible, so the frisk will be a quick sweep and a pants-leg and pocket check only. Then we can do business. The leather bomber is thick enough to let them feel for a glock, but not the wire."

"That's the part that I don't like, dude. Wearing a wire, you won't have your nine once they strip it, and no vest. This ain't good. Emotions will be running high in there, and that's when the unpredictable happens."

"Relax. It's all good."

"The van is across the parking lot," Rick said motioning to an unmarked vehicle that had blended in with the other parked cars. "You reading him? Roger that, Homicide. Don't leave my boy out here hanging, do you read? The first sign of any bullshit, we're in there. We got your back."

Forster nodded. "I know that. Wouldn't do this with anybody else but you, bro."

"Me neither," Rick said and gazed out the window. "Just look alive and stay alive in there, promise me." Then he adjusted his mouthpiece closer to his lips again. "Van, you copy, or what!"

"We copy," a voice from the van echoed into Rick's earpiece. "Didn't want to break up the tender moment between you two lovebirds."

A series of chuckles entered Rick's ear and he let his breath out hard. "Go to hell. Just be on point, dig?"

"Cool," the voice from the van replied. "You ready to rock and roll?"

"Let's do it," Rick nodded, seeming agitated. "Show time."

"I'll be fine, man," Forster said with confidence. "It's time to finally settle some unfinished family business."

"So," Reginald Hamilton said in a smug, even tone as Forster stepped into his sumptuous office, "tired of playing good cop, and now want to play bad cop?"

"Nice digs," Forster replied, taking his time to set the stage. He glanced around the heavily decorated leather and red-velvet interior, doing a quick assessment of his environment before he began to speak. He then concentrated his assessment on Reginald's arrogant demeanor, his expensive Italian suit and fine leather shoes, the Rolex watch, one-carat diamond stud in his ear, heavy silver bracelet, red Porsche on the lot . . . need for ostentation equals fragile ego, flash required; loss of money for him means a loss of power and will take him over the edge. Assessment complete. It was on, and way overdue.

"We could work something out, and it never hurts to have a stakeholder on the inside down at headquarters—somebody who can make evidence disappear, people look the other way, provide some general professional courtesies . . . what can I say?"

Reginald stood and poured himself a drink, then held up the crystal decanter in Forster's direction; he declined.

"That's right, I forgot . . . you've been battling alcoholism all you life."

Forster let the cruel comment slide and ignored the false smile the other Hamilton displayed. "And you've been battling second place all you life," he replied evenly. "So, let's just cut the crap. The old man is dead, that old bull is dead. He dogged both my mother and yours . . . so? Let's get paid."

Reginald chuckled and took a sip from his drink. "Sit down," he said as he sat. "You can leave us now," he added, motioning to two burly bouncers. "I trust you stripped him?"

When one of them produced the nine-millimeter for Reginald, sliding it across the desk for him to hold, Reginald smiled. "Then you can leave us—since now there ain't nothing between us but love."

"You got the original?" Reginald said in a threatening tone once the two men were alone.

Forster produced the document and slid it across the desk and waited while Reginald read it.

"Ain't this a bitch . . ." Reginald looked up from the will after a few moments and cast it across the desk. "The old bastard deserved everything that he got."

"I'll share," Forster said in a forced chuckle, "since there ain't nothing but love between us."

"Your mother was a drunken whore!" Reginald spat, standing now and walking back and forth behind his desk. He paced like a madman.

"Watch it," Forster warned, standing and walking to the other side of the room. He knew that he had to push past the emotion to get a confession. "Don't lose your cool, just because he always loved me better than you . . . Velda was his first love, what would you expect from the old man? Your mother was just a fill in, a rebound effort—but that's the past. I know you had to kill him."

"No," Reginald chuckled in a hard tone. "I didn't have to. He killed himself when he began taking back assets he'd promised me, as well as control of the businesses, and then concocted that senility-driven will!" Reginald's eyes glittered with pure hatred as he began toying with the gun on the wide, glass-and-chrome desk between them. "So, what do you want? How much?"

"What's it worth to you?" Forster said evenly. "Fair exchange is no robbery."

"Fair exchange?" Reginald laughed a harsh, forced, threatening laugh with ancient jealousy as its source.

"You come in here, after all these years, and try to lay claim to what I built, and you tell me about a fair exchange not being a robbery?" He picked up Forster's gun and studied it. "Hmm?"

"Well, when I calculate all the missed child-support payments that your mother sucked him dry for, and I'm sure she did that literally," Forster mused, turning up the heat on his baiting strategy, "and when you add up the fact that—"

"Your mother had nothing coming to her! She was a damned whore that my father could never quite get out of his system. She was a virus, just like you are trying to become—but I'm wearing latex, *brother*. I'm clean. So, without this will, my problems will be neatly resolved."

"You think so?" Foster said, rubbing his chin. "Guess the little problem of DeCicci's will still floating around is okay with you?"

"You found DeCicci's will?"

"Put the gun down, and let's talk about it."

"You have it?"

"Somewhere safe. Got it off my mom . . . hey, what mother wouldn't give her only son her everything?"

Reginald set the gun down slowly and his gaze locked with Forster's.

"Why don't we strike a deal . . . and leave Thomas out of this. I know you and Regina can't be that tight, since she's decided to play both sides against the middle. Bad move on her part."

"Talk to me," Reginald ordered.

"Tommy-boy won't get squat when the real DeCicci will comes out—I own Tommy's inheritance, just like I own yours . . . Regina thinks she's getting a king's ransom through his portion that he'll share with her out of misguided love, and the other half of yours that you two currently have from *my father's* hard work. But I'm the legitimate heir to both pots of gold at the end of this rainbow—courtesy my mother's colorful past life. So, *you* talk to *me,* you son of a bitch."

Tense silence strangled both adversaries as Reginald rounded his desk and stood in front of it and then leaned against it. Their locked and hardened gazes left each other's when the door to the plush office suddenly opened.

Thomas DeCicci paced in, surveyed Forster and Reginald and nodded. "Cozy."

DeCicci opened his arms wide and allowed the bouncer to do his job and take away a magnum from him.

Then he readjusted and smoothed his designer jogging suit in a huff.

"Since when do I get frisked when I walk into my partner's office? Somebody needs to tell me something real fast."

"Relax," Hamilton said through his teeth in DeCicci's direction. "You can leave us," he told the bouncer who had followed DeCicci in, and then picked up the other revolver, holding both of them in his hands like a cowboy. "Tommy . . . what's happening?"

"You tell me what the hell is happening." Thomas's gaze darted between Forster and Reginald's. "Or is this a black thing, and I wouldn't understand?"

"Don't go racial, just because your ass is now broke and got played, dude," Forster laughed with a sneer. "It ain't personal, it's just business."

"We had a deal," Thomas raged, looking at Reginald as he spoke. "You were supposed to handle the arrangements to do my old man, I took care of yours, and everything was to be split down the middle fifty-fifty. So, what is this bull?" He demanded waving his arm and sweeping it in Forster's direction.

"Your math doesn't add up," Forster interjected with a lazy stretch as he shook his head. "Neither one of you are good businessmen—no wonder your fathers left everything to me. Because you can't count. With Regina's double-crossing, game playing in the mix, she's fleeced you both out of half of your half, which makes it actually a quarter, by my count. But I was always taught that, nothing from nothing leaves nothing . . . so . . ."

"Shut up!" DeCicci yelled, crossing the room and getting dangerously close to Forster's face. "Are trying to make me believe that you got some extortionist hold on my father, messed up his brain, and got that old coot to do a stinkin' change of will with only you in it, and now you have it? You think you can take my father's assets, his business, all I own, and then make a play for my woman to scoop up her half on the Hamilton side of this, too, you greedy SOB? I'll kill you! Who the hell are you to try to take my Regina and—"

"That's my business," Forster lied, the bile of contempt for the men in the room making him taste acid, "and, it was *just business.*" He'd cut him off, hoping that he could just make DeCicci sound like a madman.

"Your damned woman just called my house, telling me to keep my Regina away from you and to expect some double cross, okay . . . so don't deny it. I'm onto you, and that's why I'm here," DeCicci pressed on, now walking in a tight circle of unspent rage. "I will kill you both first."

"Uh-uh . . . something's not right," Reginald whispered hard, now pacing with the guns in his hands. "My sister may be a lot of things, and has done a lot of men to get what she's wanted, even an old judge—our grandfather's best friend, but to do you? Blood? Her half brother? Even for Regina, that's a stretch."

"Half brother? Wait a minute . . ." Thomas DeCicci glanced from Reginald to Forster, and his shoulders visibly relaxed about an inch, even though his glare remained furious.

"You'd be surprised what some people would do for money," Forster hedged, hoping the thinning bluff would buy him time. But he would have to get out of there before Regina got there. A change of plans on the fly was in order.

Renewed adrenaline pumped through Forster's veins as he watched his words sink in without credibility. This was not good. He had to get out of there with a more solid confession on tape implicating the trio—with specifics about how they'd done the hits, and fast. The variable of Thomas being so crazed that he would say something definitive about the relationship ruse that had gotten him to the club was not factored into their hastily developed plan. They knew it was a risk, and they didn't have time to construct a plan B. If he could get them to go with him in search of the DeCicci will . . .

All hopes for a smooth exit were dashed when Regina waltzed through the door.

Flipping her long black hair over her shoulder, she walked past Forster and up to DeCicci and immediately slapped his face. When DeCicci made a fist and raised it, Reginald's glare halted the intended blow.

"You bastard!" she shrieked, circling him like a lioness would hunt its prey. "How dare you, after all I've done for you?"

Forster remained stock-still. If things went right . . .

"You pull a double cross and try to tell me the difference between right and wrong? Are you mad, bitch?" DeCicci's voice boomed and his face went beet red.

This time when Regina's palm sliced the air to collide with DeCicci's cheek, he grabbed her wrist and stopped it from connecting with her target.

"You wouldn't have any thing, if it weren't for me," she screamed, hot tears streaking her perfectly made-up face. *"I* went in there and did what had to be done. I took the risk, because you couldn't go in there and just pop him . . . what the hell was so hard about knocking the old man out and leaving him to drown to death? The Hamiltons did our part, our side of the bargain. Yet, the easy side, you sent your woman in to do that? It wasn't even worth the money or aggravation to pay for a hit that easy, that's why I did it myself—you good for nothing, cheating lowlife. It was less complicated, with less loose ends! But you left a long thread dangling when your woman called me, buddy."

"My woman, my woman—you stand here and accuse

me when your evidence of double-crossing betrayal is standing here in the middle of the floor?" Thomas walked around her, gesturing with his hands as she turned with him to keep him before her. "I will have you seen by some people that know some people, got that? And maybe I'll have them not kill you, but rearrange your beautiful face!"

"Do you think I went to law school to have to work like a dog all my life to get the things I want and deserve? Don't think that along the way I might have acquired a Rolodex of people that know some people who can disbar your stupid ass, trump up some charges within the system, and have you locked away for the rest of your life—and being somebody's else's whore, whore? Oh, don't go there, Thomas, not when your woman called me . . ."

"What woman? You're my woman! I don't have another woman!"

"All men lie . . . give it a rest, Thomas."

"Enough, Gina, " Reginald warned. "We have company . . . somebody who we've known for a long time that wants in on the party."

"I saw him when I walked in. Who cares? Kill him and be done with it," she hissed, waving her hands as she stormed toward the bar and poured herself a drink and smoothed the front of her gold raw-silk pantsuit. "Men take too long to make a decision, or a commitment," she added, glaring at DeCicci. "Do him, and have one of the boys take out the body."

"Let's not be hasty," Forster chuckled, as he worked on an escape route. "There's still the matter of the DeCicci will, which could turn up just anywhere. You don't think I just left it lying around in a shoe box, without giving somebody explicit instructions on what to do with it if I don't come home tonight? I am a cop. Use your brain and let's work out the money, honey."

Regina Hamilton closed her eyes and dug her French-manicured talons into her palms as her hand balled to a fist. "You two can't do anything right! You two cowards pay some stupid drug-addicted chump to hit Hamilton senior, promise that bum he's out in a few months, then leave him to rot and think he won't sing and get an underground buzz happening that this cop must have tuned in on—so, once again, I have to clean up behind you. Then again, don't kill him. I should just work a deal with my half brother, and leave you two broke fools to be together."

"See, I told you," Forster said, seizing the opportunity of using their half knowledge against them. He gave both men a glance, and then glanced at Regina in a way that transmitted sexual import to the men in the room.

For the moment, it worked. There was a tense silence while everybody assessed his or her position. The problem was that the ruse, and the emotion beneath it, was so distressing that Reginald had leveled both gun barrels at him.

"Let me do it," Thomas insisted in a murmur. "Let me do this skank right now in the middle of the floor. She was my woman."

"You have the gall . . ." Regina threw her head back and laughed. "You and your father give some babe a will so he won't have black grandkids, and planned to cut me out—she called me, get to that, I know all about it. My brother will never shoot me. The blood is thicker than the mud."

This was not good.

"I thought his mother had my father's will, and gave it to him?" DeCicci looked from Forster to Reginald. "My old man was crazy about that bat." He then turned his focus on Regina. "Who told you my father had problems with me being with a black woman? Some babe called you, tonight, just like one called me tonight?"

"Just like someone called me tonight," Reginald hissed.

"Something's not right." Thomas said in a distant voice. "We've been played."

"Precisely," Reginald said in a too-calm tone, as he cocked the trigger on first Foster's revolver, and then Thomas's. "Where's the will?"

"In Philly."

"Be more specific."

"Let's go, you drive," Forster hedged, buying the last grain of time he could.

"Pull him out! Do it now!" Rick yelled into his mouthpiece. "We've got an officer in trouble! You got all you need on tape!" Snatching off his communication headset, he bolted from his SUV, ignoring orders for him to wait.

The van emptied with raid-commando swiftness. Heavily armed policemen from both the South Jersey and Philadelphia jurisdictions flooded the establishment, rendering the bouncers and internal security force useless. Ahead of the pack, Rick raced through it, checking doors, kicking them open until he kicked open the one that held his brother, Forster, captive. "Freeze! Drop it!"

It all happened in slow motion. Reginald's arm swept past Forster to meet the direction of Rick's voice. Forster felt the word *no* elongate up his throat and out his mouth. A shell discharged in Rick's direction. There was no time for thought as Forster dove toward Rick. A sudden impact ripped through Forster and sent him hurling backward. And on the way down he heard another pop just as his body came to a thud on the floor. He saw Reginald fall, heard another series of pops, a woman screamed and began falling with a gun in her hand. A man yelled. Burning ice, then fire filled his chest and a warm salty fluid came up his throat and strangled him . . . then it was quiet and all of it went black.

"You lied," Lynette sniffed as she bent down to plant a kiss on his forehead. "You owe me. You were supposed to come home in one piece."

Rick looked down at the prone body of his friend. "Yeah, man. Crazy superhero stunts . . . that wasn't in the plan, bro. Just wasn't in the plan."

Dianne just covered her mouth and wept against Rick's shoulder, and Ida Graves and Velda Hamilton held each other as they encircled Lynette and two dazed little girls.

"What's the matter with everybody?" Forster whispered, opening his eyes and swallowing hard. "You act like somebody around here died." He tried to give them a chuckle of reassurance, but it hurt too much.

"Yo, man," Rick laughed. "They came to give you last rites twice."

"That's the only reason they let us all in here together, otherwise it's not allowed."

"How long have I been out?"

"Three days," Lynette whispered, moving the children closer to him so he could touch them with his fingers.

"Where am I hit? The morphine is pretty good. Tell me I can walk, dude."

"Yeah, dog," Rick laughed, relief rippling through the room, and the sound of their voices summoned a frantic nurse. "You got a hit in the lung, almost drowned on the scene in your own blood, but it passed your spine and all your vital organs. Somebody must have been praying awful hard for you, cause you're gonna make it."

Forster cast his gaze at Lynette and winked, then issued one in Ida and his mother's direction.

"Body count?" Forster murmured, fatigue making him drift off again.

"One on our side—you. Three on their side—them. Nobody left to haunt you or your mom, it hit the papers with style and class, thanks to the ladies, and you've not only got a commendation coming for excellent police work, but your ass is rich, dog. "'Scuse my French, ladies."

Forster closed his eyes with a smile. He didn't need money, he didn't need fame, and he didn't need a commendation—all he wanted was standing in the room beside him. All of them.

"Then, tell my wife," he whispered through a cough, "that I want some friend fish again for breakfast."

Epilogue

Seven months later . . .

"I just love the way it smells after a heavy spring rain," she said, breathing deeply as she nestled against his chest. "It's so pretty out here with all the trees and flowers in bloom."

He stroked the slightly damp curls away from her face and kissed the crown of her head. "Yeah . . ." he murmured into the blue-gray shadows cast by the dawn in the room. "I just love the way you smell after our storms, and you're so beautiful in full bloom."

"That's how I got in this condition," she giggled in a lazy, sexy manner. "Winter storms."

"Yeah . . . because you kept fixing me fried fish . . . told you that was an aphrodisiac, woman. My weakness."

She laughed.

"But seriously, though," he said as his gaze slid out of the large bay windows framing the room for a moment, then came back to search her eyes. "Speaking of rain . . . you think we put enough away for the baby and the girls, for a rainy day?" He kissed her again as his hand traveled down her side and came to a rest on the slight hill that had just begun to change the form of her once-flat belly.

"Are you crazy? After you sold off all those enter-prises and houses? Forster, we have more than enough."

"I just want you to be happy, and for everybody in the family to have everything they need. And, I still can't figure out why my mom and your mom wanted to keep their little homes in West Philly and wouldn't accept a daily maid, or even move up the Chestnut Hill in here with us so we could know they were all right—unless the house wasn't big enough, or something?"

"That wasn't the reason," she giggled hard and kissed his shoulder, shaking her head.

"For real . . . You sure the house is big enough for when the baby comes, and the girls, and them one day, if they change their minds? Do you really like it, Lynne? I mean, your office and everything—you like it? I don't know why they just wanted to stay where they were . . ."

"Oh, sweetheart," she murmured rolling over to blan-ket him. "You worry too much. It's about their independence. My mom and your mom are like peas in a pod, girlfriends around the corner from each other, and probably keeping company, getting into trouble, and just want their own space."

"But it took Rick and Dianne to convince them to let a cleaning lady come in their houses once a week. They wouldn't even let me put an extension on—"

"I know what your problem is," she laughed and planted little kisses against his throat, "you don't have anything to do, now that the book is done and you've retired."

"That's not true," he laughed and her tongue found his ear lobe.

"Yes it is. I'm working on my novel all day, and soon I'll have the baby to care for, and the girls have school all day, so . . . you need to find a creative outlet for your art. There is no more space on the walls here to occupy your need to gallery," she chuckled. "So, until you find a creative outlet . . ."

He squirmed and laughed in a deepening octave as her hand slid down his torso.

"Y'all women ain't right . . . even my own mother doesn't have any use for me. Velda's been in her recovery groups so hard going to conferences, and singing at them like a celeb—you can't find her . . . Ida, well, if her and Deacon Charles aren't on a cruise, then I don't know where they'd—"

"They're single women . . . I remember what that was like." She laughed, placing a kiss on the scar on his chest.

He laughed. "You'd better stop, woman. And, how'd you get so smart, anyway?"

"I am Lynette, daughter of Ida," she giggled, nipping the side of his neck.

"You'd better stop . . . before I find a creative outlet."

"Why?" She giggled. "Poor baby, I'll play with you today. Rick's gone for three weeks and has a new best friend, his wife, Dianne . . . then they'll be busy working with the contractors while the house is being finished. Ohhhh . . ."

"Stop messing with me, wait till my boy gets back and we . . . Oh, that feels good. C'mon, Lynne, stop it now, or you'll get in trouble. I'm hungry, girl."

"I guess I could feed you . . . or your could feed me . . . we could bring breakfast up here . . ."

"See, this is where trouble always begins," his laughter fused with hers as she started a lazy trail with her fingers up and down his abdomen. "There's a million things we could and probably should do today . . . but, no, you just want to start trouble."

"I've already gotten into trouble with you, that's how my belly got fat."

"I love your belly," he whispered, sliding his hands down her spine. "It's not fat, its full, there's a difference . . . and I'd love you if it was hanging down to your knees with no baby in there." His hands cupped her buttocks, and she chuckled.

"You lie so much, boy," she giggled as his mouth pulled at her lush breasts. "You'd better stop, or you'll be in trouble . . . oh, for real . . . you know that's my weak spot and that's how trouble always begins."

"I'm already in trouble."

"Your boy can't save you this time—Rick and Dianne are on their honeymoon, courtesy you, so you sent away your backup."

"True . . ." He laughed from deep within his chest. "Hmm . . . Maybe I'll call the girls for backup."

"Uh-uh . . . remember, Velda and Ida kept them last night and are taking them to the zoo later today when it's supposed to clear up. You are all alone in here with me, and on the verge of some more serious trouble."

"Every time we look up, they've run off with our kids . . . guess we don't need that much space, since most of the time it's just me and your rattling around in here with nothing to do . . . hmm . . . what is there to do—but get in trouble?"

"Want some fried fish and grits and gravy and eggs a little later?"

"Aw, see now, girl . . . you ain't started nothing but some trouble."

ABOUT THE AUTHOR

Leslie Esdaile is a native Philadelphian and Dean's List graduate of the University of Pennsylvania, Wharton Undergraduate Program. With many awards to her credit, Esdaile also holds a Masters of Fine Arts degree in Film and Media Arts from Temple University of Philadelphia, and she adds the dimension of filmmaking and visual media to her writing and other artistic and business endeavors.

After a decade as a corporate executive, Leslie Esdaile writes full time and enjoys being a wife, mother of a blended household of four children, and coping with an energetic Labrador named Girlfriend. Always on the go, she stays involved in community activities that keep her busy and well-fueled with dramatic content. She draws from life experience in her novels and adds a zany bent of humor to all her projects.